For Constance
With my wa...
and wishes
Carol...

Hidden Lives

The prequel to the Cass Diamond series

Caroline de Costa

Carol... Costa

Published by:
Boolarong Press
38/1631 Wynnum Road
Tingalpa Qld 4173
Australia.
www.boolarongpress.com.au

First published 2021

A catalogue record for this book is available from the National Library of Australia

ISBN: 9781925877854 (paperback)

Cover design by Boolarong Press

Typeset in Ibarra Real Nova 11pt by Boolarong Press

Printed and bound by Watson Ferguson & Company, Tingalpa, Australia

For Michele Moore (Hansen) with thanks for everything

I wish to acknowledge the traditional owners of the land on which the town of Cairns stands, and of the surrounding country and sea. My fictional work is set on your land and seas. I hope I have treated this country, and you as Elders and Owners, and your ancestors, with the respect due to you.

Every citizen of Cooktown was shocked to the core by the news of the Lizard Island tragedy — the death of Mrs Mary Beatrice Watson and her infant son, and the faithful Chinese servant Ah Sam, from thirst after their escape in a ship's tank from Lizard Island. The island was invaded by hostile Aborigines from the mainland; Mrs Watson, alone on the island while her husband was away beche-de mer fishing, repulsed the attack with rifle and revolver, but fearing the natives would come again, she and the baby and the Chinese put to sea in the frail craft, only to fetch up on a waterless island. The silent tragic story was told in a few pitiful pages of a diary that was found beside the poor young woman's remains — 'Nearly dead with thirst.'

Glenville Pike, *The Golden Days: Life in North Queensland in the Gold Rush Era*

From the beginning Lizard Island was a sacred place where the young people were initiated. The whole tribe would have been on Dingaal (Cape Flattery) when the Watson family arrived on Lizard Island ... The people saw smoke on the island and went over to tell them to go because they were on sacred land. However, the people could not speak English, so when Mrs Watson's friend saw them coming they began to fire shots at them and fighting broke out. They let Mrs Watson go because their intention had never been to kill, only to tell them to move away from the sacred land.

Gordon Charlie, elder of the Dingaal people, quoted in the Indigenous Gallery, James Cook Museum, Cooktown, 2000

PROLOGUE

In the early dawn it was hard to distinguish shapes. Across the passage from the beach, the edges of the island blurred into the mist. At the mouth of the river, the tea-coloured streams coming down from the mountains merged deeply with the sharp salt of the Coral Sea. Occasionally a tangled vine or a decaying log swept past, discarded by the rainforest. There was the harsh cawing of seagulls overhead, and from the scrub by the river came the morning laughter of a kookaburra.

Further down the beach from the river, the contours of a spit of rock melted into the sand. The outline of the girl blended into the shadow of the rock, and with the larger waves, disappeared altogether.

As the first rays of the tropical sun broke through the cloud over the island, it would have been possible to see the girl more clearly. Had anyone been there to do so. Her long dark hair was bleached gold at the tips. Her toenails were painted electric blue, her fingernails bitten to the quick. Her underwear was in place, but her skirt and lacy bra were caught by spicules of rock, so that, though she lolled a little with each incoming wave, she moved neither further up the beach nor back into the sea that had offered up its hideous gift. One arm was stretched up against the rock, and covered, like her legs and face, with abrasions that no longer bled. Her mouth was filled with fine white sand.

A single brown dog came padding by, sniffed a little, then moved on further down the beach to where a dead parrotfish held more interest. The sun grew hotter, and the mist lifted from around the island, so that it would have been possible to see how the rainforest reached down to the sand over there, across the bay, and how the funny candy-striped lighthouse stood on the flat slab of rock at the island's peak. Had anyone been there to do so.

The tide slowly turned and the waves receded, so that the girl lay quite still by the rock. Black flies came and began to circle about her face. A brilliant butterfly, iridescent blue, alit for a moment on one gleaming toenail.

The sun rose higher, the mist rolled further up the mountains, and on the beach huge crabs skittered forth from their hiding places in the shallows. It was another perfect day in Queensland.

1

CAIRNS, FAR NORTH QUEENSLAND
SEPTEMBER 2002

Detective Senior Sergeant Leslie Fernando hovered uneasily by a stool on the outer edge of the autopsy room, watching Dr Leah Rookwood go about her work. Well, watching was perhaps too definite a word. Leslie, despite ten years as a detective, and several more in uniform before that, had never really come to terms with the dispassionate deconstruction of the dead that earned Leah, as the region's forensic pathologist, her daily bread. The rasping of the saw through the roof of the skull, which he'd heard just now, was something that always set his teeth on edge. He fixed his gaze at a point in the middle of the white-painted window above Leah's head to stay calm. Leah herself was gently inspecting the brain she'd lifted from the opened skull. The brain of Garry Brown. Garry, a schoolboy whose family lived in the west of Cairns, had been fifteen years old.

On the marble slab by the mortuary sink, Leah turned the brain over between gloved hands as her assistant Laurie shook his head.

'No,' she said to Laurie, 'you're right. No vascular malformation, no tumour, nothing.' She turned toward Leslie. 'There's nothing here to suggest any sudden cerebral problem, no aneurysm, or bleeding into the brain, Leslie. Absolutely no sign of trauma. And anyway, we know he had epilepsy, and there's usually nothing to see with the naked eye in the brains of people with epilepsy. It's all quite straightforward, really. He vomited and aspirated, and food particles — chips and ketchup — have blocked his trachea. I could see bits of them in the bronchi. So he was asphyxiated. His tongue was blocking his airway at the back of his throat, too — we got that story from the emergency people. He swallowed his tongue, and I can see where he must have bitten on one cheek as he died.

'Yet nobody tried to help?' she asked.

'No,' said Leslie, 'nobody. Like — who was it in that Bible story? Of the good Samaritan? The priest and the Levite?' He remembered a hot, hot day in Melbourne, and a gangly Sunday school teacher with bad acne reading aloud from Luke's Gospel. Leslie's white Sunday shirt had stuck with sweat to the back of his neck and the kindergarten chair he'd been given had been way too small for his backside.

'They crossed to the other side,' he said.

In this case to the other side of the Esplanade, the wide ribbon of path, park and beach that ran along the edge of the bay fronting the town. A large proportion of the town's population passed along the Esplanade every day, running, walking, pushing strollers. Leslie himself often jogged with his girls in the dusk along the boardwalks by the water. Yet no-one had stopped when, at five o'clock on a sunny weekday afternoon, Garry, diagnosed with epilepsy when he was three, and on his way home from football practice after dropping into McDonald's for fries, had a grand mal seizure and lay helpless on the ground beneath a fig tree.

'Well, an Aboriginal kid,' Leslie added. 'You can see what they thought. On the ground vomiting. Drink, or drugs. "Not my problem." They just walked past.'

Just last night, Leslie had been in town at an ice-cream shop with Claudine and their girls. Thursday night, pay night. The girls had gigantic double cones, lime and raspberry swirl, choc-chip and mango ripple, so they'd all sat down at one of the metal tables on the footpath near City Place.

Leslie kept leaning across to steal licks from the cones, and his daughters berated him: 'Oh Dad! You're taking too much!' Both girls had their backs to the street so only he and Claudine had seen what neither of them had spoken of at the time.

Across the way a young Aboriginal kid, perhaps a few years older than Garry, than Leslie's own daughter Lily, sat sprawled against a shopfront with a four-litre cask of cheap sweet white. It was an alcohol-free zone, clearly signposted, no doubt about that.

A paddy wagon drew up and two uniformed officers, Constables Jones and Wilkinson, jumped out. They were part of a routine evening patrol; they had probably received a complaint. Wilkinson was a solidly built woman, a no-nonsense divorcee with a couple of kids, Leslie knew, and Jones a slightly porky, pink-faced lad from a small inland town, himself barely out of his teens. Both wore yellow surgical gloves with their blue uniforms. Together they'd seized the kid by the arms and frog-marched him to the wagon — not brutally, not abusively, simply doing their job. In fact, all three characters had seemed resigned to the roles they'd been given in this piece of street theatre.

Briskly, Wilkinson had ripped open the cask and poured the contents into the gutter, wrinkling her nose as she did so. Then she'd picked up the kid's backpack, which probably contained everything he possessed, slung it into the wagon, and they'd driven off. A couple of Japanese tourists had watched the whole scene curiously but without a sound. Several locals passing by took absolutely no notice whatsoever. The kid, Leslie could see, came from somewhere up on Cape York.

Leaving the ice-cream shop, Leslie's eyes had met Claudine's as each put an arm around a sleek, dark-haired daughter. The girls were laughing and chattering as together they made their way back to the car.

Remembering all this now, he thought no, it wasn't too surprising that no-one had done anything for Garry.

'Yeah,' Leah was saying. 'Someone else's problem ...' On the Esplanade, the priests and the Levites had all continued passing by as Garry stopped fitting and lay dying, until Samaritans in the form of two young Dutch girls, tourists from one of the backpacker hostels, had paused, concerned. Then, though advised by some passing members of the public not to bother — "these black kids were all the same, just pissed" — they had insisted on knowing the local emergency number and calling it on their mobile phone. Garry had been by himself, on his way to the bus stop, going home to his family. Right now, Leslie could hear his mother and other relatives keening outside the autopsy room, anxious to be able to take him back for the last time to that home.

'His blood alcohol level was zero,' said Leah. 'Of course, we didn't expect anything different, though we have to do it. As are tests for illicit substances, I think?'

She raised an eyebrow at Laurie, who nodded.

'Unfortunately,' continued Leah, 'his Tegretol level is very low. Tegretol's the main anti-epileptic drug he was prescribed. Either he'd missed taking them, or he was sick with something else, a virus maybe, and he didn't absorb them. I'll be looking at sections of the stomach through the microscope, that might help work it out. "Aspiration of stomach contents and asphyxiation following a grand mal seizure." That's what I'll write on the death certificate. Nothing to worry your department after all, Leslie. There are a few other things I could write, in good plain prose, but they're not on my list of approved causes of death.'

Leah shook her head sadly. She placed Garry's brain in a silver kidney dish and passed it to Laurie, who would make the thin transparent slices that Leah would examine under her microscope. Then Laurie would return the brain to its cavity in the skull, stitch up the incisions, and with the help of Bert Cochrane, the embalmer from the funeral parlour, smooth and restore Garry's appearance for his last farewell.

'The family should be able to take him home late this afternoon,' Leah said to Laurie. 'I'll just finish off the paperwork.'

'Right. I'll put the tissues in to fix this afternoon, and do the slides next week ready for when you come back from your break.'

'You're off somewhere?' Leslie asked.

'Not exactly,' she answered. 'Come and have a coffee and I'll tell you about it.'

She pulled off her gown and gloves and ran a tap over her hands. Grateful for a change of scenery, Leslie kicked away the stool and followed her down the corridor away from the mortuary, to the pathology department itself and Leah's cluttered office with its view of the sea. Books and papers were piled on every available shelf, chair and table. On the floor, specimen jars showed slices of liver and pancreas, a large eye with the ocular muscles dissected and strung out like gauzy ribbons around it, and a strange collection of what looked like pickled grapes: hydatid cyst with daughter cysts, Leslie read on the label. He hadn't realised cysts too could have daughters.

Leah stepped over piled autopsy reports to reach a bench with mugs and coffee. She plugged in her percolator, then tipped a stack of journals off the nearest chair.

'Have a seat,' she said. Leslie eased himself past the piles of paper and into a canvas-backed chair. *They might be plain clothes*, Leah thought, eyeing his crisp white shirt and drill trousers, his close-cropped dark hair, *but there's no mistaking him for anything but a cop.*

'Sorry,' she apologised, moving the chair towards him, 'it's even worse than usual, I know! What's happening is that I'm in the process of moving out of the flat. I'm giving up living in town altogether, renting the flat out. I'm going to live on the island all the time now.'

'You'll stay on the island even during the week?' Leslie asked. 'And commute in? It's quite far.'

'Yes. I mean, yes, I'll commute, but it's not too far. An hour, really, from the top of the island into work. I don't mind the drive, love it in fact, and it's always a straight run if I leave later in the morning. If the weather's really bad, I can stay with friends here. Or I could work at home, I can do that at any time now — with the internet and email and fax, I've everything there. You know Zak's been at uni in Townsville since the beginning of the year. I only really stayed so long in town so he could finish school. And Micky, of course, is long gone.'

The percolator began to hiccup and the smell of fresh coffee drifted across the office, masking, to Leslie's relief, the pungent odour of formalin. He'd studied biology himself at university, but it had never been a favourite. And he'd just caught sight of what appeared to be a full set of male reproductive organs in a jar, the shrivelled snail of the penis sporting a broccoli-like growth.

'Nasty, I agree,' said Leah, following his gaze. 'Genital warts and donovanosis, though he died of something else, heart failure, I think. I just took the specimen out for the medical students, it's quite an old one.'

Old or not, Leslie thought, he himself would have found it salutary as a student. 'Have you got a tenant for the flat?' he asked.

'Yes, at least for a while. Dr Hassan.'

'Hassan? I don't think I know him.'

'He's the new paediatrician. Iraqi. You know they've been
trying to find another paed for a long time now, couldn't
get an Australian to come up here. The health department's
been advertising for quite a while. Ali's some sort of refugee
from Saddam Hussein. He's got a temporary visa. Despite
the fact that he's trained in London and he's a specialist who
wants to work here, the Immigration Department has treated
him like shit. And the Medical Board wasn't much better, I
gather. His right to practise is very restricted, he can work
in the public hospital here, but not in private practice. But
otherwise I don't know much about him, apart from the fact
that he seems perfectly competent.'

'He was an asylum seeker? He came in a leaking boat?'

'Mmm ... no, by plane, I think. A few months ago. He has
friends in Sydney, another paediatrician who recommended
him. I haven't heard that he's been in one of those camps.
Behind the razor wire. But maybe he has. He certainly has
no family here in town, that I do know. Elsewhere, I have no
idea. Anyway he's moving in this afternoon, I'm meeting him
at the flat to take the last of my stuff, and I've got a few days
off to sort it all out.' Then, seeing Leslie's raised eyebrows,
she said, 'Well, sort it a bit ... you know I couldn't live
somewhere really tidy.' She smiled. 'That was a problem for
my ex.' She paused, then added, 'One of many.'

She poured black coffee into mugs, set one beside Leslie
and rummaged for biscuits in a box by the window, then
said, 'I just have poor Garry's case to dictate, and a few bits
and pieces, then I'm off until the end of next week. Why
don't you all come out, you and Claudine and the girls, the
weekend after next, it's a long weekend. We can have lunch,
and the girls can swim. Maybe take the *Dolphin* for a sail, the
girls always like that.'

'We'd love to,' answered Leslie, 'though I'd better check
the diary with my social secretary. I'll get Claudine to ring

you.' He stirred sugar into his coffee and took a welcome sip. 'Actually, Leah, while we're on the subject of Rookwood ...'

'Yes,' she responded absently. Then, as he did not continue, she turned to look directly at him, turned so that against the light from the window, her face was in shadow. For a moment longer, he did not speak.

He wanted to ask her about Brian Mitchell. He just wanted to know, well, what she thought about Brian these days. She'd known Mitchell longer than anyone else in this town. She'd grown up with him, her family had lived on the island with him when she was a child. He would ask, just generally, her opinion of Brian.

There was, though, the problem of that longstanding bitterness between the Rookwoods and the Mitchells over the fact that Brian's father wouldn't return his share of the island to Leah's father after the war, even though that had been the agreement with old Dr Thomas Rookwood, and Leah's father, who was Thomas's son, had the money by then. At least, that was how Leslie had heard it. And then Brian had built the resort, despite the protests of Leah's father, Dr Charles. Leah herself had always seemed to Leslie quite unhassled by the resort's presence on the island, but perhaps she might have reason to be biased. With allegations of a criminal matter though, she should be impartial, he thought. But then he wasn't planning to give her any specific criminal information ... well, he had very little himself. The anonymous telephone informant to the Police Department's hotline had been specific, but very sparing with the details.

'Well, not Rookwood exactly,' he said now to her. 'I really want to ask you what you think about Brian Mitchell.'

He was looking towards her as he spoke. She was still a good-looking woman, he thought, her dark hair now cut to curl about her face, which was relaxing into comfortable lines as she grew through her forties. She'd always seemed unfazed by her forensic work, so he was surprised now by her reaction to Mitchell's name. She turned sharply, and as the light caught her eyes, Leslie saw, for a fraction of a second, both fear and revulsion. Then she quickly composed herself.

'Brian?' she asked coolly.

'Yes, we've had one or two rumours reach us. I can't tell you exactly what. I just wondered, off the record, about your opinion of him.'

'Rumours of what? Sharp business practice? He's got a good accountant and an even better lawyer. He'll always stay two steps ahead.'

'Yep,' said Leslie, 'I know that. This is something different. Though definitely criminal, if it were true. I'd ask you to keep quiet about my interest in him, though.'

'I see,' she said thoughtfully, although in fact she looked perplexed. She sat down and sipped her coffee before adding slowly, 'Well, I can only tell you what you probably know already. About the Mitchells and Rookwood. Though my mother was a Mitchell, there's no love lost between the two families. Brian's father and grandfather were family solicitors to my father and grandfather. You've heard the story, more than once.'

It was all much as Leslie had thought. Leah's grandfather, Thomas, had been the son of the original John Rookwood, who'd bought the island for half nothing from the colonial government of Queensland, way back at the time of the Cooktown gold rush, when people had swarmed up here thinking the gold would last forever and Cooktown would be the Paris of the Southern Hemisphere. (And, Leah noted, with not a thought for the traditional owners whose land it had been for thousands of years.)

The gold soon ran out, but the Rookwoods kept the island. Thomas had lost virtually everything in the Depression of the 1930s except the island itself. Brian's grandfather,

Ernest, offered to buy a piece of the island to help Thomas out. It was supposed to be a kind of gentlemen's agreement, Leah explained, that if and when the Rookwoods had money again — and they had three sons then, it seemed likely they would — the money would be repaid and the land revert to the Rookwoods. But when Charles, the only surviving son, tried to get it back once he was practising medicine, long after Thomas was dead, Brian's father refused, even though Charles had offered much more than the land was considered worth at the time — and it did still seem to Leslie a surprisingly small sum. Brian's father never used their land himself, although by then he had seen that it could be valuable, which it hadn't been when Thomas sold it. Nothing was written down that committed him to giving it back. And then when he died, the land became Brian's, and Brian decided to build the resort, and there was nothing Charles could do to stop it. And the rest, as Leah said, finishing her story, was history.

'Yes,' Leslie nodded at all this. 'And Brian himself?'

'Well, as you know he's a clever businessman. He worked hard building up the resort, I'll say that for him. There were some buildings there, the lighthouse keeper's house and part of a small hospital from the war. But he worked hard renovating that, he and his first wife, Deborah. All the wives have been Deborah, or Debbie, must make it easier for him in bed ... Anyway, they established the resort, that's when I was a kid, and then they got divorced. Suddenly he moved up from being an owner–manager who lived where he worked and became a real estate entrepreneur. A real eighties thing. Now he builds canal estates and owns hotels on the Gold Coast, and juggles paper money in ways I couldn't even imagine. Around here he's still well-known because of the resort and the upmarket image it has now. I wouldn't say he's considered popular or even respectable, but that wouldn't worry him. But you must know all that, Leslie?'

'Yes, well, I guess I meant more ... at the family level? Do you get on with him?'

'In truth,' Leah answered slowly, 'I've never liked him.' She must choose her words carefully here, she thought. No need, really, to have Leslie twig that there was any more in her aversion to Brian than that family saga. It had been many years now since she'd smelt that mixture of sweat and Old Spice, or felt her stomach churn with nausea when someone mentioned Brian's name or she caught sight of him in the distance on Rookwood. No need for her to think of it all again now.

'He's certainly family,' she said, 'he must be a second cousin or something. But he's a bully, he has a really unpleasant streak in him. The time I knew him best was when I was still a child, when he lived all the time on Rookwood. He's much older than me, ten years at least.

'I'll tell you a story about Brian, it's one of my earliest memories. It would have been just when they were building the resort. I would have been nine or ten, and he was about twenty. He used to come to the house because, although my father couldn't stand him, my mother was always impressed by those Mitchells, and she even took Brian's side over the resort business. Thought it would bring "her kind of people" up here.

'I had a bird, a green parrot called Perry. I found him on the path to the beach, he had an injured wing. He lived on the veranda overlooking the sea, and at night he was put in a cage, to protect him from snakes, supposedly. One Saturday morning, Brian came up early to the house and he called me out of the kitchen to look in the cage. He was laughing like mad. And in the cage was a large diamond python that had squeezed itself in — y'know they can flatten themselves almost two-dimensional? The snake had eaten Perry, who then made such a big bulge in the snake's gut that it couldn't get back out and was stuck halfway out of the cage. Poor Perry could still be seen fluttering beneath the snake's skin. Brian was laughing as if it was the funniest thing he'd ever seen. I began to cry, I was also scared of the snake, but Brian just laughed and laughed and poked at the stuck snake with the rod we used for closing the veranda shutters. My father came out, he didn't say much, he would never argue with Brian directly, especially in front of me, but I knew he was hopping mad.'

The memory of her father flooded back, in the old army khaki shorts he always wore on weekends and a faded, red-checked flannel shirt. His feet were bare and he had carefully placed his tin mug of tea on the veranda rail before taking the rod from Brian's hands.

'I'll fix this, Mitchell,' was all he'd said, and though Brian continued to guffaw, he'd walked back down the veranda steps and off down the hill, while her father left the snake to calm down and found a gunny bag under the house.

'Dad put the snake in a sack and took it away. By then Perry had become quite still so Dad let the snake go in the bush, and later he found me another parrot, Perry the Second. But that incident always summed up Brian for me.'

'Yeah,' said Leslie, smiling slightly at this story, 'that fits with what I've seen of him. He doesn't seem to have changed much.' There were reports, Leslie knew, several of them, of Mitchell coming to blows with waiters and taxi drivers. One incident in the casino, where Mitchell had dislocated a doorman's shoulder, had almost reached court, avoided at the last moment by a large chunk of cash from Mitchell's lawyer. 'What about since then?' Leslie asked. 'I've never come across him at your place, or even heard you talk about him that I can remember. Do you mix with them when they're up here, Brian and his current wife?'

'His fourth. I've met her maybe twice. She doesn't come to the island much. Even the first Deborah, the mother of his children, I hardly knew. You'll have to be more specific,' Leah finished quite sharply. She looked hard at Leslie. 'If you want my professional opinion on something, I'll give it impartially. But I'd have to have details. And personally, I'll admit I don't like Brian, but fortunately I hardly have to see him these days. He comes and goes from Brisbane, his main home is down there, and he has some kind of large estate near the Gold Coast as well. The wives and children almost never come here. Even when he's on Rookwood he stays in the resort, takes their launch or a helicopter into town, and spends a lot of time in the casino, I believe. So it's not a problem for me. I wouldn't have him at the house, I wouldn't invite him there. But I wouldn't cut him dead in the street, either.'

Leslie drained the last of his coffee, stood up and found his briefcase.

'Well,' he said, 'I won't ask any more of you, Leah. We have heard something, but there may be no substance to it. We often get anonymous allegations against people that turn out to be absolute bulldust, and this might be one of them. Thanks for the coffee. I take it someone will fax through the report on Garry? And I'll get Claudine to give you a ring, we'll really look forward to a day at Rookwood next week.'

He waved goodbye to her and made his way to the door, down the corridor that led away from the autopsy room and out into the sunlight. There was a crowd around the street door of the mortuary. Garry's extended family. One tall, good-looking lad stood slightly aside. Leslie recognised him as Kevin Brown, a member of the Cairns Dance group. He must be a cousin of the dead Garry. Kevin was slim, with a dancer's straight build, but right now he was trembling, hugging his arms about himself, and his expression, Leslie saw, was of anger as well as grief. He seemed to be trying with all his strength to hold that anger pressed within him.

There was a general murmur from the crowd as Leslie was recognised, and some people called hello, and he nodded and acknowledged the greetings. Even Kevin slightly raised an eyebrow. Not everybody in town liked Leslie, he knew that — well, he was after all a copper — but many respected him. And sometimes, it seemed to Leslie, that he got points just for not being a whitefella. Leslie's family had moved to Melbourne from Sri Lanka when he was ten. His own skin was the same shade as Kevin's, his hair was the same close-cut curling black, though his eyes were grey-green, the light-coloured eyes of his Ceylon Burgher parents.

He climbed into his car, and on his way back to his office at the end of Sheridan Street, Leslie thought over what he had just heard. And he was convinced that Leah Rookwood could actually tell him more about the character of Brian Mitchell and his possible activities than she had so far revealed.

2

Sitting by Benjy's bed in the children's ward, Ina Frazer watched as Dr Ali Hassan moved slowly on his rounds. Slowly, Ina noted, because with each child, Ali would sit down on the bed, hold out a hand, talk and listen. Listen to the child, talk with the parents and grandparents. Dr Hassan, Ina could hear, spoke very precise English, but with an unfamiliar accent, the words running up and down almost like a song. When he spoke, he did as her own people did, not looking directly at the person he was speaking to, which was the habit of most of the white people Ina knew, but politely, slightly away, though he heard every word that was said. He seemed a gentle man, that was a good thing for a kids' doctor. He asked everyone, kids and families, where they came from, and seemed to want detail in their answers. How exactly did you get here from that island up in the Torres Strait, or that little town way out west near the Gulf, he wanted to know. Was it a jet plane and did you get to see the pilot? Do you catch a lot of fish up there where your home is? Do you sometimes skip school to go fishing?

Dr Hassan's registrar, propped against the trolley of case notes, watched, and somewhat less than patiently. She had a million better things to do. Her pager shrilled and, rolling her eyes at her boss to indicate the urgency of the call, she slipped away. Ali continued to sit unperturbed on Benjy's bed, deep in conversation, happy to finish the round on his own.

Benjy had been in the ward nearly two weeks now. Originally he'd been in High Dependency, very sick with meningitis. They had thought at first they might lose him. He'd been given the newest, most potent antibiotics in an intravenous drip. Even now, with his fever down and him eating well, there was still some question of residual brain damage. But he was completely transformed from the thin, shivering kid with the arched neck and painful stare of a fortnight before.

Ali had not previously met the elderly Black woman now sitting at Benjy's side. Her grey hair was brushed back and held with silver combs, she wore a freshly ironed print dress and, squinting through thick glasses, she'd been reading to Benjy: *How the Kangaroos got their Tails.* She closed the book as Ali arrived.

'You're Benjy's grandmother?' he asked.

'No, Doc, just a friend of the family. His Mum, family, gone downstairs, see his Mum's brother died, young, you know. He had epilepsy, he died just out on the Esplanade there, nobody realised he was in trouble until too late. So she has business to attend to. I'm here for the moment to keep an eye on Benjy. I'm Ina.'

'Well, Ina, madam, he will be ready for home in a day or so. But first the ear doctor will have another look at him. Maybe later today. We think that's where the infection came from, his ears and maybe his tonsils, and that then it spread into his head. We don't want that to happen again.'

'No, sure, Doc.'

'And he needs building up ... he's still too thin, and of course he gets asthma.'

"Yes, Doc ... we've got a special program at the school, breakfast for all the kids who come along. I'll make sure his Mum brings him. She's got a lot of kids to look after, it's hard for her.'

She eyed him placidly for a moment, then asked: 'Where do *you* come from, Dr Ali?'

He smiled slightly, now that the questioning was turned on him. 'Iraq,' he answered. It was as good an answer as any. Would she have even heard of it?

'Hmmm. Arabic is it you speak? Are you one of those refugees?'

'Well ... sort of.' He laughed, then said defensively, 'Yes, I do speak Arabic, it's my first language. But I think I can speak English too. And I can tell you I'm a properly trained doctor. I wouldn't be here if I wasn't.' No need to explain that he had the job because white Australian doctors preferred the big cities.

'Oh,' she said, 'sorry, I didn't mean anything like that. I've seen you looking after Benjy. I know you're a good doctor. I know that doctors aren't always whitefellas. And you speak really good English.'

He smiled then. 'Thank you. Actually, I've lived a long time in England. I haven't spoken Arabic much for years.'

'Ah,' she replied, 'that explains it. England. I've never been there. Seen pictures in books. Often thought about it. Now I guess I never will go.' She continued to study him carefully, and after a moment asked, 'You come in one of those boats? Spend time in one of those camps?'

'No, I came by plane ... and I have a visa, I wasn't put in a camp. Though I do know many people who are there. They are my friends.' After a moment he added, 'Most of them just like me.'

He's smiling, but I can tell he's serious. Well, you would be serious, she thought, from what she'd heard about those places. He wasn't like any white man she'd ever met, sort of sad, haunted you might say, beneath the gentleness. He was a lean man, with skin colour a bit lighter than her own, she noted, but the shape of his face and nose were different — no one up here would ever mistake him for a Black person, nor a dark white man either for that matter. To Ina, he seemed somewhere in between. The Iraqis she'd seen on television either looked just like that Saddam Hussein, fleshy and with thick moustaches, or they were covered in long white robes. Dr Ali was different again, though he did have the moustache.

She said, 'Yes, I read about all that in the newspapers. And about how that George Bush might send his army into your country too, after he's finished with those Taliban, I read about those Taliban.' She looked hard at him, then added, 'It's a funny thing, white people been coming here, just coming and walking in, for two hundred years. When they first came to this country, they just arrived and took over. With the gold, that's what brought them here first. Gold, and then cattle. Everything else followed. Never asking if they could come, just coming. Now suddenly there's people like you, from places where bad things are happening, and they're saying "No, *you* can't come", and locking them up in the desert. Did your friends come on one of those boats?'

'Some of them. I was luckier. Because I'm a doctor and I had money to pay, I didn't need to bribe anyone when I left Iraq. Which was actually quite a while ago now. And I have a friend, a doctor in Sydney, who helped me, helped me a lot.'

'You got family here?' Ina asked, and he flushed, and said no, and nothing more, so she didn't persist. She thought to herself, *Maybe they are dead, maybe I shouldn't have asked that.* He was a very good doctor, she'd seen that, calm and quiet, squatting down, gently lifting the sheets off Benjy, telling him what he was going to do before he did it, letting the little boy see the stethoscope before he put the cold steel against his thin chest. Ina had seen a lot of doctors in her lifetime and they hadn't all been good. This one took time to tell Ina what Benjy must do to stay better. He must take antibiotics each night, probably for a long time, and use the ear drops. Drink plenty of water and milk, not fizzy stuff. And eat good tucker, build himself up. *All good sensible advice*, Ina thought.

Ali opened the boy's case notes and jotted down his orders for today. *I was lucky*, he was thinking, *that I came when I did. Before the Americans decided to go into Iraq as well, which now seemed certain, just a matter of months or even weeks. Otherwise it might have been much more difficult, no matter how much they wanted doctors up here. I might be in one of those camps. Or even on the plane back to Jordan.* As it was, he'd spent many weeks in London and Sydney, with forms, interviews, more forms. The same questions, over and over again. He'd spent hours waiting, his backside numbed by the plastic chairs of the High Commission, re-reading the day's newspapers, waiting for his name to come up on the screen so he could tell a little bit more of his story to yet another disinterested face beyond a wide desk. A face whose eyes would never be raised to meet his. The eyes kept low not from respect, as people like Ina did here, and most women in Iraq always did. His wife Muna, for example, had always lowered her gaze when she spoke. No, not from respect, but from disdainful boredom, even though the face was paid well to do the job. He'd finally been given a visa in London, only to find a fresh set of obstacles to negotiate with the medical registration people when he reached Sydney. Except for the fact that he could go back each night to Colin's house, and talk to Colin and Sue, he would have given up.

'Jeez,' Colin would say, pouring them both a beer on his balcony, with its view of the beach, 'the bastards, I can't believe what they're putting you through to do this job.' He and Colin had been registrars together in England; Colin was the one who had suggested the post.

'Jeez, Ali,' Colin said, 'you're actually doing them a favour. They've been looking for another paediatrician up there for more than a year. Nobody else wants the job, yet they behave like you're an urban terrorist not a doctor.'

Passing long days in their apartment, Ali had shopped and cooked for them — all those things he'd had to learn so quickly in his first months alone in England. He prepared Arab dishes, kebabs and foul beans, lamb shanks and chickpeas — trying to repay their kindness. In the end, when he finally got his registration and the ticket north, he'd been with them four weeks.

Some days, while he was waiting for yet more paperwork to come through the fax machine or the computer, he took the train to Sydney's western suburbs, to Villawood, queued outside the Immigration Department's detention centre, and after many more hours of waiting, was allowed through the four sets of computer-controlled doors so that he could spend a few minutes with one or two of the Iraqis detained there. There was a psychologist he remembered from his days at the Children's Teaching Hospital in Iskan, and a woman whose father had taught his cousin Mehmet Ali at a primary school near Basra. So yes, it was as he had told Ina, he had friends inside. On his last night in Sydney, at dinner with Colin and Sue, they'd drunk champagne to his future in Cairns; earlier that day, leaving Villawood, he'd embraced Abduldawood, his wife Aktar, and their three-year-old son who had known no home but the detention camp, and promised he would not forget them.

For weeks though, after he'd first arrived up here, temporary specialist paediatrician to the hospital and the vast area of north Queensland it served, he could not bring himself to unpack his bag. He'd lived out of his one suitcase open on the floor of his hotel room, convinced that at any moment someone, some Australian doctor with a proper right to the job, would appear. Then his visa would be revoked, and he'd be given a one-way ticket to Baghdad. This was how he had lived in England for the past six years — always in hospital or hostel rooms, always moving on. Slowly he understood that this would not happen here, he was as experienced as any Australian graduate, his work was good. His colleagues were not unfriendly, and he began to breathe more easily.

He would get out of bed early each day, and walk on the path they called the Esplanade, along by the water, before the sun came up. Back in Jordan, in the first year of his exile, and in Baghdad where he had lived so long before that, and in the small town to the south of Baghdad where he was born, it would be the time of the first *salat*, the prayers of the day. The drawn-out call of the muezzin issued from a thousand mosque speakers: God is Great. Soon the hot rays of a brand new sun would turn the sky to gold: *al fajr* — the dawn. Ali himself did not pray like that, had pretty much abandoned public prayer once he first went to England, and given it up for good when his brother had died.

Here in the mornings by the water there were no prayers, just the cries of seagulls and an occasional jet overhead, but the early day was just as golden. There were wisps of cloud lingering on the mountains that encircled the bay, and the thick buffalo grass of the Esplanade's lawns squelched from the attention of the municipal sprinklers. A few people he saw each morning on his walk began to smile at him, and sometimes asked, 'How's it going?' which seemed to be the normal greeting here, a kind of *Salan!* though it did not seem that a reply was necessary. None of his medical colleagues had invited him to their homes — well, so what, in his last six years in England, no English person ever invited him home — but in the hospital, they drank tea or coffee with him, and occasionally asked vaguely about where he came from, though they did not stay to hear the answer. *Why should they?* Ali thought. He came from far away, he looked different, his accent was different. He was content just to sit and drink tea with these people, as he had once done in the doctors' dining room of his Baghdad hospital, to hear their talk of cricket and fishing. Politics, life beyond the town, even September 11 and the events that had followed, which had so convulsed the outside world, seemed hardly touched on in these tearoom conversations.

Today he would take another step. Benjy was the last patient on his ward round this afternoon. Ali had a few more things to sort out, then he was meeting Dr Rookwood at her flat. Today he was moving into that flat, moving to a place of his own. He would completely unpack his suitcase for the first time in six years. He, Ali Hassan, would be the tenant of an apartment in Cairns, Australia.

He looked around, but his registrar seemed to have disappeared. Never mind, he would take the trolley of case notes back to the nurses' desk himself.

'I'll see you again tomorrow, and we'll decide when you can go home,' he told Benjy, and, standing up, nodded goodbye to Ina.

He trundled the trolley towards the door of the ward, and was surprised to see Ina walking in towards him. He'd just left her sitting beside Benjy ... And in fact, turning, he saw that she was there still, and this was a second woman, so alike they must be identical twins, though Ina carried a little more weight. The second woman didn't have Ina's thick glasses. She wore a plain blue dress and carried a basket of fruit — bananas and pawpaw — and a milkshake in a paper cup, which she handed to Benjy.

From beside Benjy's bed, Ali heard Ina's deep laugh, and she called out, 'Don't worry, Doc, happens to everyone the first time they see us both together!'

He waved to them both, and their laughter followed him down the corridor in the direction of the tearoom. He was smiling himself. He was beginning to feel, just a little, like a part of this place.

3

Late afternoon, her day's work completed, Leah closed her office door and made her way to the car park, her laptop slung over her shoulder and her arms around a pile of notes she was planning to work on during her days off. She threw the lot into the back of the square yellow Land Rover — thirty years old, inherited from her father, his pride and joy. Manoeuvring out of the parking spot, she changed gear noisily and headed along the Esplanade and into the palm-edged driveway of the apartment block, where Dr Ali Hassan was hovering uncertainly on the front steps beside a single black suitcase.

'Hi!' she called through the open window as she parked the car. 'You didn't go in yet? I did give you the key?'

'Oh yes, you did — I thought it best to wait for you.'

'Come on up then.' She led the way into the foyer. 'I've only a few more things to collect, then I'll be off and it will be all yours.'

'It's most kind of you,' he murmured, standing back for her to enter the lift.

'Not at all,' Leah replied briskly. 'You're doing me a favour. I don't have to get an agent, I know you'll pay the rent, and you won't be here forever.' Then bit her tongue on her last remark, seeing the blush across his cheekbones. Of course. He was here on a temporary visa.

'What I mean is,' she added hastily, 'we hope that you'll be able to stay here and find your own place. We really need you here.'

He shook his head ruefully. 'My future here is very uncertain,' he said. 'I'm allowed to stay because it's an "area of need". Three years at the most. By which time, your Mr Ruddock apparently thinks all the problems in Iraq will be solved.' Ruddock was the country's Immigration Minister.

Ali's English was perfect, the accent almost British, she thought, but with an extra lilt. Perhaps because he spoke Arabic, which she had heard was a poetic language. 'Oh, he's not my Mr Ruddock,' said Leah forcefully.

They emerged from the lift and she unlocked the door to the apartment. It was at the front of the building on the sixth floor, with a view across the Esplanade and the bay to the mountains covered by rainforest that surrounded the town. At this moment, the apartment looked far better than it ever had when she'd lived there herself — all her clutter, and her children's, had been moved in tea-chests back to the island, and the cleaners had been in, and a painter to touch up the kitchen. The living room was literally sparkling in the afternoon sunshine.

'I don't support Ruddock at all,' Leah said, 'and I think what his department does is appalling, though it all seems a bit far away from us up here. I think you're the first person from Iraq I've ever met. Very few refugees have come so far north.'

Ali did not respond immediately. He had crossed the room and was gazing out through the locked French doors, across the terrace, at the sea.

'It is truly magnificent,' he said. Eyeing him behind, Leah thought, *When he's relaxed like that he's not bad looking.* She had met him several times around the hospital, she had shown him the apartment, but until Leslie's

questioning, she hadn't really considered him personally. He
was taller and slimmer than she would have imagined for an
Iraqi. Though her knowledge of Iraqis was confined pretty
much to the evening news, pictures of Saddam Hussein and
other stout moustachioed gentlemen. Certainly Ali wore a
moustache, but it was smaller and neater than Saddam's. He
had springy black hair, curled tight against his scalp. He wore
a dark green shirt and black trousers — more formal than
most men up here who, for the working day, donned shorts
or light-coloured cotton trousers, and open-necked shirts in
subdued checks. The deep bottle green of the shirt suited
his colouring ... Not much sense of humour, though, she
suspected.

'Yes, it's a good view,' she said. 'Open the doors, if you
like, it's yours now. And there's coffee, milk and so on that I
left in the kitchen.' She pushed open the door to the laundry.
'There are clean sheets and towels in the dryer,' she said. 'I'll
just take them out.'

She stood in the laundry a moment, folding sheets, then
carried the pile back into the living room. Ali had unlocked
the doors and stepped out onto the terrace. Warm air flowed
into the room, bringing with it the scent of the gardenias
flowering in pots on the terrace. The flowers were early this
year, the result of the hot dry winter. Leah followed Ali onto
the terrace. Beyond the Esplanade, the tide was far out. Ibis
and spoonbills stood happily ankle-deep in mud, surrounded
by their supper. On the grass, a flock of cooperative pelicans
posed for Japanese tourists, then waited expectantly for
rewards.

Leah looked down and laughed.

'My kids used to feed potato chips to the pelicans,' she
said, 'when they lived here. They do well for themselves,
those birds, I'm sure they put on a special act for tourists.'

Ali watched as a young Japanese girl held out a piece of hamburger to an inquisitive bill. 'Both your children have left home now?' he asked.

'Yes,' she said, 'my daughter's in Brisbane, and my son's in Townsville at the university. And as I think you know, I'm divorced.'

She expected him to volunteer some personal detail of his own then, but he stood silently, still watching the pelicans, and, afraid of the answers, she could not ask in turn, do you have children? A wife? Or *did you?*

To cover this silence she said, 'Your English is perfect. I suppose you learnt in Iraq?'

'Well, originally. My parents always used to listen to the BBC World Service, and made us listen too, as children, so our accents would be good. But I've been working in Britain for the past six years. And I'd been there before. I've spent ten years there altogether.'

'Oh, I'm sorry, that sounds really silly of me, then. I somehow had the idea you'd just come from Iraq recently. So you were working in England a long time?'

'Yes. Doing locums. It's very hard for non-English doctors to get consultant posts there.'

Leah nodded. She knew this was so. Foreign doctors were welcome to work away for years on the lower rungs of the ladder that led to medical specialisation, but when they tried to climb higher, found those rungs slippery indeed. 'You were in London?' she asked.

'I was mostly around the south,' Ali said. 'That's the part I knew best, from when I first went there years ago. I had a scholarship from the British Council to go to London for three months. To improve my English. I was supposed to go straight back to Iraq, but I got to know London then, and I wanted to stay. That was more than twenty years ago.'

'Your accent is really quite BBC!'

'Thank you. The British Council would be glad to hear that, if nothing else, they succeeded with my accent!' After a moment, he added with a smile, 'Despite the fact that I had a Welsh girlfriend!'

So he did have a sense of humour, Leah thought, smiling too.

'Well, when I was in London that first time, I found it was possible to stay and work there,' Ali continued. 'Visas and work permits were much easier then. They needed foreign doctors to run the National Health Service. And things in Iraq were starting to become difficult.' He stopped and looked back at her. 'You know about my country, about Saddam Hussein?'

'A little. At least, I know a bit about Hussein.'

'Well, he was just coming to the leadership at that time. It was a good time not to be in my country. And I loved London, then.' He stopped. *Then*, he thought, *I loved it then*. He'd spent four years in the city. 'Have you worked in England?' he asked.

'No — though many Australian doctors did train there. I have been to conferences ...' There had been no chance of her training abroad. Gareth had already been in surgical training in Brisbane when they had married, he had not wanted a career wife and she had only worked in a couple of resident jobs before she was pregnant with Micky.

'I didn't start my pathology training until after I was divorced. My ex-husband was — is — an orthopaedic surgeon.' Ali listened carefully to this, but asked no more.

Hesitantly, Leah broached another subject: 'Your family? You didn't marry the Welsh woman?'

'No.' His tone was muted. 'She married someone else. My family were all still in Iraq, they wanted me to go back there.' They had expected him to stay only a few months in England. 'And so, at that time, I went. For various reasons.'

Various reasons? He had finished his exams, he was a paediatrician, he was needed in Iraq. His father was arranging the marriage to Muna. The *qassima*, the marriage contract, was already drawn up. It had been the obvious thing to do.

But only one reason, really. Funny, he thought, that was still one of the hard things about being here. As it had been in Britain. Hearing her name so often. The aloneness was nothing, the aloneness he had grown used to now, after all those years waiting, in Jordan and in England. In Australia as in England, he'd found he did not particularly miss not speaking Arabic, did not miss the sounds and smells of the streets and the *suq*. But hearing her name, suddenly, unexpectedly, in the course of the working day, that was hard. Though naturally, it was never *her* name, it was simply a common name here, an English name, the name of the charge nurse in the children's ward, for example, and the girl on the switch. 'I'll just ask Di', 'Hello, this is Diane speaking.' Each time it happened, after so long, he still felt that tremor in his chest that was the sudden rise and fall of hope. In that tremor was the memory of his thighs pressing into the small of her back, and of how he'd held his arms around her and joked about her putting on weight, that last morning in the little flat behind Euston Station. He had never been able to hold his wife that way.

'My wife?' He realised suddenly that Leah had asked a question. 'No,' he said, 'I have no wife now. My wife died some years ago. I have no close family now in Iraq.'

The statement was final. Leah could only murmur softly, 'I'm sorry,' and stand beside him on the balcony, sharing the sight of the genial birds on the grass below.

This woman doctor was kind, Ali thought, but he did not know her well, and they were alone in her flat. He could not tell her about Muna, or describe even the simple facts of his life. He could not explain that there had been the accident.

Well, perhaps an accident. Out there, in the desert, beneath the merciless sun of midday, among the sandstorms, who could say what had happened? He could not talk to her of Zahra'a and his plans for her, and of how instead she had married the Frenchman.

He must keep all of this to himself.

The afternoon sun was turning the sea a deep gold. Leah said carefully, 'Looking down here, where it's so peaceful — and safe — where I've spent so much time with my own children, I cannot imagine what it has been like in Iraq.'

After a moment he answered, 'In fact, you may be surprised to learn that Iraq is also very beautiful. Even the desert is beautiful, though what you might call stark. Where my family comes from is not desert, there are lots of orchards — apricots and figs grow, and further south, dates. All along the rivers — there are two big rivers, and some smaller ones — there are wonderful palm trees. I was very happy to see so many palm trees when I came here to Queensland, they remind me of where I grew up. And Iraqi people, though they have many problems now, underneath, they still know how to laugh. The regime, and the wars, and the sanctions, they made us resourceful, those of us who were left.'

Still watching the pelicans below, he thought, *What I must do is to learn to live in the present. I cannot change the past and I do not know the future. To have a moment like this, just looking out at the sea and those birds, well, I must take it as it comes.* And, he thought, there is no need for other people who were not involved to feel responsible, as Leah clearly did. What had happened in Iraq, the Gulf War, what might yet happen, such people could not change that. Maybe whole countries could do it, the United Nations perhaps. Though he feared what America might do now in Iraq, feared it greatly. There were still cousins, in Basra and other towns, there were still the villages and countryside he remembered from his childhood. He did not want those things destroyed.

A pair of pigeons descended suddenly, dancing in the air above the balcony, and Ali, appreciating the diversion, turned towards them.

'Such pretty birds!' he remarked, as the two landed for a moment on the balcony rail and then made off again.

'Torres Strait pigeons,' Leah said. 'Yes, they are very pretty. It's spring, the time they come down here from Papua New Guinea. That's their courtship dance, all that fluttering. We often see them over on the island, they like the mangroves that grow along the coast there.'

'You have lived a long time on your island?' he asked.

'My family owned the island, most of it, for four generations, counting me and my sister. The house on the island is our real home. We lived here during the week while my children were at school. Gareth, my ex-husband, bought this flat originally — it was not my choice.' Why did she say that, she wondered. There was nothing wrong with the flat, in fact it was a very desirable residence. Funny that she still felt the need to distance herself from Gareth. 'But five years ago, my sister Mara and I gave back almost all of the island to the traditional owners, the Aboriginal people whose country is along the mainland there. Mara lives in Sweden, so I own the house that my family built, and some land around it. There's a tourist resort on one end on land that once belonged to my family. I can come and go to the island as much as I want and so can the traditional owners. My daughter works in Brisbane, and my son is doing medicine — we're a long line of doctors, I'm afraid. But they come back often, both my children. In fact, I expect Zak, my son, up here on a late flight tonight for the mid-semester break. I'm taking the last of my stuff to Rookwood now, then coming back in to collect him."

Ali turned to look at the sea. 'Can you see the island from here?' he asked.

'No — it's about an hour from here, a drive and then a boat trip. It's not far out to sea,. It's not really part of the Great Barrier Reef. It's rainforest and beach, like a little piece of the mainland. To get there, I drive up to the edge of a bay where I keep a boat to get across. The first Dr Rookwood — John — came up to Queensland to Cooktown in the gold rush in the 1870s. Cairns was just a small settlement then, it grew up afterwards, when the gold ran out at Cooktown, which it quickly did. Cooktown never grew the way it was thought it would, and Cairns grew instead, as a port for sugar and for the farms on the Tablelands, and now as a tourist destination.'

'You go by boat to the island? There is no bridge?'

'No,' she laughed, 'no bridge at all, and hopefully there never will be. It's less than a kilometre across to Rookwood, and only a very few people live on the island. There are no roads, only tracks, no cars. The resort, Mitchells, which is quite upmarket and expensive, has their own boats that go over from the wharf in town here, and a helicopter pad. That's all at the other end of the island from my house and has nothing to do with me.'

They had moved back into the living room. Now Leah, picking up the folded washing, said, 'You must come out and see the island for yourself.'

'I would like that very much.'

Leah remembered her invitation to Leslie. 'I have some friends coming a week on Sunday,' she said. 'Why don't you come too, if you're not on call?'

'Thank you,' he said. 'But how should I get there? I have as yet no car.'

'My friends could bring you, I'm sure,' she replied. 'Leslie Fernando. He's a policeman. A detective.'

'A policeman?' Ali's response was immediate and there was no mistaking the apprehension in his tone.

'Oh, it's all right ...' she began to say, and then stopped. She had been going to say 'Ali, this is *Australia*' when she remembered a scene from the previous night's television news. Iraqis behind a high wire fence. Guards and dogs. That was also *Australia*. 'What I mean is, you don't need to be concerned about Leslie's job. I work with him, he's been a friend for years. He's from Sri Lanka, though he grew up in Australia.'

Still, though, Ali looked doubtful. What, Leah wondered, had he experienced at the hands of police? In Iraq or in England?

With uncharacteristic neatness, she placed the folded washing on the kitchen bench and began to sort out tea towels from sheets. Ali watched, hesitant. He seemed so alone, Leah thought. There was just his single suitcase in the clean and ordered flat, now swept bare of the litter that had made it her city home — Micky's discarded swimsuits, Zak's empty choc-milk containers, the CDs both her children scattered about. And he won't come to the island, she saw, he thinks the invitation is only out of politeness. Had anyone else in the hospital thought to invite him home at all? People were all so busy, they had their own lives and families and relationships. He'd been here two months at least, she'd spoken to him several times about mutual cases, she'd arranged to rent the apartment to him, and yet only now had she learnt that apparently he had lost all of his family in Iraq.

It occurred to her then: she could ask him now, right now, this evening. She was going back to Rookwood, she had Zak to collect later. On this impulse she said, 'Why don't you come out with me now and see the island yourself? It's very pleasant at this time of day. We could have something to eat there, potluck from my fridge, and then I could drop you back. I have to come back in to the airport anyway, you see. *And* the invitation for Sunday week still holds!'

He did not immediately reply and she went on, 'Look, you'd be useful, I have to get all this stuff into the car, and from the wharf across and up to the house. I'd really appreciate some help.'

He brightened then. No, nobody had invited him, she was sure. And in fact, he seemed intelligent and interesting, spending a couple of hours with him, taking him to Rookwood, would not be just a rather tedious obligation fulfilled. There was cheese and plenty of salad in her fridge. And more than enough ham and sausages waiting for Zak. But Ali must be a Muslim. No pork. Some smoked salmon, then, in the bottom of the fridge, she remembered. And beer? Did he drink? He did seem quite, well, westernised, and he'd lived a long time in England. She could offer.

'Well thank you. If you are sure I can help you. I haven't really been out of the town since I arrived.'

She pointed to the cartons of books stacked by the front door.

'Seriously, I could do with your assistance. Can you bring those down to the car? We'll need two trips in the lift. Then we'll lock up here and be off.'

4

Leah took the wheel as Ali climbed into the seat beside her, glancing to take in the contents in the back of the vehicle. The Land Rover was piled high with cartons from which books and assorted goods spilled.

Leah laughed. 'It's been much worse than that,' she said.

They drove out through the suburbs and onto the highway leading north, past the Cairns airport where the Flying Doctors' tiny Beechcraft was just coming in to land. The noise of the car's old engine made conversation difficult, but Leah pointed at the little plane and raised her voice to remark to Ali, 'More work for somebody!' He smiled, turning to take in the view of the wide expanse of the Barron River once the airport was passed.

It had been an unusually dry winter, which meant that flowers were everywhere. Bougainvillea dripped purple and gold blossoms onto fences and verandas and climbed the eucalypts on the straggling roadside nature strips. There were pink lacebarks and scarlet flame trees. Dry brown grass showed how long it had been since any real rain had fallen.

'Within a month or so,' Leah said to Ali, 'the rains will start and that will transform all this, the grass will turn bright green and the sugar cane will shoot up.'

The suburbs were strung out beside the highway. Older houses, comfortable timber Queenslanders on stilts, stood high above new estates where breezeblock walls supported iron roofs of kookaburra blue and sunbird yellow. Then suddenly the houses ceased altogether and they were in the midst of sugarcane fields. Many fields had already been cut to stubble, and some were still smoky from burning-off so that the smell of warm caramel hung in the air. Ali stared at the cane trains standing at the edge of the fields on miniature rails, their trucks piled high with the chopped sweet sticks awaiting the mill. He had the use of a hospital car only when on call, he had explained to Leah, so he'd seen no more than the town itself.

Now mountains loomed up on their left, rainforest on their peaks, dry scrub on the lower slopes, with the cane fields spread at their feet. They crossed several khaki-coloured streams, the water sluggish at the end of the dry season. Every river and creek had its red and yellow crocodile warnings in English, German and Japanese. To their right were intermittent glimpses of the sea, and sometimes of mangrove swamps. There was little traffic to slow them down.

Looking sideways, Ali was able to take in more about Leah as she drove. Slim and tall, in her mid-forties he guessed. Not much make-up. Dark hair with a touch of grey at the roots. She'd slipped off her working clothes of earlier in the day —high-heeled sandals, a black jacket and skirt — and now wore a purple T-shirt with black trousers. Her feet were thrust into comfortable sneakers for driving and she'd wound a silky purple scarf around her neck. He thought she must have been a very pretty woman when she was younger. Well, she was not unattractive even now. She was self-assured, but not overly so, like some Australian women he had met and found intimidating. Of course, she was in her own land, driving her own car, to her own island, naturally she was self-assured. She was a good pathologist, he knew. He'd had several occasions to consult her and had found her willing to think carefully about an unexpected diagnosis. And she was very kind. He was well aware that his rent was below the market value of the flat, however easy and reliable a tenant he might prove.

They drove for more than half an hour, then Leah turned off to the right. A wide area of mangrove swamp soon gave way to a chocolate-coloured river — the Cassowary, she said. The road was bitumen but narrower than the highway, so they drove more slowly now. He was able to take in the occasional houses, all built high on the stilts common to the Queensland countryside, in deference to the climate, whose seasons he had learnt were just The Wet and The Dry, both of them very warm. These houses were brightly painted — terracotta, lolly-pink and peppermint — and surrounded by outbuildings, with tractors and cars and children's bikes scattered in the yards. The signs of normal family life. For a moment Ali felt his throat tighten. On their left, the bank of the river was close now, on their right a line of hibiscus formed a crimson hedge over which hung dark-leaved mango trees in vigorous flower.

Then the land on their left widened out, and Ali saw a café with a huge cement crocodile outside. Shops and a few houses huddled together by a bus shed, and road working equipment stood in a council depot behind a wire fence.

'This is Cassowary village,' Leah explained, 'our nearest town!'

She slowed and waved to a blonde woman of ample size walking a dog outside the café.

'That's Renee,' Leah explained, 'she and her husband Bill run the Big Croc café.'

Renee wore the largest pair of shorts Ali had ever seen. She smiled broadly and waved back at Leah. Leah did not stop, but drove on through the little township and onto a graded dirt track running parallel to the river's south bank. They bumped their way along for a kilometre through tall trees with papery skins. The river's muddy banks were now further apart and giving way to sand in some places. Finally, they came to the end of the track where a timber wharf jutted out into the sea. Leah stopped the car, and in the sudden silence, Ali looked out at all around him.

First he took in the beach. Stretching for miles back in the direction of Cairns was a wide swathe of white, clean-washed sand as fine as caster sugar. There was coarse shrubbery down to the edge of the sand, but no litter, no sign of urban existence, just waves washing in and retreating. Not real breakers because the sea here was sheltered by the reef a few miles out, Leah explained. About two hundred metres away from them was a rocky outcrop where a woman threw sticks for a dog, otherwise the beach was empty. It was, thought Ali, a place of immense peace. To walk here each day must surely be balm for the soul.

And then Rookwood Island ... Ali got out of the car and stood on the wharf, taking in the island as the claret-coloured rays of the sun setting in the west began to light up the clouds beyond Rookwood. The island rose straight from the sea about half a mile away. Ali could see how it must have appealed to Leah's ancestors. It appealed to him here and now.

It was a perfect size and shape, crowned by a funny red and white striped lighthouse on a flattened shelf of rock. There was a white beach, with a small wharf near a rocky headland at the right end of the beach. Mermaids Beach, Leah said, though no mermaids have ever been seen there. On the left, she pointed out the whitewashed buildings of the resort she called Mitchells, largely hidden by palms and bougainvillea. From the edge of the sand and rising almost to the island's peak was the tangled green of the rainforest.

Tied to the wharf where they were standing were several small boats, and a larger one painted bright red. Leah now climbed across into this and began hauling on a rope to bring it in close to the side of the wharf. Ali watched in some consternation, knowing nothing of boats, but she simply said, 'This is the *Argo*, Ali, we use her to go back and forth on this side of the island. She has a motor, but sometimes we sail her as well.' She gestured at the single mast. 'If you can start passing me some of the boxes, we'll load up.'

So all he had to do was unstack the car and pass the boxes across to her.

The task gave him the chance to look at her more closely. She looked beautiful in this evening light. She was completely at home, he saw, perfectly balanced in her boat; this was what she did every day. She explained that *Argo* was the name of the boat of some mythical person called Jason, a Greek, and that there had once been a children's radio show in which Jason and his crew had been important. When she was a child, she and her sister had always listened in, and she'd named the boat after Jason's boat, and painted it red because Jason's *Argo* had been vermilion. She also owned another boat, on the other side of the island, called the *Dolphin*, after the first boat her great-grandfather had brought to the island.

'That one's anchored in a place called Turtle Beach on the far side,' said Leah. 'And there are turtles there!'

The *Argo* was soon full.

'We can't take everything across now, we'll leave some and Zak will help me bring the rest when we come back again later,' Leah said to Ali. 'Sit down there in the stern — the back of the boat — and just stay looking forward so you don't feel seasick,' she added kindly. 'I'm used to it, but it can be choppy. We do have ginger tablets and peppermints in that locker there, but it's a short journey, keep breathing in the sea air and I think you'll be all right.'

He turned to do as he was told and she grinned.

'My bedside manner's wasted in pathology,' she remarked, casting off and expertly coiling the line at her feet, and he couldn't help noticing, as she lifted the rope, how the material of her T-shirt clung to her breasts, and how the colour purple suited her complexion.

He moved to sit down in the stern, and that was when he saw the sign.

Attached to a large rock by the wharf, in colours of red, yellow and black, the sign was a memorial to fifteen Aboriginal people who had been murdered in 1882. Murdered right here at this beach. Five actually on the beach, two young boys in a canoe on the water offshore, and eight on adjacent land. The Cassowary River Massacre, it was called. Ali read that the sign was part of a national program to document massacres of Aboriginal people by British colonists across Australia, and that there was more information about the tragedy in the Cairns Museum.

Leah watched as Ali stopped and took in this information, then looked again at the beach, calm and perfect in the evening light but once the scene of shocking brutality.

'Those people,' he asked, rocking unsteadily as he turned back to look at her, 'they didn't have names?'

'They had names,' she said, 'but those names were never recorded. It's a terrible story. I'll tell you about it when we get to the house, if you like.'

He sat down and Leah started up the motor, then steered the boat away from the wharf and out into the sea, where they began to bounce across toward the island. He looked back at the boxes left sitting on the wharf, but she reassured him.

'Don't worry, nobody will touch them, everyone knows everyone else around here.'

'Your ancestor, the one who bought the island first,' he asked, 'he came here from England?'

Conversation was clearer above the noise of the boat's motor than it had been with the engine of the car, and he felt that if he kept talking it would be easier to ignore the definite nausea that was welling up in his guts with every thud of the boat against the waves. Leah casually kept a hand on the tiller as she turned to answer him, and her scarf blew sideways, shimmering in the wind.

'John Rookwood? From Ireland, Northern Ireland. His wife, my great-grandmother, was Irish too, though they met and married here. At least, in Cooktown, further up the coast, when it was the centre of the gold rush. Cooktown was booming, which is why they both came here.'

The sea air rushed past him, carrying her words with it. Now Ali began to feel how to move with the motion of the boat, his sickness suddenly disappeared and he felt exhilarated by the trip. He had never before been anywhere like this.

'The gold soon gave out,' Leah was explaining, 'and most people left, but because John was a doctor, he stayed on.'

'So you have all been doctors?'

'Pretty much — John's son Thomas, who was my grandfather, and then my father, Charles. My father had two brothers who both died in the Second World War.' Ali looked up, concerned.

Leah went on quickly. 'Not many Australian families lost two sons in that war, it was a statistical blip. But in the First War, many families from around here lost two or three or even more sons. Huge numbers went from Australia to fight in Turkey and France and other places. Have a look at the war memorial in the centre of Cairns, dozens of names, and it was only a small country town then.'

Ali, clutching hold of the side of the small boat, said: 'It was after that war that Iraq was founded, you know.'

Leah thought a moment and then said, 'Really? I thought Iraq was much older than that.'

'The people were always there, the Arab people, but it was Turkish for hundreds of years.'

They had come into the lee of the island. Leah slackened the motor and they chugged more smoothly now towards the wharf on the south end of the beach.

Ali asked: 'Your own father, he escaped the war?'

Leah took some time before she answered. Then she said, 'Well no, he never really escaped it.' She stood for a moment in the stern as the *Argo* rocked gently towards the wharf. 'He was about to start medical school when the war began. He dropped out and enlisted straight away before his father could stop him, which I believe he would certainly have done.'

Thomas himself had spent two years in France during the First War, and rarely spoke of it, Charles had told Leah. 'I know my Dad hated it,' Charles had said, 'he had to watch so many men die that he could do nothing for.'

'My father went to north Africa, then to Borneo and the Philippines,' Leah now told Ali. 'He didn't do medicine until the war was over, as a mature student. And he'd lost two brothers.' The older one, Leah knew, had been the most important person in her father's life when he was growing up, and the younger one was her grandmother's favourite.

'So my Dad spent the whole of his life feeling guilty about being alive himself.'

Survivor guilt, it was called now, fashionably. It had taken her many years to realise how it had affected her father. She was not sure he had ever understood it himself.

If she looked up, Leah thought, she could see the flight of steps Charles had built from Mermaids Beach to the top of the island. He'd brought the concrete mixer across to the island by boat, together with bags of cement, and each weekend for months he'd fought his own personal war with the rainforest, dragging boulders out of the bush and cementing them into place to form a stairway. It must have been soon after the resort was finished, all that stair building. While Dad worked away, Leah and Mara had run through the rainforest, made cubbies in hollow trees where they'd kept their tea sets and dolls, and spied on the first resort guests, who'd been disappointingly boring. The stairway was good and necessary, a quick way to the top of the island. Only much later did Leah understand her father's determination to get it finished. It was a monument to Philip and young Thomas.

Ali was silent, and Leah paused, remembering their conversation on the balcony, conscious that perhaps she had already said too much. Then she added carefully, 'My experience is second-hand. But I do understand that war, even if you survive unscathed physically, affects the rest of your life.' Now that the *Argo* was close to the island's wharf, she threw a line over a bollard and made it fast.

In fact, Ali was surprised. He had not expected an Australian woman, in a place like this, to know such things. *The guilt of those who survived.* How well he was acquainted with it. After Muna's death — once he had accepted that she really was dead — he had held that guilt fast inside himself, refusing for years to let it fade. Obtusely, he knew that the guilt would have been less if he had loved her more. Well, if he had loved her at all … What had he thought earlier? That he should live for the moment? He must believe this. This was what he must try to do.

And the moment was spectacular. The rainforest rose steeply from the edge of Mermaids Beach. At the farther end of the sand, the same fine white sand as on the mainland, could be seen the thatched cabins of the resort, surrounded by clumps of red-trunked palms. Immediately beyond the wharf, a flight of rocky steps led directly up from the beach into the rainforest, while to their right a wide path of beaten earth disappeared around the southern point of the island. He could hear the calls of unknown birds from the trees close to the beach. Expertly, Leah jumped onto the wharf and turned to face him.

'Welcome to Rookwood!' she said, as Ali climbed cautiously from the boat. 'There's a good walk now,' she said. She seized a handcart like an overgrown wheelbarrow, which was lying on the wharf. 'You're not feeling sick?'

He shook his head, no, especially now that he was off the boat.

'This is where the work really begins,' she continued. 'You'll earn your supper!'

Another handcart was at the end of the wharf. She fetched that too, and between them they loaded the boxes into the carts.

He followed her onto the pathway which began to climb the side of the island.

'We have to bring everything in this way,' Leah explained, 'so the path is not too steep or rough, it zigzags up the hill and isn't too bad really. The steps go straight up to the house, for when we're not loaded down. I promise you a great view as we get to the top! But you can see why us Rookwoods are all so fit!'

Ali was already breathing heavily as he hauled his handcart behind her. By the third turn in the path, it was possible to see above the rainforest far across the sea to the south, to where a few lights close to Cairns glimmered. Seagulls swooped and shrieked overhead and the setting sun had turned the sea to burgundy. Leah pointed out the sensor lights, which would come on to light the path for anyone wanting to use it at night.

'When I was a kid, we only had torches and there was always the possibility of standing on a snake.'

'Are there many snakes?' Ali asked quickly.

'Nothing really poisonous. Pythons and tree snakes mostly. We always make a lot of noise as we walk and they keep out of our way. I don't like them either, once a python ate a parrot I had as a pet. But my younger sister kept a snake for years in her bedroom, a carpet snake called Axminster. She adored him. He's buried in the family cemetery at the top of the island near the lighthouse.'

'Your sister lives in Sweden now? She comes back to Australia?'

'Sometimes. Not often. We get on well when we see each other. She's one of the few Rookwoods who is not a doctor, by the way! She left when she was very young, seventeen. To get away from our mother, who was a difficult woman. Mara ran away to sea, from an expensive boarding school in Brisbane. She joined the Swedish merchant navy, saw the world, lots of it, and now she lives with a Swedish engineer on their own island in Sweden.'

This information was intriguing, but Ali was concentrating hard on breathing enough just to keep going as fast as Leah did to the top of the path. He pushed his barrow behind hers up the final incline to a grassy area where she had stopped. And catching up, found an impressive sight.

5

Earlier that day, after his meeting with Leah in the hospital, Leslie Fernando had returned to his own office on the sixth floor of the Police Department building at the bottom of Sheridan Street. Sunshine spread like warm butter across the streets of the town, and Leslie was unhappy at the thought of spending his afternoon in air-conditioning. At least there was the consolation of having his desk by the windows at the front of the building, so that as he contemplated the solving of crime he could gain inspiration from the mountains spread around the bay, and the little white boats making their way along the inlet, and the sea stretching all the way to the horizon.

After eleven years, Leslie felt part of this town. Soon after he and Claudine had arrived here fresh from Melbourne, they had bought a house, the kind of house they would never have been able to afford in the city down south. This house sat easily on a hill overlooking the town, a Queenslander that seemed as though it had always been there, a house into which he and Claudine and their daughters had grown.

The town had grown too, and changed a great deal, even in the time Leslie had been here. People were still flooding in, looking for cheaper housing and a place in the sun. Mostly, like Leslie, from the south. Cairns had been more of a sugar town when he'd first arrived here. From the side window of his office he could still see, between the new housing estates, fields where this year's cane plants were starting their climb towards the sky. Many of the cane farmers were Italian, and they had brought pasta and pizza and good coffee to the town, and a taste for wine, and a volatility lacking in the earlier Anglo-Saxon inhabitants. Now the bottom had fallen out of the world's sugar market, none of the kids wanted the family farms, and tourism had taken over as the town's main industry.

Tourists had brought wealth and a demand for more sophisticated leisure pursuits and entertainment. They had also brought more crime, a different and more international kind of crime.

Which brought Leslie back to the present, and to Brian Mitchell.

The message had been a phone call to the 1800 number of the Police Department, Crime Stoppers. 'Don't give us your name, just give us your information' the ad for Crime Stoppers ran. And that's what they'd got. 'Brian Mitchell gets drugs from Justice and deals them through Cassowary,' the messenger had said. A young male voice, Australian accent. That was all.

Leslie had a fair idea what Justice was. Or rather, who. Justus Lee. The trouble was, the feds and Customs had once already boarded Justus Lee's boat, the *Hyacinth*, a luxurious ocean-going cruiser for which Mr Lee had paid a cool thirty million of apparently legitimately earned US dollars. They'd had a search warrant and they'd ripped out panelling, sniffed and poked and probed, and found nothing but a few bottles of Scotch behind a locker. Not surprisingly, Mr Lee had been furious. He'd been in Manila at the time, but he was soon on the phone, complaining and threatening every official, parliamentarian and businessman in north Queensland that he knew, who were considerable in numbers, and finally getting an official apology.

Justus Lee was rich, rich at celestial levels. He was an Australian citizen of Filipino Chinese ancestry who'd made money in construction — the construction of cheap apartments for the poorer citizens of Manila, as Leslie understood it — then branched out into shipping. Mr Lee was one of those gents always just one step ahead of the law, well, there were a few of those. His connection with Cairns was the casino. Lee liked to gamble. He was a high-roller. Only a few such people came here, most preferring the greater sophistication of Sydney and Melbourne, and Leslie was happy that they did so.

Mr Lee always got extra special attention at the casino. Sometimes he took a suite in the casino hotel, but he also quite often stayed at Mitchells over on Rookwood Island, taking over all the accommodation for his friends and staff. He could keep his cruiser moored out there and use its launch to come into town, or he could come across to the casino by helicopter. Whether he'd come to the resort first and then met Mitchell, or the other way around, Leslie didn't know, but the two men were now old friends. Justus and Brian. Brian and Justus. They had common business interests and common leisure interests — Brian took Justus game fishing, and Justus had invested in some projects on the Gold Coast. The normal activities of well-heeled businessmen.

The question was, were there also common criminal interests? Certainly Brian Mitchell enjoyed a visibly opulent lifestyle, as well as supporting three ex-wives. Much of the property he had acquired had been made over to these women in various divorce settlements. Mitchells itself had been divided between Brian, the first Deborah and their two children. So although Brian liked to refer to the resort as his, he really only had a quarter share. Other properties, Leslie's investigations had shown, were quite heavily mortgaged. Yet Mitchell was often seen, at the Cairns casino and on the Gold

Coast, spending up. Could there be sources of funds other than the obvious ones?

Lee's activities merged the legitimate with the highly questionable even more than Mitchell's, but that was all largely beyond Leslie's jurisdiction. The feds and Customs had had some intelligence about Lee. That he had ships legitimately trading around the coasts of Papua -New Guinea with copra and coconuts and goods for general stores, but that other substances were also sometimes aboard. That there could then be a discreet transfer of goods at sea, for instance into Lee's own boat, which would then sail calmly down to Queensland and anchor, for example, at Rookwood Island. If Mitchell organised a transfer from the resort onto shore somewhere, at arm's length, he and Lee could and would deny all knowledge of what their underlings were doing if they were pressed. But depending on what was brought in, such a venture could nicely supplement their already substantial incomes with some handy tax-free cash. It was this intelligence that a few months earlier had led to the disastrously unsuccessful raid on Justus Lee's boat while it was in Australian waters.

Leslie stood up and crossed to the window, gazing down at the scene on the town's main wharf. A hydrofoil from a reef trip had just slid alongside, and four hundred sunburnt tourists were being disgorged back onto land. At the marina beyond the wharf, dozens of boats were docked, craft of all kinds, sailing boats and high-powered cruisers for game fishing, catamarans and speedboats. Nearly all of them were capable of easily making the trip from the Australian coast across to PNG or Indonesia and beyond.

That there was a steady trade of high-grade weed down across the Torres Strait from Papua New Guinea was general knowledge around these parts. New Guinea Gold was a top-class product. The official view was somewhat disingenuous,

Leslie felt. It was OK to be in possession of modest amounts of weed, but not to deal. It was years since Leslie himself had smoked even tobacco, but he had to admit he'd enjoyed getting stoned at Melbourne student parties, and he still had a sharp nose for a smoking joint anywhere he came across it. Alcohol was the real problem drug in this town. What did concern Leslie, and Leslie's federal colleagues, was the fact that the dope, in larger amounts, was often traded for guns, semi-automatics even, which made their way back into Moresby and the PNG highlands and were responsible for increasingly violent crime. Many of these guns arrived from small Asian or Pacific ports.

What would concern Leslie even more would be if Justus Lee, or persons known to him, were shipping other drugs, heroin say, to some point on the high seas not too far off the PNG coast, and transferring it to another vessel with easy access to the Australian coast. The seas in theory were surveyed and overflown — in practice, if it were planned carefully, people could and did get away with murder, off the standard shipping lanes and away from the busier ports.

The Torres Strait was a direct pathway from Asia into Australia. *Well, more a six-lane highway than a path*, Leslie thought. Five large islands and hundreds of smaller ones were spread across the sea between PNG and Australia, and there were many more islands, some just like Rookwood, down the east coast of the mainland. Local people, with family both in PNG and in the Australian islands, slipped back and forward in small boats, without question; identity papers and Medicare cards changed hands easily. Goods of many kinds went on into Indonesia, and other goods came back. Anybody with a boat, some local knowledge and determination could bring into Australia what they wanted, in modest amounts, across those straits. If they then had contacts in the nearest big town, almost anything was possible. And that town happened to be Cairns.

Leslie's thoughts turned to Cassowary village. Just recently, Charlie Angell had been selling weed in large amounts; he'd been pulled in and charged with having in excess of two hundred grams. Well in excess. Charlie had been around north Queensland for years; his mother was a woman from Thursday Island, his father the Irish skipper of a prawn trawler. Charlie had numerous half-brothers and -sisters scattered throughout the region. He'd been known as a dealer for a long time, but usually on a small scale. There were people who'd sell you weed all over the place, up there north of the Cassowary, but mostly modest amounts that they grew themselves out on the backblocks and in the forests. Everyone knew everyone else's turf, and it seldom caused too much trouble. Magistrates and judges were fairly relaxed, often seeming to Leslie to allow the possession of more plants than might be considered strictly necessary. But all of this was a very different scene from the heroin trade.

As Leah had said, Brian Mitchell was not a person to trifle with in this town. Though he knew him only slightly, Leslie, like Leah, could not say he liked him. Smooth in business surroundings, Mitchell could be abusive and threatening in other situations. Leslie had seen him on several occasions when he was drinking and losing in the casino.

Leslie had discussed Mitchell with Drew Borgese.

'What do you think of him?' he'd asked, and Drew had been blunt:

'He's a bastard.'

Detective Senior Constable Drew Borgese had recently been transferred to Leslie's division, and Leslie was pleased by the transfer. Gradually the Detectives Division was being integrated, the all-white spots coloured in. Drew's maternal grandmother was from Fiji, his father's family from Sicily.

Drew himself had grown up on the Tableland. At six foot four, he towered over Leslie, though he was lean and wiry with it, and he had dark orange curly hair. His nickname at school, he'd told Leslie, was Giraffe. Leslie himself was fit and he held a black belt in taekwondo, but still he found Drew's presence reassuring at times when they conducted interviews together with certain people.

Drew had worked the casino and the tourist quarter for more than two years when he was in uniform.

'Mitchell,' he said, 'yeah, I often saw him around. Pushy guy, feels he's gotta make an impression on everyone. It's all about who he knows, more than money even. I was there that night he punched the doorman. Just a little bloke, he was, the doorman, Chinese–Australian, and he was just trying to tell Mitchell that the limo in the driveway was booked for someone else when Mitchell completely lost it and slugged him. Amazing. Anybody else, they'd have got two years minimum for aggravated assault.'

As well as that incident, he'd more than once just escaped charges of offensive language. A bully, Leah had said. Well, bullying was how he'd got where he was in business. Even though his business up here was now confined to the resort — Leslie had checked this — he was well-known for his developments in the south-east of the state, and for the kind of people he brought up for fishing vacations at Mitchells. Every now and then, the photo of some minor film celebrity or sporting star would be on the front page of the Cairns newspaper because they were visiting Mitchells for game fishing, and Brian would always be somewhere in the picture. He was still an impressive looking man, if a little heavy. He had a full head of dark hair, which appeared to be his own, and a dominating expression. He was not someone to make accusations against without a very firm foundation.

Or even to question. One would need very hard evidence indeed to nail Mitchell.

Leslie sat back down at his desk and opened a file. He would just make a call to a mate of his over at Coastwatch and have a bit of a chat.

6

The sun was slowly disappearing behind the mountains on the mainland as Leah and Ali reached the top of the island. All around them was the wrinkled dark satin of the Coral Sea, sparkling in a thousand tiny places as the last shafts of sunlight caught the tops of the waves. Here and there was the gleam of a fishing boat still out on the water, and back towards Cairns, the glow of the town's lights rose into the sky. Then, looking to the left, Ali saw the house.

Leah's house stood on the eastern cliff of Rookwood Island, with a view of the sea on three sides. The house was a single storey, spread across a flattened area near the top of the island — a traditional timber Queenslander, lowset on piles and nestling into a niche of rock to protect it from the cyclones of the Wet season. Surrounding the house was a wide veranda on which cane chairs and couches sprawled. Green-painted corrugated iron covered the roof and formed water tanks at either end. Bougainvillea, deep red in the dusk, clambered over the veranda railings. Buffalo grass stretched in front of the house, and three poinciana trees marked the point where another path led from the cliff edge down to the beach on the island's eastern side — Turtle Beach, Leah called it, pointing it out to him, 'our favourite swimming spot'.

'And that's the *Dolphin*, moored down there.' Ali could just make out the shape of the boat, her sails furled and tied against the mast, riding at anchor about twenty metres from the shore.

Leah continued. 'On the north side is another beach called North Beach. Not very original, I admit. That beach is more open to currents and mud from the river so it's not so good for swimming, but there's good fishing. The path going down starts just over there' — she pointed into the darkness — 'but it's dangerous, there are falling rocks and a sheer drop down into the sea. It's actually called the Devil's Path. To get down that side safely, you really have to go back down the hill and through the resort. So we don't use it much. That's our lighthouse, of course.' She pointed to the very top of the island where the striped lighthouse stood beside a wide shelf of rock.

'It's not used any more,' she said, 'but we love it. My father bought it from the government when it was about to be dismantled.'

Ali stood still for several minutes, slowly turning his head to take it all in.

Leah stood beside him, smiling. Then she said, 'Yes, it's wonderful, isn't it? I always enjoy coming back home.'

'I can see why you want to come back to live here,' said Ali, 'even with the long drive, which itself is charming. To wake up every morning and see this ...' He stopped, feeling he had overstepped himself, and blushed — fortunately, he thought, it was too dark for her to notice.

In a single movement, the sun dropped below the horizon.

'Come on in,' Leah said to him. They left the barrows by the veranda steps, and she led him across a veranda and through French doors to the living room, switching on lights as she went.

'We have our own generator for electricity,' she explained.

Against an inner wall stood an upright piano, covered with family photos in a variety of frames. Sofas and armchairs were strewn with books, magazines and discarded clothing, including, Ali noted, a black lace bra. Two Burmese cats were curled up together on a sofa, but leapt to their feet when Leah approached, and rubbed their backs against her legs, purring loudly. On the right, close to a doorway leading into a large kitchen, was a long dining table covered with a blue cloth. On this were piles of notes and folders, a computer and several pathology specimens in jars: Leah's home workspace.

'What can I offer you?' Leah was enquiring. She asked hesitantly, 'Do you drink beer?'

Ali laughed. 'I do' he said. 'After so many years in England, of course.'

Leah handed him a Carlton Cold and took one herself.

'Cheers!' she said. Ali took a long appreciative draught.

'You're not a strict Muslim then?' Leah asked.

He hesitated a moment, then said, 'I am a believer, but not strict in practices. People who live in non-Muslim countries often don't understand that not everyone in a Muslim country is actively religious. My father's family was originally Shia Muslim from Basra. And many Shias are very traditional in what they believe and do. But my family was more liberal, like many people who live in Baghdad. There are many things wrong with Iraq, but religion is not compulsory, it's not an Islamic state. If I have to fill in a form, I put Islam as my religion. Like many people here and in England who I've met who would describe themselves as Christian, but hardly ever enter a church. There are many good things about Islam — in its original teaching. But much of that teaching has been neglected, or changed by other people since, for their own benefit. In Iraq, and in other countries as well.'

'I know practically nothing about Iraq's history,' Leah said. 'There was a lot of British influence when you were growing up?'

'It was Britain that put Iraq together after the First World War. With the Americans and French.' He hesitated a moment, unsure of her political views, then, remembering what she had said of the Immigration Minister, went on, 'Not out of love for us, of course, but because they wanted our oil. And they just believed they could have it. They cobbled up a country out of three separate groups — Sunnis, Shias, Kurds — and they gave us a king. Nobody in Iraq wanted this king, but the British held an election and the king got more than ninety per cent approval, supposedly. So you see, Saddam really is simply imitating the British.'

'What happened to the king? There's no king now, surely?'

No, he's gone. His family live in London. We had a revolution in 1958. On 14 July. But unlike the French, we didn't end up with our liberty.'

He had been three years old. His earliest memories were of that time. His grandfather had been a lawyer, but also a poet and a nationalist. Ali could remember that, after the revolution, the house was filled with people, happy people, day and night. All talking, singing, dancing. He had been allowed to eat as many dates and sweet cakes as he liked. There had been the reciting of many traditional poems and also of his grandfather's poems. Everyone seemed very happy, and it had seemed that this happy life could go on forever.

But then his grandfather had fallen out of favour with the new regime. One morning, Ali had woken up and found that everything had changed. His grandfather was gone, no-one would tell Ali where, or anything about him. The other people, the friends who had been so numerous, were not there either, and there was an atmosphere of fear that even a small child could feel.

He realised now that his grandfather was suspected of having communist sympathies. In fact, he almost certainly did have communist sympathies. There was so much poverty, how could a poet not have communist sympathies? And the government had been determined to crush the communists. He had never heard what had really happened to his grandfather.

He could imagine, though. He knew very well what had happened to his own brother.

'But you went to school in Iraq?' Leah asked.

'Oh yes. And to the university in Baghdad. Those things were still possible for us. I did my internship and my military service, and it was then that I got the award to go to England, in 1981. Saddam was only just in power. England was still highly regarded in some circles then, and the ability to speak English was a plus. My mother's family had many contacts with English people when she was growing up. They were Sunni, that's the other kind of Muslim faith. I come from a tribe that has both Shias and Sunnis. There were many intellectuals in my mother's family, and they were even less religious than my father's relations. So it was quite natural that I learn English, and eventually, go to visit England.

'The English organised Iraq so that there are lots more Shias than Sunnis. But Saddam is Sunni, and the Sunnis, some of them, are very powerful. The Shias have suffered a lot because of this.'

He seemed disinclined to say more, though there were many things she wanted to ask: 'Why did you leave Iraq when you did?', 'What happened to your wife? And to the rest of your family?'

He swallowed the last of his beer. 'This island seems like paradise,' he said. The warm night air was very still, the only sounds the soft hum of the distant generator and the waves washing gently onto the sand of Turtle Beach.

'Yes, in many ways it is. We can sit here in peace and safety. But as you've already seen this island has had quite a chequered history.'

'You said you'd tell me what happened ...'

'Let me get you some food first, and another beer.' She would find the salmon and some salad, there was plenty for them both. And there was an hour at least before she needed to set out for the airport to collect Zak.

7

The same evening, as Leah was telling her story to Ali, Ina Frazer sat with her sister Ivy on the veranda of the home they shared in the western suburbs of Cairns.

Ina had lit the kerosene lamp the two women used outside at night. Every evening she would trim the wick and clean the lamp and fill it. Then she would strike a match, and the light would flare briefly as she stoked the flame before turning it down to a soft glow whose drifting fumes kept insects at a distance. They could have turned on the electric light, but the lamp brought back memories of the cottage Ina had shared with her husband Albert, many years ago, on the cattle station over towards the Gulf where they had both grown up. Her kids had been little then; now they were grown with children of their own.

Ivy had made a big pot of bush tea in the blue enamel teapot and the two women sat together as they liked to do at this time of night, filling and refilling their cups, talking and then falling silent. Earlier Ivy had cooked supper, and they'd sat down together at their kitchen table, but they'd only picked at the meal. Neither had much appetite after the events of the day.

Garry Brown's family had wanted to bring him home as soon as they could. His spirit would be restless until his body was back with his people. So once the autopsy was complete, Bert Cochrane had set to work and by five o'clock the procession was ready to start.

First went Garry, closed into a simple wooden coffin, driven in the back of a white ute belonging to his cousin Kevin. Kevin drove slowly, his headlights on, with Garry's Mum and his sister Lucy together with him in the front seat. Then followed a line of seven more cars, battered Holdens and Toyotas in various states of repair, some with wires hanging loose. Packed in were the members of the Brown and other families who had spent the past two days waiting for Garry outside the mortuary and the funeral parlour.

Ina and Ivy had shared the back seat of the final car in the line, Des Farrell's blue Kingswood, circa 1980. This car now emitted a cloud of black smoke with every gear change, but nevertheless had lasted time and distance. Lucy's son Benjy was still in the kids' ward, so Ivy had co-opted her sister-in-law to stay with him for the evening. The doctor had said he could come home tomorrow, but he was too little anyway for funerals and sorry business.

The cortege had moved solemnly along the streets and laneways of the part of Cairns where the homes of the Brown, Frazer and other families stood, coming to a halt outside the Brown family's house, where Garry had lived with his Mum, Lucy, Benjy and two uncles. The uncles and two cousins, together with Kevin, shouldered the coffin, and they carried it up and into the front room where a trestle had been placed to receive it. The uncles unscrewed the lid, and Garry's mother Shiloh placed around him the armfuls of flowers her neighbours had brought. Tears poured down her cheeks.

Bert had done his job well. Garry lay serenely, his eyes closed, among frills of white cotton. All traces of foam, blood and saliva had been removed and the autopsy sutures neatly concealed. His mother's final memory would be a peaceful one.

Once all was in order, people began to arrive. In the backyard, the uncles set out plastic chairs and tables, and there was beer, but there would not be too much drunk in that house tonight. In the kitchen, women made tea, and thick sandwiches of bread and meat for those who needed them. Most were there simply to hug and hold the family members, and to weep with them. Ina and Ivy were among them, wearing their good black dresses and carrying a large bunch of flowers from the frangipani and hibiscus in their garden.

In the front room, the mood was sombre. People sat on chairs of all shapes and sizes, talking in low voices, and the air was heavy with the scent of frangipani and the smoke of candles and cigarettes. After a suitable time, Ina and Ivy had been relieved to fold their arms around Shiloh and then take themselves away. There had been so many scenes like this over so many years. And tomorrow there would be the full funeral service to cope with, before Garry's departure with his family for his burial on country out west.

All this was in their minds as the twins sat together on the veranda. But so was something else. Kevin Brown and Ebony Passmore.

All their mob was proud of those two, but especially Kevin. Kevin had gone right to the end of Year 12 at the high school. Then in a short space of time he'd become one of the lead dancers in the Cairns Dance Group, which performed in the cultural centre in town, and he was soon to appear in the town's theatre in a work he'd created himself.

Ebony was his girlfriend. At least, that was what everyone had thought. She'd been going with him for the last two years, since she was fifteen and still at school. Browns and Passmores were close, but those two were not related by blood so everyone approved their being together. Ebony had dropped out of school last year, but still she'd got herself a place in the dance group and seemed to be doing all right. She was a beautiful girl with long dark hair bleached gold at the tips. As a dancer, she was not as good as some of them, but recently, extra girls had been taken on because Mr Mitchell over on Rookwood Island had hired some of the group to perform in his resort. Ebony was one of those working at the resort while Kevin worked in town. And it seemed like working over there had changed Ebony quite a bit.

Brian Mitchell paid well for the dancers, and he'd got a couple of girls jobs in hotels down on the Gold Coast, but he didn't like the kids hanging about near the resort where his guests might see them. So the dancers were picked up each evening from the Cairns wharf by the resort's launch, and dropped straight back to Cairns when their two shows were over. This included Ebony.

The previous week, Ivy had been standing in the post office in a line behind Ebony, waiting to buy two stamps. She couldn't help but notice when Ebony opened her billum — her string bag in bright red, yellow and black, knitted by her aunty up on the Cape — that inside, in her purse, not even zipped up, Ebony had more money, in new hundred dollar bills, than Ivy had ever seen at one time in her whole life up to that point. Ivy had quickly averted her eyes so that, when Ebony looked up, Ivy seemed to be intently studying a notice about passport photos, but her mind was racing. *What was that girl doing with so much money?*

'My Lord, sister,' she had said to Ina, on arriving home within the half-hour, 'I swear there was at least two thousand dollars just there in her bag.'

Ina had shaken her head. 'It's good the kids got work over there on Rookwood,' she said, 'but not if they fall into bad ways. I fear somethin' gonna' happen to that girl.'

Then the following day, late in the morning, the sisters had been walking together through the neighbouring park, wheeling their groceries home. From behind a bushy area, raised voices could be heard — Kevin and Ebony, arguing.

'It doesn't mean anything,' they heard Ebony say. 'Anyway, you can't tell me what to do.' There was a slap, and a cry, and then Ebony had stumbled out of the bushes and down the path away from the park, oblivious to the concerned gazes of Ivy and Ina.

Now Ivy squeezed them both a final cup from the pot. 'That girl's got herself into something over her head on that island,' she said. 'Maybe Kevin too.'

Ina nodded. 'You're right,' she said. 'In my bones, sister, I feel something bad's gonna happen to that girl.'

8

In the house on the island, Ali stood up and moved towards the kitchen.

'Let me help you,' he said to Leah. 'Living in England has made me domesticated. In Iraq I never did anything for myself. But once I left there, I had to learn to cook just to survive!'

'Well, we'll happily put you to the test,' Leah answered, 'and get you to cook us Arab food any time you like.'

They carried plates of salad and fish back into the living room. Leah pushed a pile of books and newspapers from one end of the table, set two places and they both sat down. Then she began her story.

'My great-grandfather John Rookwood bought the island from the Queensland government in 1878,' she began. 'Nobody had any use for islands then. They were interested in the cattle country, and then in gold, and silver and tin, anything that could be mined easily, mostly around the rivers. Islands were only used for locking people up, Black people and lepers. If you'd suggested that millions of Japanese would one day pay good money to come here in large flying machines to take their holidays on some of these islands, you'd have been marched off to the lunatic asylum.'

That John Rookwood had ever come to far north Queensland, Leah knew, was pure chance. He'd taken a post as a ship's doctor, sailing out of Liverpool for New South Wales, in 1875, newly qualified as a physician, and intending to set himself up in the sheep country west of Sydney. But reaching that colonial capital, he'd found something he could never have imagined. Leah's father had explained it to her. 'I'm damn sure you couldn't call yourself Dr Rookwood in Sydney in those days,' he said, 'or in New South Wales anywhere.' Rookwood was the name of the huge new cemetery just laid out to the west of the city. Every day, black steam engines drew carriages hung with crepe and loaded with coffins at a respectful five miles per hour along the line, from the Gothic arches of Mortuary Station to the rolling paddocks beyond the city limits and the newly built necropolis. 'He might just as well have called himself Dr Death,' Charles had said. 'I don't suppose he had any idea of it before he left Ireland.'

Now Leah explained to Ali, 'When John Rookwood first came here, the island was used for fishing and turtle hunting by local Aboriginal people from the mainland, but they didn't often stay overnight here. Some families traditionally have always come over here, and North Beach was an important place for them because there's good fishing there, but they've never liked that north-eastern corner of the island, and tended to avoid it. Pieces of the rock fall off there without warning. As far as I know, there were no established camp sites on the island. Not that it would have worried the government, or even John himself, at the time if there had been Aboriginal people living here. The British just thought they had a right to the whole of Queensland ... as you've said they did in Iraq.'

'As they did in Iraq,' Ali agreed.

'Anyway, for the first few years in Cooktown, John was very busy setting up in medical practice. He came to Queensland with very little and didn't even own a house in Cooktown for several years, although houses must have been cheap. He bought the island first. He's always struck me as a rather enigmatic character. Interesting enough to come halfway around the world to a gold rush town and buy an island. Yet he comes down the generations as very stern, very rigid.'

'Did he leave a diary, or something like that?'

'No, no letters or diary. No journal that he confided his thoughts to, like a lot of people did then. Just his medical records, some of them are in the Cooktown museum and some still at the hospital in town. I have them in my office. Very precise, beautiful handwriting, the way the Victorians did it. And he wrote a little textbook, a monograph really, published in Sydney, on the treatment of tropical ulcers. He saw a good many of those in the Cooktown population. There are also some family photos. A few of his personal books, the most interesting is his copy of *Robinson Crusoe*. We often say that he must have bought the island because he liked Crusoe when he was a boy, but no-one really knows now. There are a few stories my grandfather passed on to my father. Though I think many of those have been embellished by my Dad, who was always fond of a good yarn.'

Leah stood up and moved across to the piano. 'And I know even less about my great-grandmother. Adeline. At least about what she was like. The story I am going to tell you is really about her. John married her in Cooktown. She had been his nurse. A pretty typical thing for a doctor to do!' Leah picked up a silver frame from the top of the piano. 'This is their wedding photo. 1879.'

Adeline was sitting bolt upright, wearing a wedding dress that covered her ankles with a frill of broderie anglaise, but was otherwise severely cut and high-necked. Her hair was braided and pinned up, her gaze gentle but unsmiling. Her matron of honour was similarly dressed. The new husband stood at Adeline's side, one hand resting delicately on her full-length sleeve. Narrow-shouldered, in a dark three-piece suit, wing collar and black tie, John must have been sweltering in the Cooktown heat. He sported a small neat moustache but no beard, unlike the best man and the minister, both of whom displayed fine examples of hirsutism. John Rookwood was bespectacled, and appeared slightly defiant. Certainly he was not the image of the tough frontiersman. Even allowing for the unaccustomed stress of the occasion and the demands of the photographer, the portrait conveyed little sense of spontaneous enjoyment of the day.

'None of them look like they're having much fun,' Leah commented.

'No. It lacks ... passion.' Ali thought of his own wedding. In the blazing heat of a Baghdad late spring. 1986. Muna in white silk, elaborately beaded, her hair veiled. She had been beautiful. Himself, in a dark English suit and tie, sweating hard, and not just from the heat. He had stood awkwardly in just such a pose as John Rookwood. Without passion.

'Yes — exactly. Hard to imagine a satisfactory consummation,' Leah laughed. She was thinking that, by the time she'd married Gareth, their sexual relationship had been well-established, even though they'd never lived together. The sex had been the best part, though he had always wanted to be in control. Wouldn't let her take the pill. Insisted on condoms. Until the night of Micky's conception, when he'd insisted on not using them ... Then it struck her that the conversation was taking a slightly risky turn. She was alone here with this man, but she certainly wasn't interested in him sexually. Definitely not. Sex was something she always kept within very finite boundaries, by having very short and casual affairs outside of Cairns. This had been her pattern ever since her divorce, and it had worked very well, thank you. As far as Ali Hassan was concerned, she was just being friendly. She'd made it clear from the beginning that she was returning to the airport to collect her son.

'I was about to tell you their story,' she said quickly, stepping into the kitchen for more bread. She sat at the table again and continued the tale.

'Well, John owned the island outright after paying the government the enormous sum of fifty-five pounds. At first, he came here only very sporadically. Then he acquired a boat, the first *Dolphin*. He had learned to sail in Ireland, and he began to come here more often. Mostly on weekends for picnics with friends. Adeline would come, and after their son, who was Thomas, my grandfather, was born, he came along too.

'From the moment he first saw Rookwood, John had decided to build what he called a summer-house, so that he and his family could stay overnight. It was really just a cabin. He'd already built a wharf just where my wharf is now, at the southern end of the beach where we tied up. You can still see some of his original piles. And on that point of land, he put the cabin and a separate kitchen, very simple buildings of logs, and fenced off from the rest of the island so that the fence closed in the wharf as well. There were no proper pathways up here then, just rough tracks in the bush, so building right up here wouldn't have been possible.

'The summer-house was finished and the family spent weekends there. In October of 1882, they went there again for several days. Just John, Adeline and the baby, and their Chinese servant, Lee Chin.'

By then there were thousands of Chinese in Cooktown for the gold, Leah explained. A lot more Chinese than white men were at the diggings, and they were not popular with the white miners, who called them Chows, but they weren't as despised as the Aboriginal people were.

'John had arranged to go fishing with another doctor from Smithfield, which as you'll know is now a suburb of Cairns At that time it was a small port. He set out on the Saturday morning very early to meet Dr Fitzgerald, sailing the *Dolphin*. He expected to be back before dark.

'He left Adeline with Lee Chin and two dogs for protection. She also had a shotgun, which she knew how to use. But there had never been any problems since they had come to the island, and probably she was just planning to spend the afternoon playing with her son on the beach.

'Now the story I was told when I was growing up was that, as soon as John disappeared over the horizon, a group of marauding blacks came around the point and attacked the cabin, and Adeline and Lee Chin, unprovoked. Certainly, that's how it was always portrayed in Cairns and Cooktown.'

They'd finished their salads. Leah gathered up the plates. 'I'll bring some fruit,' she said, disappearing into the kitchen. Returning with a basket of grapes, she went on with her story.

'More recently, in the new museum, the other side of the tale has emerged from some of the descendants of the Aboriginal people over on the mainland, people whose country this has always been. And it's a version that seems more likely. That story is that a group of local people, mostly men but at least one woman and a child, had come across to hunt turtles at North Beach. One of Adeline's dogs escaped through the fence around the cabin, made its way to the people on the beach and attacked the child — not badly, but frightening it a lot, and the people were angry. A group of them came around the point at the north end of the landing beach to complain.'

'That's where you showed me the resort?' Ali asked.

'That's right,' Leah said. 'Lee Chin saw them coming and ran to warn Adeline. They locked the gate in the fence and put Thomas in the cabin, and Adeline got out her shotgun. So they were already in defensive mode. The Aboriginal people I'm sure didn't speak English, and Adeline didn't know about the dog hurting the child. Tempers rose rapidly, there was a lot of shouting, and to scare them Lee Chin took the shotgun and fired it into the air. Unfortunately, the shot ricocheted off a tree and grazed one of the men, not wounding him badly but inflaming the situation.

'Spears were produced and it looked as though the men were going to try to burn down the fence. Adeline decided that they must try to escape by boat. They had just a small rowing boat tied up to the wharf, which was of course inside the fence. She grabbed Thomas, and while Lee Chin held the shotgun, she made the boat ready and put Thomas in. Then Lee Chin got in too, but as he did so he was injured by a spear. Nevertheless, he began to row — the Aboriginal people couldn't follow them immediately, even if they'd wanted to, since their canoes were back at North Beach. Adeline just had to hope that they wouldn't be pursued.

'Lee Chin had begun to row towards Smithfield. Adeline had fled without any real plan except to get away, but she thought that they would be helped by the tide. Mainly, though, she was expecting to meet John on his way back. She calculated that she and Lee Chin would only have an hour or so at most to row before he picked them up. She was sure they would then all go back to Smithfield for the night.

'When John had reached Smithfield though, he had discovered there was an outbreak of spinal fever. Many people had come down with it very quickly, and Dr Fitzgerald, the only doctor there, was flat out coping. John also realised that there was a storm brewing and that it would be unwise to set out for the island in the evening. He knew Adeline was safely with Lee Chin and the dogs, she had enough food and oil for one night, and he thought that once she saw the weather, she would understand that he had decided not to come back until morning. So he rolled up his sleeves and set to work looking after the fever victims.

Though since this was before antibiotics, I'm not sure what he did that was very effective.

'Lee Chin rowed for about an hour and he rowed right into the storm, without any sign of the *Dolphin*. Then the storm took the rowing boat out to sea. Adeline had to rip her petticoat into strips to tie herself and Thomas and Lee Chin to the boat, which began to take in water, and they were very lucky they weren't swept overboard and drowned. This went on for several hours and the boat was taken further and further from the mainland. Just as they were despairing totally and it was getting dark, Lee Chin spied a tiny island, a cay of sand and rock, and with a superhuman effort managed to row across to it and beach the boat there.'

Ali was plucking grapes and eating them, but all his attention was fixed on Leah.

'Lee Chin had been wounded in the chest and had lost quite a lot of blood, so he was very weak,' Leah told him. 'Adeline dressed the wound with another strip from her petticoat and they prepared to spend the night on the cay, not knowing what the morning would bring, or even if they would survive until then,' Leah said. 'The only water they had was rainwater in the bottom of the boat, which was very salty, mixed with seawater, but they all drank some of this, even the little boy.

'They spent the night there, very dark because of the storm, exhausted and terrified, I imagine, not knowing if a larger storm would wash them away or if they'd be able to see in which direction the coastline was when morning came.

'In fact the land wasn't visible the following morning. They'd drifted right out to the reef. The storm was over, but it was very hot. Lee Chin was still weak from blood loss, but he wanted to try to row. Adeline wouldn't let him. She thought it was better to stay put. There was quite a lot of shipping along the channel between the reef and the mainland. Hopefully, somebody would see them and come to the rescue. She used the remains of her petticoat to attach to one of the oars to try to attract attention. Apparently, in the first few hours of the morning, they did see some ships but they weren't seen themselves. Of course at that stage no-one knew they were missing.

'John got back to the island in the early afternoon of that second day and found they weren't there, and was frantic. Firstly he ran all over the island calling Adeline. The Aboriginal group had all gone, understandably. The island was empty of human life. Then John realised the rowing boat was gone. And he's said to have discovered traces of blood — Lee Chin's — on the wharf, which is quite possible. The story later got more and more lurid, as it did the rounds in Cooktown — that there were two Chinese servants lying murdered, in pools of blood, that kind of thing.

'He did the only thing possible, sailed back to Cooktown to organise a search party. This was just being got together when a ship called the *Ariadne*, whose captain was a man named Jackson, hove to across the horizon with all three of them safely on board. At least, very shocked and dehydrated, I should imagine, but alive. Jackson's watch had seen the flag that Adeline had made, and the ship sent a longboat across to get them. The *Ariadne* was on her way into Cooktown anyway.

'The story up to this point was always part of folklore in Cooktown. The old museum had photos of John and Adeline and Thomas, though not of Lee Chin, and an account of how they were heroically rescued by Skipper Jackson. What wasn't told was the sequel.

'The story spread rapidly around the district that Dr Rookwood's wife had been savagely attacked by wild blacks on the island — on the doctor's own property. A posse of armed men quickly got together and planned to go and revenge what was seen as an outrageous attack on white civilisation and property. The leader was a local butcher.

'They set out by sailing boat the following morning, seven or eight men armed to the teeth, and soon came to Rookwood. They searched the island but could find no-one. They got into their boat again, and on the sea between the island and the mainland, where we came across just now, they found two young Aboriginal boys fishing from a canoe. Both the boys were shot dead. Then the party landed on the beach over near where we parked and set out this evening. Some local people appeared, initially just curious, not knowing what had happened to the boys on the water. Again the avenging party opened fire and killed five people, including three women. Then the Aboriginal men began to fight back, spears were thrown, and the white men got back in their boat. They turned their guns on the men again, killing eight of them, before they headed back to Cooktown. They received a heroes' welcome back in Cooktown.

'So fifteen Aboriginal people were murdered in and around the beach that day.'

Ali shook his head. 'That's terrible,' he said, 'terrible. This has been the history of my country also. Did your ancestor, that first Dr Rookwood, go with those men?'

'No,' said Leah, 'he didn't. And I don't know whether he approved of the party setting off. Certainly there's no record of his trying to stop it, and he would have been well aware of what was being planned and where it would lead. It was considered perfectly all right to shoot Aboriginal people then, with no thought of law or decency. As far as I know, there was never any investigation or complaint or police involvement into what happened here that day.

'But every Aboriginal person for hundreds of miles around learned what had happened here, and passed on that knowledge to their children, and their children's children and grandchildren. And so, when the new museum was set up, local people came across with their side of the story, and now it's told, too, along with Adeline's.

'There's not much, though, about Lee Chin. No record of what later happened to him. Many Chinese died in epidemics, especially from typhus, and ultimately those who survived mostly went back to China. What Lee Chin did I don't know.'

Leah knew there was something more to the story, but she would not tell that now. After all, it was only a rumour. And it seemed so unlikely ...

Some of the documents recently unearthed by the museum had suggested a liaison between Adeline and Lee Chin. There was a newspaper report that hinted that an affair had begun on the cay that stormy night, and had continued after their safe return to Cooktown. Leah, despite her forensic training and her knowledge of the world, still found that hard to believe. However reserved and distant John and Adeline Rookwood seemed now, she felt that they must have lived on together happily enough in Cooktown right up until John's death in 1900, though they had no more children. She could not fit Lee Chin into this picture. This was not part of the family she knew.

So she stopped there, and they sat in silence for a moment, Ali absorbing the story. Moths fluttered in the glow of the table lamp and tiny geckos pattered, upside down, across the ceiling, in pursuit of even smaller insects attracted by the light, for the French doors were open to the veranda.

'Thank you for telling me all that,' Ali said finally. 'It's a very moving story. There are similar stories of the English in Iraq, shooting and dropping bombs on people in the cities in the 1920s. Innocent people. These are important stories. And you are a very good storyteller. In Iraq we would call you a *hakawati*. That's an important person for Arabic speakers!'

Leah smiled. 'It's something I got from my father,' she said. 'He had lots of stories about the island, which he swore were true.'

'So after these events the family didn't come here for a long while?' Ali asked.

'Actually, that's another story altogether,' Leah answered. 'I'll have to save that one for you, Ali. In fact, John did come back soon after, and he continued to come, and bring friends for picnics, for years afterwards. Then something else happened. Of course, you must come here again, and if you're really interested in all this, I'll tell you some more of the Rookwood stories. But now I'm going to make you some coffee, and then we'll have to go. Zak's plane is due to land at eleven and I'll need to drop you back to the flat first.'

'You'll go and come back here in the dark?'

'We've a very sophisticated system of lights now, down the steps, which will come on as we go down, and we'll take a torch anyway. And coming back, well, I'll have my strapping son with me.'

9

L eah edged the Land Rover into a parking spot between a Pajero and a Toyota Land Cruiser. It was Tuesday, lunchtime, four days following her evening with Ali Hassan. Zak had arrived, and they'd sailed and swum and talked about the malarial parasites that Zak was currently studying. Just now she'd dropped him off to catch up with some schoolfriends, while she shopped at the mall in the centre of the town and called into her hospital office to sign reports.

The large air-conditioned shopping mall had completely replaced the rows of small shops that she remembered from her childhood, shops with wooden verandas sprawled right across the pavement. Their demise was, she supposed, inevitable, though around the mall the old timber homes had been preserved. The tall Police Department building across the street from the mall looked down on the gingerbread balconies and balustrades of those heritage houses.

Leah crossed the parking lot and passed through the sliding automatic doors that separated the mall from the warmth of far north Queensland. She made her way down past Katies, Just Jeans, Sanity and the doughnut shop, heading for the supermarket. She was thinking that she'd have to come back to town on Friday to the market for vegetables and fruit, and fish too, but she could stock up now with everything else she needed. She had guests to cater for — Leslie and his family on Sunday, as well as Zak for the whole of the holiday weekend. She was so busy making a mental shopping list that she collided with a man standing in front of CostLess Shoes. Reeling back, apologising, she saw that it was Ali Hassan, and to her surprise she began to blush. He was holding several pairs of sandals

'Oh, I'm sorry! Looking for a bargain?' She smiled, trying to sound casual.

He smiled back, and momentarily put a hand on her arm to steady her. His shirt today was a rich dark merlot red, a good colour, and his fingers on her arm were slim and supple, their backs covered in fine dark hairs.

'Many bargains actually,' he replied. Then she saw that he was also holding at least a dozen footprints made of cardboard, of different sizes and shapes.

'These are the feet of some Iraqi people in Woomera Detention Centre,' he explained. 'They cannot get out to buy their own shoes, you see. They have sent these to me, so I can try to match them.'

A large saleswoman with a label saying CHRISTINE was hovering nearby, apparently expecting Ali to make a bolt with a dozen left-foot sandals.

'I'll help if you like,' Leah volunteered. 'What exactly are you looking for?'

'I thought one pair of sandals and one pair of sneakers each,' he explained. 'I'm told the ground gets very hot between the buildings in the summer, and there are no trees. I think these sandals with the straps with holes are best, they can be adjusted to suit the width of the foot. And these sneakers with this white tape on them.'

'It's called Velcro.'

Christine hovered nearer. 'Can I help you? These are for people who can't try on their own shoes?' she asked incredulously. 'What people?'

Ali looked across at Leah. 'They're in a detention camp in South Australia,' she responded crisply, her composure now restored. 'They're asylum seekers.'

'Oh.' Christine looked Ali up and down. 'You're from the same place?'

'Yes,' he said shortly. 'Iraq.'

Leah said quickly: 'Dr Hassan is working in the hospital here.' Immediately Christine's expression changed. Leah could see her thinking, *Gee, a doctor, not one of those refugees after all. People who can't buy their own shoes, I never thought of that.*

'We've more size 10 in the brown out the back,' Christine said, 'I'll go and get them.'

In a short time, Ali and Leah had selected thirty pairs in assorted sizes and colours. Ali pulled out his wallet and found $400 in notes, a good proportion, Leah thought, of his pay cheque this fortnight.

Christine packed the shoes for them, then leaned her bulk across the counter and said to Ali, 'Sorry, but I never thought about stuff like that before. When you send the shoes, you send those people my best wishes as well.' She flushed as he smiled and bowed.

Leaving the shop, Leah said to Ali, 'Why don't I drop you to the flat? My car's close by.' She could shop some other time.

'Well, thank you, I had been going to walk, but ... there are a lot of these.'

'My car's in the parking lot on the Police Department side. I'll lead the way.'

And so it happened that Leslie Fernando, glancing out the side window of his sixth floor office, while contemplating the possibility of arranging a chat with Mr Brian Mitchell about certain matters, and thinking also of his lunch, observed his old friend Dr Leah Rookwood come out of the shopping mall, together with an unknown man of Middle Eastern appearance. Both of them were laden with an extraordinary number of shoes. They climbed into Leah's car and drove away. Even from this distance, Leslie could see that Leah was laughing and talking happily with this stranger. *Could that be the Iraqi doctor?* he wondered. *How intriguing, I must tell Claudine tonight. And we'll be seeing Leah anyway on Sunday.*

10

Zak sat at the dining table devouring pancakes as fast as his mother could fry them in the kitchen. He wore khaki shorts and a T-shirt, and his long legs — his father's legs, not that Leah had ever seen much of those — stretched out beneath the table into unlaced sneakers. His nose, too, was his father's, broad and flat. His dark hair was spikily cut and gelled. In Leah's opinion he needed to shave, but she had gathered from her son that the three-day stubble was in fact carefully planned.

A languid electric fan above the table stirred dust particles through the air. The weekend papers from the southern capitals — Sydney and Melbourne — were spread across the dining table. It was a warm Sunday morning, a week following Zak's arrival home. He had lazed around for most of this week and was due to return to Townsville on Tuesday.

'So who's coming today, Mum?' he asked.

'Leslie and Claudine. And their girls. And the Iraqi doctor I told you about, who's taken the flat. Ali Hassan.'

'Oh yeah. Isn't he a Muslim though?'

'Well, yes and no. He is a Muslim, but not a very strict one. And why should that make any difference to his coming to lunch?'

'No, it doesn't I guess, just that we don't get many Muslims up here.'

'Well, I can assure you he's very nice.'

Something in her tone made her son turn around to look at her. She was bent over the sink, turned away from him, but the back of her neck was blushing crimson. Zak raised an eyebrow. *Something going on here?* he wondered. Leah was concentrating on washing out the mixing bowl. She decided not to mention that she had lunched three times with Ali Hassan during her holiday week, since each time she'd told her son she was 'just catching up' at the hospital. As a result, no reorganisation of her household had taken place at all. The items she'd brought with Ali from the flat still sat piled in the barrows at the side of the veranda.

After the encounter at the shoe shop, which had led to them lunching together, she and Ali had met again twice. 'I've just got to drop into the hospital tomorrow,' she'd said each day to him, and so they'd agree to meet again for lunch. And on each occasion, they'd decided against the hospital café, and instead crossed the road and walked on down the Esplanade together to find another place, away from the interested gazes of colleagues.

He had told her a little more about himself. He made it clear that, while he would give her the facts, he wanted no great show of sympathy in response. She now knew that he had made an arranged marriage, had a daughter, been a specialist paediatrician in Baghdad. Then something had happened, something involving his older brother, who had been killed. He had been forced to leave in a hurry. His wife and daughter, and his younger brother, had died while trying to join him. This was as much as she knew. Oh, there was also his sister-in-law and her children. They had recently been able to leave Iraq and she had married a Frenchman.

Whether he had found anyone else, someone still in England, say, who might come to join him in the flat, she did not know. But why should this concern her? He was just a friend.

'So are they coming up together?' Zak now asked. 'I'll go across and pick them up if you know what time.'

'Yes, Leslie's bringing Ali. He said they'd be at the wharf soon after twelve.' Ali had been finally reassured by her defence of Leslie, and agreed to come up to the island with him and Claudine.

'All that stuff, Mum, that you brought back last week — that's still sitting outside. Can I do something with it before these people come, like get it out of the way for you? I know you won't let me chuck it out!'

'No, don't throw anything out!'

'What about moving some of it up to the lighthouse? Where you put all our old schoolbooks, mine and Micky's, that you're saving for future museums.'

'Well, you never know. I think they're interesting. I wish some of the first Rookwoods had left us a few things like that. The lighthouse is a good idea. There's certainly no room left in my study, in fact, I haven't been able to get into it to work for months.'

'I'll do it straight after breakfast. Is the key still hanging above the stove?'

'Yes. I'll come with you. I love the lighthouse, but I hardly ever go there when I'm here on my own.'

After breakfast they set out. Zak piled the barrows with more items Leah couldn't bear to part with, as well as many books. They followed the path which led around the front of the house and up to the highest point on the island, the flat rock beside the lighthouse. At a distance, the two cats followed, disdainful but curious. They wore bells around their necks to warn native birds of their coming, and tinkled softly as they walked.

An enormous blue sky stretched above the island. Seabirds swooped and cawed, watching for food on the rocks way beneath them. Across the passage between island and mainland was the mouth of the Cassowary, with rivulets of honey-coloured water spreading outwards into the sea. The mountains on the land were sharply etched against the bright light of mid-morning. The red and white lighthouse stood a little to their right. Leah looked at it with affection. She had been happy that, when its services had been made obsolete, the Rookwood family had been allowed to buy it.

'It's just a big toy,' remarked Zak. 'It must have been fun putting it together. Like giant Lego!'

The pieces had come out by steamer from Lancashire in 1910, part of an order from the Queensland government that had kept a whole factory in work for a year. It had been assembled on the site and the light began flashing in 1911. There was a notice explaining all this attached to the front door of the lighthouse, which was arched like that of a tiny Gothic chapel. Occasionally, guests from the resort made the trek up the hill for the view and the history. The lighthouse had become fully automated, the notice further explained, in 1939, with the outbreak of war. There was only ever one lighthouse keeper, Ronald Greentree, a veteran of the Sudan and South African wars, who'd been nearly ninety when he was pensioned off, protesting, in 1939. Leah's father had known old Mr Greentree well. 'Never missed a day filling and cleaning the lamps,' Charles had once said. 'He loved his work.' By 1960, the lighthouse was no longer needed — coastal shipping had more accurate ways of detecting Rookwood Island. The machinery was dismantled and the engineers no longer appeared twice a year to service it and take dinner with Leah's parents. Now the only function of the lighthouse was the storage of Leah's overflowing possessions.

To their left was the family cemetery.

'Want to go in for a moment?' Leah asked, and Zak shrugged, why not. White and orange bougainvillea spilled over the railings that surrounded the graveyard, and a lime tree flourished in a corner. Steps of stone cut out and carried from the rock above the cemetery led up to the graves themselves, which were on a flat area slightly raised above the surrounding ground.

In the centre, with his own low-railed grave, was John Rookwood. 'Born in Tullymore, County Down, in the country of Ireland, 4th April, 1842. Died on this island, not one hundred yards from where he now lies, 21st April, 1900. *Requiescat in pace.*' Thomas lay on John's right, 1880–1940. In front of Thomas, two of his sons: Charles (1919–1989) and young Thomas (1924–1944). Young Thomas had been brought up here in a coffin from the flat mallee country outside Mildura, where he'd pancaked his plane the second week of his Air Force training. He'd volunteered for overseas service but never left Australia. His gravestone was the white cross with the Rising Sun of the Australian Imperial Forces.

Philip was beneath a similar white cross in a war cemetery on Malta, Charles had once explained to Leah. Philip Horton Rookwood, 1913–1944. Twice Charles had made the solitary journey to that site. Mercifully, the older Thomas had not known the deaths of any of his sons. But his wife had seen them all. Rose Margaret Rookwood (1892–1989) had gone to meet her maker just a few weeks after Charles, still sharp as a tack and living on Rookwood at ninety-seven. And both she and Thomas had known together the loss of their only daughter. Rosemary, 1st–9th August, 1923, lay in a tiny plot by the cemetery gate, with its own marble angel. She'd been born with a hole in her heart in an era before cardiac surgery.

There was — as Leah's sister Mara had frequently remarked to her when they were children, and Zak's sister Micky sometimes remarked to him — still plenty of room left for them all. Perry the Second and Axminster and other pets were interred in a small plot behind the human graves; Axminster had required folding several times into a sack so that he could fit into the hole Charles had dug for him. Mara herself was unlikely to leave her mortal remains here, Leah thought. She'd probably want a dramatic burial at sea.

It was their father's dying in 1989 that had brought Mara back to the island, and to Leah, for the longest period since the day she'd sailed out of Sydney Harbour as a mess-girl on the *Kristina*. When Leah had sent for Mara to come from Sweden, Charles had waited, uncomplaining, reduced by then to a small dry chip of a man. He'd lain softly in bed in the main room of the Rookwood house, with its view of the sea, refusing until his second daughter arrived to use the morphine drip Leah and others had set up for him for the pain of his prostate cancer. Once Mara was there, though, he'd gripped her hand tightly and consented to the soothing trickle of narcotic into his veins, though not so fast that he could not spend a final fortnight lingering with his daughters, who moved quietly about him.

Gran Rookwood had sat in the warmth of her cane chair on the front veranda, watching the sea, just barely aware that her last living son was dying. She slid away peacefully one night just eight weeks later, and Leah had been free then to take Zak and Micky to Brisbane, and complete her specialist training.

After Charles' death, it had been a simple matter to transfer him to his lasting resting place up the hill, and for many evenings after his funeral, while Mara stayed on Rookwood, she and Leah would bring glasses and a wine bottle up to the cemetery, and sit by Charles' fresh grave, and talk about the separate courses their lives had taken.

It was Mara who'd explained to Leah how Charles had felt about surviving the war. Especially when the Mitchells built the resort, Mara said, he thought he'd let his brothers down, and Leah realised she was right. If his brothers had been here, it would never have happened, her father always believed. Somehow they would together have wrested the land back from the Mitchells. And his brothers would have stopped him marrying a Mitchell, Mara added. Mara still hated to speak directly of her mother. *Then* we *wouldn't have been born*, Leah had thought, but this was not an idea to produce at that point for Mara.

It was during one of those talks that she'd first told Mara about herself and Brian Mitchell. Mara had been furious — 'It's not too late to do something, bring a charge, even now,' she'd said — and Leah had known this was so. Only she'd have to have been more like Mara to do it, and if she had been more like Mara, then maybe nothing would ever have happened anyway. Considering all this now, standing with Zak by her father's grave in the Sunday morning sunshine, Leah had the feeling that Leslie, the other day, with his questions about Brian, might just have gleaned something of this episode in her past. She would have to think hard about whether to tell him at least some of the story, if he asked her again.

Now Zak plucked a handful of white bougainvillea flowers and placed them on John's grave. A little mockingly, but only a little, Leah saw.

Then he looked puzzled. 'Mum, who was John's wife?'

'Adeline. Adeline Horton.'

'But she's not here.'

'No. Because ... um ... yes, I remember. She married again after John died, and she went to Sri Lanka. At least, Ceylon it was then. She married someone with a tea estate, a planter. And lived to a ripe old age and I guess died there. I think she lived almost up to the war — the second one.'

'Did you ever meet her?'

'Zak! I wasn't born until years after that war was over ...'

'Yeah. OK. Just getting my generations mixed up again.'

'Your grandfather met her. My father, Charles, who's right here. Who you barely remember, of course. He was taken by his father by ship to England in the 1930s and they stopped over in Colombo. You've seen those old postcards of elephants ...'

But Zak was losing interest. 'Let's go to the lighthouse,' he said. 'I always like the little staircase.'

They pushed the barrows up the final incline and Leah produced from her pocket the large brass key marked 'Government Property' that had always opened the lighthouse door, and which Ronald Greentree had reluctantly surrendered in 1939. The door creaked slowly open. Old Greentree would have been horrified at the lack of oil.

The interior was dim, lit only by two small windows halfway up the cast-iron spiral staircase that led to the light itself. There was a smell of warm dust. Piles of cardboard boxes contained books, newspapers, shoes, past school prizes, riding hats, broken bicycle wheels and cracked terracotta pots. Zak looked around despairingly. Where the hell were they going to fit the latest lot? And would his mother ever get rid of any of this?

'We'll just shove these things a bit further in, for the moment,' Leah said, sensing his reluctance. She gave the nearest box a hard push, and with a squawk a bush rat raced out from the back of what had clearly been a cosy home, and shot up the staircase.

In a flash, one cat leapt through 180 degrees from the doorway and up the stairs in pursuit. Bells tinkled furiously. There was a mezzanine floor above them, which the engineers had used to work on the machinery of the light, and the cat could be heard slithering across this. The second cat remained disdainfully behind, her back arched.

'Poor Ratty!' said Leah. There was a bang from above, and the crash of something heavy falling, followed by a piteous cry, feline rather than rodent. Zak and Leah stood for a moment, listening.

'She's stuck somewhere,' Leah said. 'I'll have a look. I hope it's not a python.'

'I'll come too,' Zak offered. 'And it won't be a python, not a big one, it couldn't get in.'

He led the way around three full spirals and into the upper storey.

This level smelt faintly of mould and was even dimmer than the floor below, but in the corner, the back half of the cat could be seen emerging from a small space in the inner wall of the lighthouse. The chase had dislodged a lamp and an old yellow oilskin, which had fallen over the cat, whose front half was now well and truly entangled. Laughing, Leah lifted off the oilskin and fished out the cat's shoulders and paws, so that her head could emerge as well. She shook herself crossly and hissed. Leah let her down. There was a rustling inside the lighthouse wall; somewhere in there must be the rat, his heart beating furiously, but a triumphant smile on his face.

There was something else wedged in the space in the wall, Leah now saw in the half-light, so shadowy that the outline was barely visible. A box.

'Help me get hold of this, Zak,' she said, and he reached over and helped her prise it out. It was heavy, and about the size of a jewellery box.

'It's brass,' she said. 'Quite solid. Tarnished, but I'm sure it's brass. I've never seen it before.'

'It looks Indian, or Eastern,' Zak said.

'It would probably polish up nicely,' Leah remarked. 'Can you open it?'

There was a dusty key in the lock, but it would not yield. There were more scuttling noises from inside the lighthouse wall, and the cat began to hiss again. It was so warm that sweat was trickling down the back of Leah's neck.

'Let's take it back to the house, Mum,' Zak said. 'It doesn't open easily. Probably nothing much inside anyway.'

'OK. Come on, Cat,' Leah said, starting back down the stairs. 'We'll just pile the rest of this up down here. I promise I'll come back and sort it all out soon!'

11

Back in the house, Leah set the brass box on the kitchen counter and then glanced at the clock.

'Zak! It's half past eleven already, you'll need to go now to get across to pick them up. And I'll need to get a move on with the lunch.'

Zak took the keys for the boat, pushed sunglasses onto his nose, and went off out the door. Leah opened her fridge, found lettuce and avocados, baby spinach and fresh pineapple. She oiled the tuna steaks and chopped limes and onions for salsa. She checked the ice-cream supply for Lily and Larissa. There was not too much more to do. She had a cake baked, wine in the fridge. Things seemed under control.

In her bedroom, she pulled off her jeans and T-shirt and slipped on a silk shirt and cargo pants. She brushed her hair, tried on one pair of heavy silver earrings, checked them in the mirror and changed them for another. *I am* not *nervous about seeing him again*, she told herself. *It is* normal *to want to look good. Well, the best you can, baby. Be honest!* The previous evening she had done her hair colour and painted her toenails scarlet.

She wandered back to the kitchen. The clock read quarter past twelve. It would be another half hour at least until her guests arrived back with Zak. Her eyes fell on the box again and this time she picked it up. There was a keyhole, but the key was rusted to the lock and wouldn't budge. She took a kitchen knife and gently inserted it between box and lid. From beneath the sink, she unearthed a can of WD-40 and sprayed the lock. She tried the lock again and with a protesting squeak, it turned a semicircle, there was a click inside the box and the lid sprang free.

The interior of the box was lined with stained red silk, and contained a collection of old papers and cards. There were hand-coloured postcards of Ceylon and Singapore — elephants, the Mount Lavinia Hotel, the Tiger Balm Gardens, a P&O steamer. There was a bundle of letters in faded brown ink that was barely decipherable, tied with a ribbon whose colour had long ago become indeterminate. And tucked beneath the ribbon were a couple of newspaper cuttings. Intrigued, Leah found a spot at her dining table and sat down to untie the ribbon. Carefully she unfolded the first cutting.

'*Cooktown Herald and Palmer River Advertiser*, 25 April, 1900,' she read.

> It is with deep regret that we announce the death last Saturday of one of Cooktown's best known and respected citizens, Dr John Rookwood.

'*Known and respected*', Leah thought. Not 'loved', as a town's long-time doctor might be described in the final evaluation before he went to meet his Maker.

> Dr Rookwood had been visiting his property Rookwood Island for a picnic with friends. It appears he had walked alone along a narrow cliff track on the north-eastern corner of the island. At an overhanging part, he apparently slipped and fell some 200 feet onto the rocks below. That part of the pathway is notorious for falling rocks and Dr Rookwood had cautioned previous visitors to the island against taking that route, which is the quickest way to the beach on the north side. He himself had intended to visit the north beach in

search of a large male turtle recently seen there, whose shell he hoped to add to his collection.

One of the ladies picnicking, Mrs Howe, heard him cry out as he fell and the gentlemen of the party were quickly on the scene. Messrs Woodall and Dunlop dove into the sea and recovered the doctor, but sadly found him already deceased.

Doctor Rookwood was born in Tullymore, County Down, Northern Ireland, and took his medical diplomas from Dublin. He had practised in Cooktown for 24 years, to the enormous benefit of so many of our citizens.

He is survived by his wife Adeline and his son Thomas, a medical student in Sydney. A memorial service is being postponed to enable Thomas and his mother to return from Sydney. A further announcement will be made by Cochranes' Embalming and Undertaking Services when arrangements are in hand for the memorial service. All at the Cooktown Hospital and in the town extend their deepest sympathy to Dr Rookwood's family.

Of course she had known the story. That was why she and Mara had never been allowed to take the Devil's Path down to North Beach when they were children, though sometimes Mara would do it for a dare. Nor had she allowed Micky or Zak to go that way, though she was sure that Zak had done exactly as Mara had. Not Micky, she was much more sensible than her brother. Leah had never seen the story recorded though, and she was sure her father had not known of the newspaper cuttings. They must have been hidden away in the lighthouse for more than sixty years.

There was a second newspaper cutting from the *Cooktown Herald*, two weeks later. Leah now studied this.

'Sinister secret behind doctor's death?' it asked.

Rumours are circulating in the town that on the day of Dr Rookwood's death, blacks were seen on Rookwood Island by members of the picnicking party, and one lady, who wishes to remain anonymous, noticed a rustling in the bushes above the pathway from which Dr Rookwood fell. This area is visible from Turtle Beach where the picnickers were gathered. This lady believes that a heavy stone, thrown from above the pathway, put Dr Rookwood off balance, causing his fall. The same informant states that she definitely saw blacks in the bush above the rock overhanging the cliff pathway earlier in the day.

We note that Rookwood Island, the site of the tragedy, was the scene of the regrettable incident some years ago in which Mrs Rookwood was forced to flee with her son Thomas, then an infant, after being attacked by blacks. Subsequently, a party of Cooktown gentlemen carried out some reprisals, although whether any lives were lost amongst the blacks is not known. Police at the time were unable to determine the number of casualties. Our current informant goes so far as to suggest that Dr Rookwood's death was not at all an accident, but deliberately planned and executed by the blacks frequenting the island in revenge for the raiding party nearly 18 years ago. This seems to us unlikely as the native mind is not able to retain such memories. Nevertheless we hope the Police will fully investigate these claims."

Unable to determine the number of casualties? Leah thought. Every Aboriginal person in the district knew the number of casualties, and passed that knowledge on so that it was recorded even today in the Cooktown museum. It did not seem that the police investigations could have been very thorough. The family story had always had John simply falling off the cliff. *Was* it possible that he was murdered? Very possible, when she thought it over. A big stone rolled down towards the cliff path at just the right moment would sweep anyone on that path over and down to a certain and hideous death on the rocks below. *What's more*, Leah was thinking, *the person who did it could then easily slip away unnoticed through the rainforest* ... She was mulling over this when she realised that her mobile phone, left on the kitchen bench, was ringing. Her mind still on John Rookwood, she crossed the kitchen and picked up the phone. 'Hello?'

It was Zak, on his own mobile, breathing heavily.

'Oh, hi, Mum ... I think you'll need to come across. There's a ... body ... on the beach. I found her. It's a girl. An Aboriginal girl. I was waiting for Leslie and walked along the beach. To those rocks. Then thank God Leslie turned up, and your friend, that doctor. Can you come across in the little tinnie?'

12

It was her own fault, really.

Things had been fine between them, just fine ... why did she want to break that up?

He recalled her hair — like a curtain of dark silk down her back, it was, with just the ends gold-flecked. He remembered a piece of that hair straying across her earlobe once when he'd nuzzled it, and she'd laughed and flicked it back as his tongue moved down towards her nipple. She'd wriggled and giggled beneath him. Even now, after all that had happened, he grew hard just thinking about it.

What made her change like that, really? There'd been so much in it for her. For both of them.

And then the taunts. That's when he knew he had to do something. Who did she think she was?

13

The tinnie was a small metal dinghy, with a temperamental outboard. If it gave up on her she'd have get out the oars, hope Zak was watching, and call him on her mobile to come across to get her. But fortunately the motor cooperated for the occasion. There was a breeze blowing over this side of the island, a chop to the sea, so the tinnie bumped its way hard across the waves.

Leah had hastily put salad and fish back into the fridge, pulled on a hat and sunglasses, and run straight down the steps to the wharf, where the tinnie was moored. As soon as she was well out into the channel, she looked across to the beach, where unusual activity was immediately obvious.

Next to her own Land Rover was a police car, which must have been somewhere nearby to have arrived so soon, and Leslie's car beside it. Then she saw two more blue and white police cars arrive — they must have come screaming up from town, and she watched as Leslie's car drove away. About twenty people were gathered near the wharf and two uniformed cops moved to keep them back. Further down the beach, to Leah's left, she could see the tiny figure of Leslie — Claudine must have been driving their car then — and she thought she could see Ali as well, plus several more blue-uniformed men. In the distance, out towards the main road, she could just hear the sound of another siren. All around her the sunlight shimmered on the water, and it seemed impossible that a young girl should be lying dead on that beach. An Aboriginal girl. At the site of the massacre.

Leah shivered — after so many years, she could still be upset by death in young people. Her thoughts, always, were for their mothers.

Now as she steered the tinnie, Leah had time to consider. A local girl? Had she drowned? Kids here could swim before they could walk, bobbing around like corks in the sea in the Dry season, and in mountain streams in the Wet when the stingers spawned in the ocean and beach swimming was perilous. *Don't jump to conclusions, Leah,* she reprimanded herself, *just because she's on the beach doesn't mean she drowned.*

Leah cut the motor as she came up towards the wharf. Zak ran along and the uniformed cop, recognising her, also came to help. Constable Jones. A bit overweight, young, pink, close-cropped blond hair, sweating slightly in the warm sunlight. A solidly built policewoman, Constable Wilkinson, was keeping the curious at bay at the other end of the wharf, standing in front of the memorial to the massacre victims.

Leah threw her line to Zak and he and Jones pulled her alongside the wooden wharf. Zak looked calm now, but it was clear he was not far from tears. Leak climbed from the boat and put her arms around his shoulders.

'Zak ... what an awful thing to happen.'

'Yes. And I know who she is now. Ebony. Ebony Passmore. I walked back and ... had another look. I'm quite sure it's Ebony.'

'What about her family?'

Constable Jones answered quickly. 'A car's been sent to the family in Cairns, Dr Rookwood.' He gestured down the wharf.

'None of these people know yet who she is ... until the family's informed, so ...' He gestured meaningly and Leah nodded her head.

'I understand.' She turned to Zak.

'Where's Claudine? And the girls?'

'Claudine took them in to the village to wait for a while.' He dropped his voice. 'Lily must have known her too, but she doesn't know who she is yet. She must have been in Lily's year, I think. But she left school much earlier.' *As most Aboriginal girls did*, thought Leah.

'You stay here,' she said. 'I'll walk down and talk to Leslie. Sit down on the wharf.'

'Yes, mate, you've done all you could do,' Jones said. 'Sit there and take it easy.' Zak sat down and put his head in his hands.

Leah walked down the beach towards the rocky point. The smooth shingle had been washed clean by the incoming tide. Both Leslie and Ali came towards her, their faces sombre.

'Bad news,' Leslie said. 'She's been in the water a good few hours I'd say, by the look of her skin, but not much longer than that.'

Ali nodded. 'I came straight along when we met your son,' he said by way of explanation to Leah, 'but I saw at once there was no hope at all.' It was clear that, though he had seen many deaths, he was still moved by that of the young stranger.

On a sand spit beside the outcrop of black rocks lay the girl. Her once beautiful face was bloated, blue and water-logged, covered with strands of dark hair bleached blonde at the tips. There was sand in her mouth and bubbling foam dribbled from her nostrils. She lay on her side, the incoming waves rocking the body a little in the shallows. Had the tide brought her to where she now was? Or had she been dumped there? Leah noted a ring near her navel and a tattooed snake on one shoulder. Her toenails were painted electric blue, her fingernails bitten short. Her skirt was rucked up around her waist, but her pants and bra were still in place. A lacy top was torn and partly hanging from one shoulder. A folded body bag waited on a dry area of beach. Already two policemen were methodically searching the area around the body.

'Very tragic,' Ali said softly behind Leah. 'Someone has gone to find her family. I believe they are in Cairns.'

'Yes,' Leah said.

She squatted by the body. One arm was stretched out towards the rocks, the other was folded beneath her. There were abrasions on the face and both arms that looked like scratches from sharp sticks. It was hard to be sure, when the skin had been in the water, but she thought the abrasions were post-mortem. Which was interesting.

There was the squeal of brakes. Leslie's colleagues had arrived at the wharf. Three men in white shirts and dark trousers, looking incongruous on this tropical beach, leapt from the car. Leslie waved to them and they set out along the sand. One of them was Drew Borgese. Leslie had been pleased to find Drew was on duty that morning. All three seemed surprised to see Leah there before them, already at work on a Sunday afternoon.

'Afternoon, Doctor.'

'Afternoon, Drew, John, Joe ...'

'It was Leah's son who found her,' Leslie explained. 'We're supposed to be having lunch with Leah on the island. In fact, that is just what we will do when we have this sorted out. Her folks are on their way from Cairns. I guess they'll identify her as soon as they get here. Bad business this, whatever's happened to her. Oh, this is Dr Hassan from the hospital.' The detectives nodded and the men briefly shook hands. One detective unpacked a camera and began taking photos of the scene.

'Any ideas yet, Doc?' Drew asked. He towered above his solid middle-aged colleagues, his height and energy seeming barely constrained by the business shirt and sober navy trousers his new role demanded.

'None yet,' Leah replied. 'From immediate inspection, she does appear to have drowned, no obvious major trauma. And it must have happened not far from here or she would have just gone straight to the bottom. But a young girl doesn't go swimming in the sea fully clothed on a Saturday night, which is when this seems to have happened, without some compelling reason.'

Drew nodded. 'Yeah. Alcohol maybe. Or something else.'

A cloud of fine sandy dust, and another vehicle had arrived. An old battered blue Kingswood with a stinking exhaust, at which the uniformed cops cast a speculative look. A young man jumped from the driver's seat, followed by three older women. Constable Wilkinson moved quickly to bring them across the beach towards where Ebony lay. Leah walked back to join them.

'Hello — I'm Leah,' and they nodded, yes, the doctor from the island. 'You're ... her mum?' Leah addressed the first, youngest woman.

'Aunty,' she replied. 'Violet. Mum's dead. She lived in my house. She really dead? How come? From what?' Tears ran down both cheeks and the other two women also began to cry.

Now Leslie and Drew joined them and silently shook their hands. Leah was aware of Ali sadly watching the scene. Leah took Violet's hand and led her across to where Ebony lay.

'We're thinking she drowned, but we don't know how yet.'

Violet wailed and threw herself down beside Ebony's body, and the detectives drew back and did not interfere. The young boy, the driver, also began to howl to himself, 'Shit, shit', and to pace away up the beach.

Leslie turned to another of the women, the more composed, and asked, 'Is her father in Cairns? Has she been living at home?'

'Daddy dead too. Longtime now. She in the dance group. You know. Been dancing in town and over there.' The woman indicated Rookwood, in particular the resort end. Leslie looked at her keenly.

'She's been working at the resort?' he asked, avoiding using the dead girl's name. 'At Mitchells?' The woman nodded. Leah noted Leslie's expression and remembered the questions of the week before. What had Leslie heard about Brian Mitchell?

'They been working there ten–twelve weeks now. Mostly nights. Their boat bring them back at night. All the girls. Mitchells' boat.'

Leah could see the questions forming in Leslie's brain. Who were the other girls? Did they all go back together last night? Or did Ebony not join them? If not, why not? Had she a meeting with someone else? But he simply said, 'We'll be wanting to ask about all this in good time of course. And I'm afraid we'll be having to move her into town, to the mortuary in the hospital, until we've made sure what's happened.' The woman looked distraught, so he added gently, 'We must find out what happened, you know. And then she'll be able to come home.'

Various questions were forming in Leah's mind also. What might she find if the body were turned over and the back of Ebony's head examined? Or elsewhere? Had she been sexually assaulted? What were the blood levels, not only of alcohol but of various other substances that might make a girl like Ebony do what she might not otherwise have done on a Saturday night? Did she have a boyfriend?

Another car drew up, an old red Cortina, and Leah saw emerging a woman she knew well — Ina Frazer, tidying her hair and then bending to help an elderly man out from the back seat. At least, he appeared elderly, but Leah knew he was probably less than sixty.

'Grandpa Farrell,' said the woman on the beach. 'Her dad was a Farrell.' The two came slowly across the beach, Ina helping the old man, who limped painfully. When they reached Leah and her group, Ina hugged the other woman and then Leah in turn, and Leah held out her hand to Grandpa Farrell.

'I'm sorry,' she said simply.

'Yeah,' said Ina, 'we don't know anything about why this happened yet. Seems she didn't come back from work last night. That's all we know.' Leah thought of how many premature deaths, in young and beautiful people, Ina had seen in her life. Ina worked hard for the community, but this death rate had not changed much in the twenty years she had been in Cairns.

Ina turned and saw Ali, and to Leah's surprise, nodded bleakly to him. 'Hello Doc!' she said. Then she too went across to where Ebony lay and squatted down beside Violet, and remained there some minutes, with her arms around Violet, weeping silently.

'You've met Ina?' Leah asked Ali.

'Yes, she comes in to our ward to see Benjy, she and her twin sister. We've had some good talks.' Then he added, 'It's very good she's here, for the family, she's a very strong lady. But what about your own boy, he must be very upset.'

Leah shook herself guiltily. Of course. Zak. 'Come with me,' she said, and impulsively held out her hand to Ali. He reached for it, and Leah was abruptly conscious of a current of emotion, sharp as an electric shock, running between them. He continued to hold her hand for a few seconds as they walked across to where Zak was still sitting. Looking back, Leah saw Leslie regarding them both with interest.

At the wharf, a large blonde woman had arrived, and was sitting down with Zak. Ali recognised her from outside the Big Croc café, and Leah made the introductions.

'Hello, Renee — this is Ali Hassan. Zak, you already met Ali ...' Zak stood up and Leah was surprised and pleased to see Ali lean forward and hug Zak briefly.

'You couldn't have done anything more,' he said to Zak. 'Whatever's happened, it happened a while ago, during the night probably.'

Renee turned to look down the beach and nodded and sighed.

'Do you think she ... died here ... on the beach?' she asked Leah.

'I understand what you're asking, Renee,' Leah said. Leah had known Renee all her life. They'd shared a desk in the primary school in Cassowary village, when Renee's father farmed sugar cane on a property near the highway. Renee had gone away down south to work for a while, then come back married to Bill, and for years they'd run the shop in Cassowary village, and later opened the Big Croc. Renee had a heart to match her considerable size; she would not like to think of a young girl, a local, dying alone in the sea so close to her own home.

'It's not clear yet, Renee, what happened, whether she drowned or died some other way. You know she was one of the dancers from the group in town. Ebony Passmore. Apparently she was working at the resort last night. May have been working, I guess, maybe she didn't turn up there. And the kids in the dance troupe usually got taken home by boat afterwards. But you'd think that if she'd been with them and somehow fallen overboard, that would have been noticed immediately, and she would have been pulled out of the sea straight away. She must have been able to swim well anyway, and she's only got a few clothes on, she certainly hasn't been attacked by a shark, and the sea's not cold. And if for some reason she did fall off and they couldn't get her back on board, or see her, you'd expect an emergency call straight away, and for every boat from miles around, and the Rescue Services, to be out on the water there until she was found.'

Renee nodded agreement. 'Yeah, we heard nothing until we saw the cops coming through, and then Claudine turned up with the girls and told us what happened. I put Claudine and the kids in the café for the moment and came to see if I could do anything to help.'

She sighed again. 'Too many kids dying, Leah, still.'

Zak was standing a little to the side. Leah turned to him and said briskly, 'Zak, could you take Claudine and the girls across to Rookwood in the *Argo*? You'll need to tell them it's Ebony, it'll be common knowledge anyway soon, and they'll be upset. You'll be a good person to talk to them. I'll come when I can with Leslie, it shouldn't be long, all the technical people are here and plenty of support for Violet and the rest of the family. The body ... Ebony ... will have to be taken into the hospital.'

She paused for a moment, and then added, 'Maybe you would take Ali too?'

'No,' said Ali. 'May I wait and come with you in the small boat?'

'Yes,' said Leah quickly, pleased he wanted to stay with her. 'Leslie will come with us as well, I think.' It seemed that on the car journey to the wharf, Ali had warmed to Leslie. Certainly he seemed unconcerned about the police presence around them.

Zak was happy to be able to do something and get away from the death scene. He handed his mobile to Renee so that she could call the café to get Claudine to drive back to the wharf. Two more carloads of Ebony's family from Cairns arrived just then, and began to spill out onto the sand, and now the police came over and began to move them back.

'We'll need a couple more minutes folks,' she heard Drew say. 'We're not sure what's happened and we need to make some checks. Her aunty and grandpa are with her, and that's enough for the moment.' A couple of Cassowary locals started to drift away. A white van drew up — the hospital's mortuary van.

'We won't be long, Zak,' Leah said. 'You find drinks and things for Claudine and the girls.'

She leaned over and hugged him, and said more softly, 'And try not to be too upset. I think it's going to turn out to have been some kind of accident that no-one could have done anything to prevent.'

But this was not her private opinion.

14

Of course he planned to act shocked when it was realised she was gone. He didn't know exactly how he would come to hear the news. Maybe even in Cairns itself, her family, they'd think she'd just left to go down south, they knew that's what she'd been planning. Maybe they wouldn't miss her for quite a while. That would be good. Maybe no-one would be able to remember exactly when they had last seen her. That would help him.

He couldn't act too shocked though. He was a good actor, he knew that. He'd be sad, and sorry for her family, of course. Wonder how she was getting on down south, if that's where she was.

Say she'd probably get in touch, in time ...

If he had to talk to the police, and that might happen, that was the line he'd take. Not a bad dancer, but not very responsible. Probably just upped and left. Thought she could make a career by herself, down on the Gold Coast somewhere. He rehearsed it over in his mind. Yes, he was a good actor. He could convince any copper.

15

H alf an hour later, Leah started up the motor of the tinnie in which Leslie and Ali sat. Claudine had been happy to accept Leah's suggestion and go with Zak and her daughters to the island.

Scenes-of-crime officers were still taking photos of the body and the beach around it. Already some relatives had set out for the hospital, and Ebony herself would follow soon. There was blue and white police tape stretched widely around the scene, and the local crowd was starting to disperse.

Leslie took the line from Constable Jones and Renee waved them off. Nobody spoke until they were well out onto the water, each enjoying the peace the sea brought and the sight of the island in front of them, and in Ali's case, dealing with a distinct queasiness induced by the tinnie's movement and not helped by the tragedy of the morning's events.

Then Leslie, looking toward the resort end of Rookwood and trailing his fingers through the clear waters over the side of the tinnie, said, 'About half a mile from where she's supposed to have been last night — though we'll have to check that, of course, that's Drew's job for today, I'm officially off duty — half a mile to where Zak found her. Is Zak OK by the way? He must have had a hell of a shock.'

'Yes,' said Leah, 'I'm afraid he did.' She looked back at Ali.

'He's really grateful to you, I think, even as a medical student he hasn't seen many dead people, and to find someone you've known like that must have been terrible.'

'What I'm thinking,' Leslie continued, 'is if she did dance last night, and didn't go back home, as seems possible, *someone* must know where she did go. And *someone* must have missed her. But they didn't raise any official alarms. Drew told me there've been no missing person reports the whole weekend.'

'Exactly what occurred to me,' Leah agreed. 'Of course, the autopsy may tell us a lot more. Which I won't be doing till Tuesday, by the way, tomorrow being a holiday. But the sea where she was found is too shallow to drown in easily, and if she drowned farther out, she would have sunk until there were enough post-mortem changes to bring the body back to the surface, which would take several days if sharks didn't get it ... somehow it doesn't seem like a straightforward accident, though I wouldn't say that to Zak.'

'No,' Leslie agreed. 'Or the girls.' He turned to Ali and gave a smile. 'We've already seen how curious Lissa can be.'

'Oh, that's all right.' Ali looked embarrassed.

'She asked Ali a million questions about Iraq on the way up here,' Leslie explained to Leah. 'Do Iraqi women wear headscarves, do they take them off at home, do they go to school, can they be doctors, can they be teachers?'

'It's good she is so interested,' Ali smiled. 'And she thought all my answers to those questions were good ones! Iraq is a bad dictatorship, but it has been a secular state, women have been able to study and work much more easily than in other places like Saudi Arabia. And although many women wear the scarf, it is not compulsory. Despite all the other problems of life in Iraq.'

'Yeah,' Leslie agreed. 'That Saddam seems a nasty piece of work by any standards. Do you think the Yanks will get him out eventually? Or that there will be an uprising and he'll be overthrown?'

Leah looked across at Leslie. Was he aware that Ali had lost most of his family in Saddam's Iraq?

'Not that,' Ali answered. 'He is too powerful, he has too many cronies in high places and he has killed anyone who could be an enemy. Eventually something may happen, he might even die, and there will be change. I fear what America may do, since 9/11 they have just seen all of us Muslims as the enemy. And it is difficult to see how we would ever have a good government in Iraq. I would like that to happen very much, perhaps I could go back to work there then. Although as I told you, most of my family are gone.' So he had spoken of this already to Leslie.

They were coming in closer to the island now. Leslie studied the thatched roofs of the bungalows at Mitchells, scene of last night's dance performance. The resort lay tranquil behind its red-trunked palms. There was no suggestion, from this distance, that whatever had happened to Ebony had in any way affected the guests. One of the resort's launches was just coming in to their own wharf after a morning trip to the reef.

'It certainly looks peaceful and innocent,' Leslie commented, although Leah saw that he was watching the shoreline carefully. There were several small boats moored there, belonging to staff from the resort, who could take themselves across to the Cassowary wharf, or fishing, or even to Cairns if they wanted to. Just as there were quite a few inhabitants of Cassowary village who had boats moored near the wharf on the beach, or on the river near the village. Had Ebony been taken by someone, somewhere, in one of these boats, during the night?

And what, Leah wondered, did Leslie know or suspect about Brian, and did he really imagine she knew anything more? In fact, everything she knew about Brian was in the distant past, though she had come to realise that those events had shaped the course of much of her life until now. She was suddenly aware of Ali asking a question.

'They are mostly foreigners who come there?' he enquired, indicating the resort.

'Mostly,' Leah answered. 'Plus rich people from Sydney and Brisbane. A fair number of Japanese and Filipinos. They divide their time between the resort and the casino in town. There's a resort launch to take them in to the casino and bring them back, and even a helipad and a helicopter service if they're in a desperate hurry to get rid of their money. But also there are Germans and other Europeans, people from all over the place.'

Ali thought for a moment, then asked, 'Your ancestor sold the land for that place?'

Leslie looked directly across at Leah. They were coming in to her own wharf now. Big copper-coloured crabs were frolicking in the shallows of Mermaids Beach. Leah cut the motor and Leslie gathered up the line ready to throw it over the bollard on the wharf. The *Argo* was already tied up neatly. Leah manoeuvred the tinnie close in beside the *Argo* and scrambled up onto the wharf.

'My grandfather,' she replied to Ali's question. 'Rather unwillingly. It was the 1930s and he was in financial trouble. He had hoped to get it back. But that didn't happen.'

'Ah,' said Ali. So there was bad blood there. The land had somehow been taken from Leah's family by these Mitchell people. But the tinnie was rocking quite violently, and he needed to get out of it and onto the wharf without falling into the sea. The rest of this story would have to wait.

Leslie jumped out, and leaned to help Ali from the heaving tinnie up onto the wharf. Then he turned to them both and said, 'So for the moment we are treating this as an accident, especially for conversation this afternoon?'

Leah and Ali nodded and the three set off up the stairs towards Leah's house. As he climbed, Leslie made a conscious effort to relax and take his mind off both Brian Mitchell and the clammy skin of the dead girl, subjects which might or might not be related.

'You've been up here before?' he asked Ali, who was panting a little beside him. 'The view just gets better and better as you go up, I always find.'

'Yes,' Ali agreed, 'I think it must be the most wonderful place in the world to live.' Then, conscious of Leslie's small nod and smile beside him, he blushed and fell silent.

'We must take you to the reef,' Leslie said quickly, to cover Ali's embarrassment. He was about to add 'while you're here' and stopped himself just in time. Leslie had been vaguely opposed to the government's actions against asylum seekers, but up until now they had seemed far away from north Queensland. Meeting Ali had given an added dimension to his ideas on the situation.

'I would like that,' Ali replied,'although I am not a good swimmer. Not many Iraqis swim much.'

As they came up towards the veranda of the house, it was clear from their tear-stained faces that both Lily and Larissa knew that it had been Ebony on the beach. Leslie hugged his daughters.

'We don't know exactly what happened yet,' he told them, 'but her family are with her now.'

Zak had poured a brandy for Claudine, who was also wiping away tears, and had found himself a beer. Now he stood up and got drinks for the new arrivals, hesitating for a moment in front of Ali.

'Yes,' said Ali, 'I'll definitely have a beer.'

They sat on the veranda with the view of the sea before them. The mood was uneasy — to resume the day as it had been planned was impossible. Then Zak stood up and suggested a boat ride to the girls and they ran off down the path to Turtle Beach with him, promising to be back within the hour for lunch.

As soon as they were gone, Claudine turned to her husband. 'You think there was an accident, Leslie? How could a young girl like that end up there?'

'You're right, Dina, we were just saying all that coming across here. At the moment, there are a lot more questions than answers. Drew will be getting on with the case this afternoon, in fact, right now I'd say. There may be a very simple explanation.' He paused for a moment. 'Or it may be very unsavoury indeed.'

Leah, wanting to lighten their mood, remembered the brass box. She stood up and fetched it from inside the house. 'I've something to show you,' she said, 'nothing to do with what's happened.' She put the box down and opened it.

'What is it, Leah?' Leslie asked. 'It looks Indian, or even Sri Lankan.' And Claudine exclaimed, 'Yes — look at those elephants!'

'Yes, I think that must be right,' Leah answered. 'Zak and I found it this morning. There are letters in it, and newspaper clippings about John Rookwood's death that I've never seen before. I think the box must have belonged to John's wife. Adeline was her name. After John died, Adeline married a Ceylonese tea planter and spent the rest of her days there. In fact, I think she ran some kind of guesthouse with her sister after her second husband died. I suppose eventually someone sent some of her things back to my grandfather after she died herself. That must have been more than sixty years ago. The letters have probably been in the lighthouse all that time.'

Leslie looked hard at Leah, and then said, 'A guesthouse ... Claudine, don't we know that place, on the Kandy Road? In Kurunegala? We've passed it several times when we've been back to Sri Lanka. Where my mother used to stay as a child, she knew both those old ladies. Emily and Addie. They were formidable! We've old photos of my mother standing between them on the front steps.'

Claudine nodded, saying 'Yes, I remember that house, it's part of a teachers training college now.'

Leslie said, 'You've never told me about your Sri Lankan connections before, Leah!'

'I barely know about them myself, Leslie. Adeline was my father's grandmother. She never came back here after her second marriage and I think my father only ever met her once.' She passed the bundle of cards across to Leslie.

Ali said to Leah, 'You haven't told me the second bit of that story yet ... why your family left the island.'

'No. I'm not sure it's the right story for now, Ali, but Leslie and Claudine know it already, and in fact, it's in these newspaper cuttings. Rookwood certainly comes across as having a bloody history.' For a moment all were silent as they studied the postcards and read through the newspaper reports.

'The obituary doesn't say much about his wife,' Leslie remarked, 'it seems she wasn't at the picnic. It was someone else, this Mrs Howe, who saw him fall.'

'That's true,' Leah said, 'but I'm sure she did come back to Rookwood with John after the incident here, and the massacre. She must just have been away from Cooktown at the time he died. The picnics resumed, obviously, after the massacre. I'm afraid the fact of Black people being killed didn't loom large in the minds of the citizens of Cooktown at the time — shooting them was normal then. I have a few photos from the 1890s that I'll find.' She crossed back into the living room and took a scrapbook from a shelf, conscious of Ali's eyes on her back.

The scrapbook contained faded photographs of genteel picnickers, the ladies in hats and full-length dresses with leg-o-mutton sleeves, the gentlemen in suits and ties, boaters the only concession to the pleasure of the day's outing. It was possible — just — to recognise the beach by the landing stage on Mermaids Beach, and the flat rock near where the cemetery now stood.

'Strangely enough,' Leah remarked, 'none of these do show Adeline, although there are a couple of Thomas, here and there.' She pointed to one of Thomas in a sailor suit, aged about six, and another, self-conscious, in his early teens, with his father. John was dressed correctly in white jacket and trousers. He had put on weight, though, since his wedding photo, become more round-shouldered and myopic; in his hand he held his usual clay pipe.

'Thomas was sent to school in Charters Towers,' Leah added, 'so I guess he wasn't here much. It seems a pity for his parents to have had their only child leave home so early, but I suppose it was the way then. When we were kids, Mara and I went to school in Cassowary village and spent all our free time playing in the bush here, or on the sea, and so did my Dad and his brothers, but it's hard to imagine Thomas ever did, looking at those photos.'

She had taken Micky and Zak with her to Brisbane when she was completing her specialist training, after her divorce from Gareth. It had required constant juggling, getting work and study done, being there to pick up the kids and supervise music practice and make sure the ratings were suitable on the television shows they watched, and everything else single mothers did. But she couldn't have imagined doing it any other way. Gareth had access visits to Micky on alternate weekends, but he'd largely lost interest once he married

Jackie, and more often than not she had both children those weekends too. She would have hated to send them to boarding school. Once she was a qualified pathologist, they'd come back to Cairns, and lived in that flat during the school weeks, coming back to Rookwood for weekends whenever possible, and school holidays. So as kids, Zak and Micky too had spent all their free time playing around the island.

Now Claudine looked up from the second newspaper story and asked, 'They're saying somebody pushed the first Dr Rookwood off the cliff? I'd never heard that before, I thought he'd just fallen off the path, it's quite dangerous over there.'

'Well, I had never heard that before myself,' Leah answered, 'but maybe someone pushed one of those large rocks down onto him, or distracted him, so he fell off down the cliff. A perfect murder, if no-one sees you, especially in the pre-forensic medicine era.' She looked across at Leslie. 'Even today, if no-one saw you,' she added.

'Yes,' he said, 'if you were hit by a rock that then knocked you over the cliff, the injuries you'd get at the bottom would account for everything the pathologist would find. Whether the rock lands on the ground or falls into the sea makes no difference.'

'Rocks sometimes just fall down that path anyway,' Leah said. 'If someone down on Turtle Beach saw a rock fall, it could have been just coincidence. There's a warning sign at the start of the path in case any of the resort's guests wander up that way, though they rarely do.'

'So did the police investigate this story, was anything ever proven?' Claudine, a policeman's wife, now wanted to know.

'I don't think so,' Leah answered. 'It may have just been an accident, but it may have been deliberate, in revenge for the massacre. Local people wouldn't have known that John himself wasn't in that raiding party, but they would have known that he was now the boss of the island and came there regularly. And he was a whitefella. And,' she added, 'if that's what someone had in mind, and they had to wait eighteen years for John Rookwood to walk along that path, maybe that's what they did. Just waited. Eventually, it could be worth it.'

'So then John was buried on island,' Leslie remarked.

'Yes,' said Leah, 'he was the first in the cemetery, which was then built up around his grave. The boat for the picnic was quite small, and it was decided that it would not be appropriate for the ladies of the party to have to share it with a corpse, and a disfigured one at that. Nor did anyone wish to remain for the night on the island with the body! The men of the picnic party wrapped John up in the picnic tablecloth and carried him to the cabin, and locked him in there. At that time, they had planned to return the following day and bring him back to the Cooktown cemetery. However, his will was found that night in Cooktown and it specified his wish to be buried on the island. I've always thought that made him seem more human, somehow, more warm-hearted, wanting to be buried here. Some of the men returned with the Protestant minister, and no doubt several shovels, and chose the site for the grave on top of the island. So the cemetery was there before this house was even thought of. The island was virtually abandoned then, after John died, at least by white people, until the lighthouse was being built, and then Thomas, who was by then in practice in Cairns, came back here and built this house.'

She turned more pages in the scrapbook. 'There was a service for John in the church in Cooktown,' she explained, 'but it was a memorial service not a funeral. There's a copy of the order of the service. John obviously liked order, he'd set out exactly what he wanted in his will. Hymns. And Psalm 138. He couldn't have imagined,' Leah said, 'how inappropriate this would be.' She read it out aloud now:

If I shall walk in the midst of tribulation, Thou wilt quicken me, O Lord; and Thou wilt stretch forth Thy hand against the wrath of my enemies, and Thy right hand will save me.

'The Lord must have had his back turned on John on his way to North Beach then. I think it was after John died there that the track was named the Devil's Path.'

At the back of Leah's mind was the thought that perhaps Adeline *didn't* ever return to the island after the incident with Lee Chin, and the massacre. Why had she needed to come from Sydney for the memorial service? Could she have left Cooktown years before? Maybe the rumours of the liaison with Lee Chin were not as far-fetched as Leah had imagined. But it was unlikely that she would ever know the truth.

There was the sound of several voices on the path from Turtle Beach, Zak and the girls returning. He'd taken them in the *Dolphin* right around the island, using the engine rather than the sails. Then they'd swum off Turtle Beach.

'We saw five turtles!' Larissa said, as the girls stood dripping in their tiny bikinis on the lawn. 'Five!'

'We saw the big old man turtle,' Lily added. 'He was swimming up and down, looking at us wondering what we were doing in his territory!'

'He's at least fifty years old,' Leah told them. 'I know from my Dad that he was there before I was born, and he was already grown up!'

Claudine chased the girls in to change for lunch. Leah gathered up the scrapbook and photos, deciding that for the moment there must be no more talk of death on Rookwood.

Barbecued tuna and wine mellowed the mood of the afternoon. The discovery of Ebony had made lunch much later than Leah had planned, and when the meal was finished, nobody wanted to swim. It was easier just to sit on the veranda, watching the sea and letting the conversation drift. From time to time, Leah was conscious of Ali's glance resting upon her, and her skin tingling in response, but she was careful to avoid his eyes.

As the afternoon lengthened, Leslie stood up to leave. He would drop Ali home as well. Zak announced that he too would go into town — could he take Leah's car? He'd be back later that night. Leah walked with all of them down the steps to the wharf where the *Argo* waited. Across on the mainland, police tape could still be seen at the spot where Ebony's body had been found. Leah was glad that Leslie and Ali would be with Zak when he went across there now.

In a flurry of thankyous and goodbyes, she felt Ali's hand touch hers, and his lips brush her cheek.

16

As Zak departed in the *Argo* with her guests, Leah slowly climbed the pathway on the south side of the island, thinking about Ali Hassan. She pressed her hand against her cheek, still burning where his mouth had touched her skin. Halfway up the path was a stone seat, and she sat down on this, looking out across the sea. In the distance were hydrofoils returning to Cairns from reef trips, and closer to the island she thought she could make out a family of dolphins. There was no beach on this side of the island; beyond a protective railing, the rainforest dropped straight down into the water.

This seat was the place where Gareth had proposed to her. It had seemed romantic at the time. She hadn't realised then that he was less in love with her than with the idea of the island and what it could mean for him. As her mother had been more infatuated with the idea of a man with an island than with the man himself ... though her mother never even laid eyes on Rookwood until after she was married, and soon lost interest in the island once she had to live on it. When her parents divorced, her father had arranged that Rookwood would go to Leah and Mara, not his ex-wife, who was otherwise provided for, and anyway much preferred the Gold Coast. Leah had kept her own name when she married. For a while Micky had her father's surname, but after her parents' divorce, she demanded herself that it be changed to

Rookwood. By the time Zak was born, Leah was divorced, and anyway, Gareth was not his father.

Gareth's ideas about the island had been rather different from Leah's mother's. Soon after their marriage, he had suggested to Leah that they borrow a large sum of money and put a second resort where the house stood. The views from that point were the best anywhere on the island, he said, and among the best in the whole of Queensland. The zigzag path could be widened and guests brought to the top of the island in motorised buggies. Of course, the house itself would have to be demolished. Leah couldn't believe what she was hearing.

'No!' she had said fiercely. 'We will never do such a thing. Mitchells is bad enough.'

Years later, Leah felt that if she had to pick a moment when her marriage with Gareth had started to disintegrate, it would be the moment of that conversation.

Now she closed her eyes for a moment and thought of Ali. He'd had an arranged marriage. He had not discussed it more, but she had the impression it may not have been very happy, and that he felt guilt about his wife's death. He had spoken lovingly enough of his daughter, but rather distantly. He had spent a long time in England after his wife had died. What had he done for sex there? Had he left someone behind who he was involved with still? Somehow she had the feeling that this was not the case, but that might just be wishful thinking. Maybe there was someone who would come to join him in the flat.

She felt the sudden surge of a strange emotion. Jealousy! Jealousy at the thought of Ali in the bed in her flat, her bed, with another woman. This was ridiculous, she told herself, you hardly know the man.

This sudden flowering of passion was the last thing she had been expecting, the very last.

Zak had been the product of a casual encounter following a conference dinner in Brisbane. Already her marriage was faltering, and in the following week, she would discover Gareth's affair with Jackie. On her own at the dinner, she'd found herself drinking whisky with the star speaker at the conference, Professor Ted Davis, internationally famed virologist from London. Soon they were in bed in his hotel room. At some stage he mumbled that he supposed she was taking the pill. She wasn't, but she figured she was near the end of a cycle, so it was OK.

In the morning, after a further intense encounter, he'd ordered breakfast from room service, and they'd chatted pleasantly over coffee and croissants before he'd told her, politely but firmly, that she must leave, as he was giving one final workshop for the conference then taking a flight to New York.

Three turbulent weeks later, after a showdown with Gareth, and when she'd moved herself and Micky into a Cairns hotel and found herself a lawyer, she realised she hadn't had a period in quite a while.

A pregnancy test hastily bought from the hotel's downstairs pharmacy showed two blue lines.

There was a week in which she just could not decide what to do. She didn't want an abortion, but how to cope with work and pregnancy? What to do about Gareth? What to do about *Ted*? She barely knew the man ... should she let him know? Could she continue a pregnancy without telling him? If she had his child, that child should surely know his father ...

Then one day at lunchtime, she went to the hospital library to look up Ted's name in the UK Medical Register, just to find some basic information about him. How old was he? Where did he work? Where did he live? While she was waiting for the librarian to bring her the heavy tome recording the details of every medical graduate working in

Britain, she picked up the airmail copy of *The Lancet* for the previous week.

It contained Ted Davis's obituary.

Covered with goosebumps, barely able to focus on the print, she learned that soon after arriving in New York City, Professor Theodore Davis had stepped out of a taxi into the path of an oncoming truck.

So just twenty-four hours after leaving her.

There was a great deal in the obituary about his qualifications, his brilliant career, his academic success. The world of research into AIDS, and into the lymphadenopathy-associated virus that seemed to be the cause of it, had suffered an enormous loss, the *Lancet* writer said.

From the obituary, Leah discovered he'd been brought up by his West Indian parents in South London, an only child. He was survived by those parents, and his wife Sarina Noble. Apparently no children.

But although he never knew it, and nor did his parents, who had both died by the time Leah was able to travel to London with her son when he was ten years old, he also left Isaac Theodore Rookwood.

Leah had recognised Sarina Noble's name. She was one of the first Black fashion models. In various women's magazines, Leah studied photos of the tall and strikingly beautiful Sarina.

On the same London visit where she did not meet Ted's parents, Leah tried to contact Sarina. She was hard to track down, Leah only ever had a phone number. Sarina's personal assistant was frosty on the phone, clearly disbelieving Leah's story and assuming she wanted money and fame. Sarina, she said, had remarried, retired from modelling, and refused any further communication or information about other living relatives, in the UK or Trinidad.

Leah had engaged in a few flings over the years since Zak's birth. The last, Nathan, had moved to Canada a year ago. Since then there'd been nobody else, but this had not bothered her unduly. She had many male friends here who were her colleagues, like Leslie. She had plenty of female friends. She had her family. Falling for an Iraqi refugee was not part of the agenda. She'd let the flat to him because she'd heard he needed a temporary home, asked him to dinner because he seemed so alone. Nothing more. And now here she was, trembling like a teenager when his hand touched hers.

And anyway, what about Ali? she asked herself. She might be making the whole thing up. Though she remembered Leslie's expression, on the beach, seeing her and Ali together. Leslie, she was sure, had observed her wearing a silk shirt and rather more make-up than was usual for her on a Sunday. Leslie didn't miss much. Nor did Claudine.

This brought her uncomfortably back to Leslie's questions about Brian Mitchell. What had he thought of her answers? Certainly she'd tried to deflect the conversation away from any discussion of herself and Brian. How much of this had Leslie discerned?

At university, she'd had a couple of boyfriends before that first night with Gareth. None of what had happened with these boys had been very interesting or pleasurable, but she'd done some reading and convinced herself that there must be more to this sex business than she'd come across so far. It was just a matter of finding the right man. Gareth was already a doctor, a surgical registrar, when she'd met him at a party in her fifth year at medical school in Brisbane. Somehow she'd lost the fellow student who had brought her to the party. Anyway, Gareth had seemed older and much more glamorous than her date. He'd found her a Coca-Cola, a drink she'd never been allowed as a child and therefore associated with sin, and from his pocket produced a half bottle of Bacardi, from which he poured a generous measure into her Coke. Somehow, soon after that, they'd ended up in his parents' house with a wide view across the Brisbane River. Somehow his parents were away for the weekend. Somehow he didn't have to work in the hospital until Sunday evening, and somehow she soon found herself with no clothes on and Gareth teasing parts of her that none of the other blokes seemed even to have known existed, and herself making sounds that she'd never known she was capable of. Thirty-six hours had passed in a haze of sex, sleep, warm baths together and take-away food. By then Leah had had more orgasms than she could count and she was hooked.

It was several years later, when they had moved back north and were living on the island, that he would turn on her and say, 'I knew what kind of girl you always were, look at you, you had sex the first time you met me! You had sex with that Mitchell guy, your swimming coach, when you were thirteen, you told me so yourself. Don't tell me he talked you into it! And you expect me to believe you haven't been having affairs the whole time we've been married?' He then listed the names of a dozen men he accused her of sleeping with, all married or partnered with other women. All, in fact, just good friends, of both hers and Gareth's. Some of them were her colleagues at work, some lived far from the town and would have been physically impossible to conduct affairs with even if she'd had the interest and the time, which she hadn't. Since that first night with Gareth there'd been nobody else. She was hurt and bewildered.

The week following the Brisbane conference, she'd discovered what many people had known for months: Gareth was having an affair with a theatre nurse. Confronted by Leah, he merely agreed it was true, and said that he was moving out to live with Jackie. 'Hell no,' she'd said, 'I'm moving, and I'm taking Micky.'

In fact, once it had all happened, she found being free of Gareth an enormous relief. She was shocked by Ted's death — but she barely knew the man. She had to move quickly with divorcing Gareth, so settlements were in place before her pregnancy was noticeable, but once this was done her whole life opened out. She could start her pathology training, get paid while she did it, not have to ask anyone's permission to do so. Mara came from Sweden for Zak's birth, and stayed for months with her sister. The only sadness had been their father dying. She would have loved to have spent more time with him.

It was clear to Leah that Ali was someone who'd had more than his share of sadness and drama in life. He'd been caught up in political events, but more than that, he'd known personal tragedies. Though he'd joked about the Welsh girlfriend, she had the impression he'd been hurt by her, and maybe by other women. And he was, after all, an Arab male. What did he think, deep down, about Western women?

As well, his stay in Australia could only be a limited one. He had said he would return to Iraq if the political situation changed. That was understandable, it was his country. She herself would never leave Rookwood. Well, she supposed that she might do so for a short time, but she would never leave the island altogether. The final resting place in the cemetery near the lighthouse she hoped was a long way off, but she certainly thought that was what would eventually happen.

She stood up and began to climb the rest of the way back to the house, touching the glowing spot on her cheek, and thinking about the fine dark hairs on the backs of Ali's fingers. She thought about those fingers stroking her skin, and then sharply reminded herself that absolutely nothing had happened between them. Apart from anything else, she was forty-four years old. Men her age were invariably interested in much younger women, in her experience. She was probably completely mistaken about his feelings.

At the top of the path, she looked back towards the mainland. She could just make out the *Argo* reaching the wharf, and the tiny figures of her passengers disembarking. She saw Zak start up the Land Rover. Then Leslie's car drove away, followed by Zak. Hell, she'd have to do Ebony's autopsy on Tuesday. Of course she'd done many such cases before on people she had known. It was a small town. But still she did not look forward to it. Zak, she knew, had gone to see schoolfriends who had known Ebony. She hoped they would be able to talk it through together. At least tomorrow was a holiday, and she could spend more time with her son if he needed her.

She walked back into her house, gathering up glasses from the veranda as she did so. In the kitchen, she turned on the radio to catch the evening news as she stacked the dishwasher. The national round-up was just finishing. The Prime Minister, she heard, was shrilly dismissing international complaints about the detention of asylum seekers on Nauru. Then the local news items began. The first report was of the body washed up on Cassowary Beach. Ebony Passmore had been identified, the newsreader said calmly. She had been seventeen years old, a dancer with a local theatre group. Police were investigating ... Leah snapped the radio off and finished the dishes in silence. Then she sat down at her computer, where reports awaited her, and worked away for a couple of hours. She poured herself a glass of wine, and at that moment remembered the letters in the box she'd found in the lighthouse. She retrieved the box from the veranda, set it down on her work table and took out the bundle of letters.

The first was addressed to Mrs Robert Mossop in Stanmore, Sydney, New South Wales, and bore a Cooktown postmark and a stamp for one penny. From the envelope, Leah took several sheets of frail white notepaper covered with a practical hand.

17

East Coast Hotel
Charlotte Street Cooktown
21st October 1878

My dear Emily,

What with arriving here on the steamer, overseeing the unloading of my trunk, arranging my accommodation (which is both spacious and comfortable, I have both a sitting and a bedroom, and for this the purser of the *Dundas* must be thanked) and starting almost at once at Dr Rookwood's establishment, a whole ten days has passed without my putting pen to paper. I know though that you received my telegram. It is hardly believable that the telegraph line goes all the way south, 1500 miles, and then eventually to you! What a truly wonderful and modern invention the telegraph is, it is an invention that I cannot imagine will ever be surpassed, and it is a great comfort to know that I can be in touch with my dear sister almost *at once*, should ever it be necessary.

I can hardly think where to begin to describe this place to you. It is fortunately still the Dry season, and would be very hot, but the town has a fresh breeze from the south-east from early morning, and so it is quite pleasant to walk in the streets for most of the day, although when the rains start to come I am sure they will be a *quagmire*. Five years ago there was nothing here but the bush, and mangrove swamps by the edge of the river. Now there are wide streets which are being properly finished off and gutters of granite blocks. These streets are filled all day and a large part of the night with men and horses and dogs. The most noticeable thing is how there are so many more men than women, of course, that was to be expected. Most of them are quite rough-looking fellows in from the diggings which are about one hundred miles away. There are more than sixty public houses in Cooktown! Many of these men walk into the town covered from head to toe with dust and mud, but with only one thought in their minds — to exchange their gold for money in the Government assay office and find the nearest public house. The results you can imagine, the men frequently ending up in intimate contact with the newly-built gutters. However I have found it quite safe to walk in the street, I am already being known as 'the Irish Nurse' or just 'Nurse' and greeted by the shopkeepers and their children. Some of the miners do have their wives and children with them too. Many are camped just on the edge of town, but some have put up more solid bush-timber huts where their womenfolk can stay while they are up at the diggings. Most of the houses in the main street are of a single storey, built from planks, but a few have an upstairs as well, and balconies like Sydney houses.

There is every sort of shop imaginable, to supply the diggings, and one can buy *exactly* what one wants as in Sydney, although often from off a dirt floor or out of a sack! The Royal Mail steamers come in twice a week direct from England, through the Torres Strait from Singapore, so we can have all the newspapers and journals from home just as quickly as you can do in Sydney! The shops, like the houses, have all been built from planks, some of them leaning very precipitously against one another, but now some of the more established merchants are staring to build with bricks which are being imported from the Sydney brickworks, so the town will soon look more established and less ramshackle. Already the Bank of New South Wales is finished and there are several other respectable hotels apart from this one. You can see I am starting to sound quite *proprietary* about the place after just a short stay!

Dr Rookwood seems quite a pleasant kind of man though reserved and not given to talking a great deal. Yes, he is unmarried. As we both knew, he did his medicine in Dublin but he is from Ulster (the County Down) and so far, I would have to say, seems to lack that Dublin *sense of humour* as a result. But he is very fair. I shall have my dinner and my supper with his housekeeper and in the mornings do rounds with him as required and see to such of his patients who need a nurse. In the afternoons I shall be free to hire my services to those who need me. He will pay me three guineas a week and for my afternoon patients I will be free to charge fees as I see fit, depending on the time taken and the difficulty of my tasks. It is expected that there will shortly be a start to a hospital for the town and it is sorely needed. At present there are two rooms behind Dr Rookwood's surgery where those needing bed rest can be accommodated but only for a short time. Just yesterday Dr Rookwood lanced a large abscess of the groin for one of the miners, under chloroform, I assisted with the boiling of the instruments and holding the mask. He has a good deal of new equipment from London and I am pleased to say is very fussy about cleanliness, he told me he had heard Dr Lister speak when he was in Dublin. I would much have preferred to keep him (the patient) a while, but there was no room. His 'mate' took him off on his horse to their camp, he was swearing and shouting a good deal from the pain, poor man, and even when he came back today he was needing more laudanum. It would be much better to have one or two wards for males, with night nurses as well as day, the night work could soon be learnt by any respectable woman, not necessarily trained as we are, and I am sure that there will soon be a need for a female ward as well, as the town grows in size — in short, a proper hospital.

You will see, my dear Emily, from all this, that I am quickly settling in here and occupying myself fully, and I do not believe that I have made a mistake in answering the advertisement, or in leaving the Sydney Hospital and coming here. At the very least I shall stay the year I promised originally to Dr Rookwood, without any difficulty. There are plenty of suitable entertainments here (and even more unsuitable ones, from what I see going on in some of the streets, but of course that was to be expected). There are to be picnic races, and a circus is coming by steamer from Brisbane. Every day newcomers arrive from the south and from England, and many of the men go straight off to the diggings, even though the Palmer River gold is said to be less now than what is being found on the Hodgkinson River further south. Dr Rookwood says he is sure that even if the gold does not last there will be cattle-raising and farming inland here, and Cooktown will become a great city.

I would like you to arrange to send me the red cedar chest with the linen inside it, I am sure I will use it after all. It will be much more economical than making new purchases here. Please use some of the notes I left with you and not your own money. It will take not more than three weeks to be here with the steamer.

Embrace my 'sweet little maid' for me, and give her lots of kisses. I am sad that she will be so grown up when next I see her. And to you, dear Emily, and to Robert, I send my warmest love, you know that even though I am far away here my thoughts are still so often with you all. I will write again on Sunday.

Affectionately, Adeline.

Leah studied the letter, fascinated. So her great-grandfather had advertised for a nurse, and her great-grandmother had responded to that advertisement and come to Cooktown in order to work for Dr Rookwood, four years after the town was established. When it was still seen as a prospective city in the north. Even though by then all the easy gold was gone from the Palmer. John Rookwood had been partly right — there would continue to be a demand for his services throughout his life, but the pastoral industry would develop more to the south. The Botanic Gardens, the wide streets lined with granite, though, they were all still there, a reminder of what the town might have become. Leah picked up the next letter, in a similar envelope, also addressed to Mrs Mossop, and unfolded the fragile sheets.

Hope Street Cooktown
10th December 1878

My dear Emily

I hope this reaches you all before Christmas and that you all enjoy a happy festive season. Of course my presents for the little ones were sent on the steamer last week to be certain of arriving in time.

I will be taking Christmas dinner with Dr Rookwood and Mr and Mrs Chapman. We shall attend the Christmas service in the morning and not plan to dine until mid-afternoon in view of the climate. It is now very warm throughout the morning, it rains a good deal but we do have the south-east breeze to cool us down from the middle of the afternoon. There are chickens and geese freely available from the butcher's and Mrs Chapman's Chinese cook has made a plum pudding under her explicit directions. So it will all be very much like home.

It will be very pleasant to have a few days holiday. Since the new gold was discovered at Lukinville and Coen, inland about two hundred miles, there are new men arriving every week. As a consequence, the doctor is always very busy, and so am I. He does take some time on Saturdays to go sailing, and latterly I have been included in the sailing parties. The doctor is planning to buy an island about five hours sailing time from here, to the south of Cooktown. Apparently he first saw it on his voyage up here from Brisbane and was much taken by its aspect.

Emily, he *is* a man of some contradictions — when he speaks of the island he is positively *loquacious*, but most of the week, at meals and in the course of our work, he will say no more than is absolutely necessary. The housekeeper, Mrs Mulligan, and I must chatter away like starlings to fill the void. He does however always escort me to the service on Sundays, which is very pleasant, and he is more conversational on these occasions. And he is very well respected in the town, especially since an incident last year, when he stopped a horse which was bolting with a buggy containing a butcher's wife, almost certainly saving her life.

Cooktown itself continues to grow. It seems that there is still plenty of alluvial gold just waiting to be picked up out of the streams inland — waiting to be picked up though by men who have to walk in with all their food and tools on their backs, savage blacks always a threat, and competing with the 'Chows' who outnumber white men five to one here. The Chinese are very much disliked by the white miners — really because they are so much better at keeping their money. They have their own shops, and vegetable gardens, and a temple. Everything in their shops comes direct from China. Parts of the town are just like Shanghai I'm sure, the huts huddled together, and in the shops are the strangest herbs and dried foodstuffs. Very occasionally one comes to try Dr Rookwood's medicine, usually on his last legs. There is a Chinese cemetery as well as a Christian one but they do not mark the Chinese graves.

Emily, would you believe that there are whole sections of this town which are *filled* with opium dens and other places of iniquity. Opium is very freely imported from China. Though the public houses frequented by the white miners are just as bad in my opinion. It is a dreadful thing that men can come so far, risk their lives and work and live as they have to at the diggings, then come into town and go straight from the Government Assay office with their money to the closest public house, and often stay there until they've drunk the lot. Dr Rookwood is then responsible for patching them up when they get into fights, something which happens often. Especially on Friday nights there are bruises and broken bones aplenty. The men are all very stoical — just last week we attended to a poor man who had his hand and part of his forearm blown away with blasting powder up at the diggings, his mate brought him back by horse, the horse was speared from under him by the blacks and the men themselves were lucky to escape with their lives. They had to leave the poor horse who was no doubt found very tasty by the savages. Dr Rookwood had to amputate at the elbow, the patient had a high fever for nearly a week, which is only now settling. I am glad to say that I believe we shall soon have our hospital ...'

Here the writing faded away before Adeline's final signature. Leah felt sleep overcoming her. The remaining letters could wait for another day. Leaving a light on for Zak, she climbed into bed and was asleep almost immediately. Later, briefly, she was awakened by the sound of her son returning. On her bedside clock, she saw that it was two in the morning, then she fell deeply asleep again.

18

That same evening, after Leslie had dropped him at the front steps of his apartment block, Ali opened the doors leading to the terrace of the flat and moved one of Leah's cane chairs out onto the edge of the balcony. The tide was in, and though the moon was only a half, the length of the Esplanade was bathed in silver light. Couples strolled along the pathways and the occasional jogger could still be seen. Ali sat in his chair regarding his view and smoking a rare cigarette. And thinking about Leah Rookwood.

Why was he letting himself fall for another unattainable woman? It was ridiculous to think that a woman in her position, an established woman, with property, a profession, a family, would be interested in a foreigner like himself with no permanent job and no prospects of one. There was no chance of anything meaningful developing between them. Nor could he envisage a casual sexual relationship with her. There had been some encounters of this kind in several of the places where he'd held jobs in England, encounters which had produced very brief spasms of excitement and relief, but which ultimately had been regretted by both sides. He certainly wanted nothing like that with Leah. He must be very careful or he could make a fool of himself. He might even have to leave Cairns.

He must make himself think rationally about this. His obsession with Diane, the sad shame he had for so long associated with his marriage to Muna, and finally his preoccupation with Zahra'a, had all been such negative emotions. Leaving England, with the possibility, small though it was, of a different life in Australia, he had resolved to put all these feelings behind him. And certainly not to commence any new relationship.

Muna. He thought of their wedding night. She was a virgin. Of course. He tried to spare her pain, but there was blood on the sheets, he had torn her hymen. Well, she thought it right, had been told to expect it.

Obediently, she'd turned her face to him as soon as they were alone in the hotel bedroom. The guests would dance all night in the ballroom below. To tell the truth, he hadn't been sure that he would want her so easily, hadn't known at all how he would feel. Then he had discovered that his body could be separated from his mind, he could allow desire just to flow. At a lower level, not connecting to the brain, not letting himself think too much. 'Muna!' he said, kissing her neck. He'd said it loudly, then softly, and she'd giggled a little. She'd slipped off her silken layers and come into his arms. Then shut her eyes.

She always shut her eyes, shut him out. Only much later, after she was dead, did he learn from his cousin Mehmet Ali, a distant relative on his father's side, that she had wanted to marry her own cousin on her mother's side, Aziz. But her father had been adamant.

'A doctor like Ali Hassan will make a much better husband for you,' he had said, seated no doubt at the head of the family at dinner, 'and bring honour to the rest of us as well. He has much better prospects, a medical specialist, you'll have a fine house, maybe in Al-Mansour or some good part of Baghdad.'

Her family were from the small town to the south of the capital where Ali himself had been born. They were merchants and dealers, not members of the professions like his own immediate kinsfolk.

He'd never given her any credit for imagination. It had hurt him when he realised that, throughout the labour of his love-making with her, while he, when he thought of anything, thought of Diane, she had probably survived by thinking of Aziz. Not because he was jealous of Aziz, not at all. But if he'd bothered to learn more about her they could perhaps have had greater communication, and they might have made a better life together. But he had thought only of himself, believed that only he was capable of finer and more complex feelings.

On that first night, and the many that followed, he found in fact that he did have to think of Diane, to make it go on happening. To think of Diane's skin and smell, instead of the sweet and innocent flesh of the woman he was with, to think that he was back in the flat behind Euston Station, with outside the braking of the No 38 bus and the tinkling of a milk bottle kicked over by an unsteady drunk going home late from the Crown and Feathers on the corner. The distant smashing of glass was a sound Ali would forever associate with arousal.

He'd stroked and caressed Muna as he had Diane, but she didn't sigh as Diane had always done, let her thighs fall easily apart as Diane did, reach out a hand to grasp and guide him in at the right time, cry out at her moment of ecstasy then almost immediately burst into giggles at herself. No, it was just a release, for him, and an act of obedience for her.

And then ... He could hardly bear to think, even now, of what happened next.

After fifteen months, Muna was not pregnant, despite menstrual cycles of twenty-eight days, as regular as the moon, and conjugal liaison at least three times a week.

Ali took her to a private clinic in the centre of Mansour, across from the Alkarkh Basketball Club. He had a sudden remembrance now of that time, and of how after the visits, he and Muna would go to one of the fast food places that had sprung up in that glossy new clinic building, for tea and American hamburgers with fries. She loved that. Was that building even still standing? Most of those doctors were gone now, to Jordan, Egypt, the States if they'd been able to get there. That's what Mustafa had done. He was in Philadelphia, no doubt as cocky as ever.

It had been to Mustafa that Ali had taken Muna. He'd grown up with Mustafa, in the same town. They'd been to school and medical school together. Mustafa moved swiftly through specialist training and was soon a rich and sought-after gynaecologist with good connections to the government.

Ali had never really liked Mustafa. Once, when they were both six, Mustafa had been brought for the day to play with Ali, at Ali's grandparents' house outside Baghdad. They'd stuffed themselves with mulberries from the family's tree and then Ali had taken Mustafa to play in the depths of the apricot orchard. At first all had gone well, they'd climbed the biggest, oldest tree that reached to the top of the wall of the family compound, and built a lookout over the alleys of the village behind the house. But then Mustafa had turned mean, shoving Ali so hard that he almost fell from the tree, grabbing a lower branch just in time. Later, Mustafa had caught two of the family's cats and tied their tails together. All his life Ali had remembered the look of triumph on Mustafa's mulberry-stained face as the two cats struggled to get free, then turned to fight each other. One cat had subsequently died. But it was Ali, not Mustafa, who had got into trouble and been slapped by his grandmother.

Later, at school, they played soccer together. Mustafa had been mean then too, but it had been good to be on the same team with him.

He'd spoken to Mustafa before the consultation. Over tea in his office, Mustafa offered Turkish cigarettes. Ali declined but Mustafa slowly breathed in the rich tobacco fumes. Then winked.

'Doing it right, Ali old boy?' he'd asked. 'And often enough?'

'No doubt whatsoever.' In his English suit and tie, Ali felt urbane and confident.

'And she's menstruating regularly? No previous illnesses?'

'Very healthy, man. Young. Twenty-two. My father's cousin's youngest daughter. She's had her appendix out is all.'

'A very pretty girl. And I'm a good judge — with my opportunities.' Mustafa had winked slyly. *Maybe I am lucky*, Ali had thought. *Maybe I should think more about my luck.*

'Ali, it's good practice, you know,' Mustafa said, 'to test the bull first!'

'Well, that's what I wanted to tell you. But without her knowing. I've had a child already, in England.'

Mustafa raised his eyebrows, smiled slowly, then blew out a perfect smoke ring.

'Ah! English girls!' he sighed expressively. 'I was a year in Leeds, you know. "Got lucky"' — Mustafa dropped into English here — 'as they say, several times. You see this kid, write to its mother, you have to pay for it? What goes on?'

'No.' Ali hurried over this bit. 'I didn't even find out about it until we'd separated.' No need to admit that Diane had left him. 'She eventually married someone else who seems to have taken the — boy — on. We have no contact at all.'

He recalled the pain, of finding the note, and the flat empty of her things. The pain of finding that she'd gone off with David Llewellyn.

'A son!' Mustafa marvelled. 'You have a son you haven't seen!'

'Well, apparently.' He'd calculated that the child had been born seven months after Diane had gone from the flat. He'd had to go on snatches of conversation overheard in the doctors' tea room, and a bit of information from one of Diane's nursing friends, who clearly felt sorry for him.

'I think she was worried about going back with you to Iraq,' Emma had said, 'she'd heard stories of English women who'd married Arab men and gone to the Middle East, then later been divorced and lost access to their children. I know you've been here a long time, Ali, you even seem sort of English, but once you were back in Iraq, well, I think she thought she'd have no control over what happened to her family.'

They needn't have returned to Iraq, he wanted to say, we could have stayed here, gone to America, whatever she'd wanted he would have done. But he knew it was more than that. The affair had worked itself out. She hadn't wanted to spend her life with him.

'Yes,' he said stiffly to Mustafa, 'yes, a boy, he's with his mother, I have no contact.' He added then, 'She wasn't the sort of girl I could marry.' It was unfair, deeply unfair, to Diane, he had longed to marry her, but Mustafa would understand such a remark, and indeed Mustafa nodded sagely and changed the subject. Muna would need a laparoscopy, he said.

This had shown widespread adhesions where Muna's appendix had burst when she was seven years old, blocking her fallopian tubes, though her ovaries were healthy. Mustafa suggested the new treatment, IVF. A visiting specialist, Professor Spalding, had been working in Mustafa's private clinic. In cases such as Muna's, results were good.

First, Ali should have a sperm count.

Two days later, in a small cubicle in Mustafa's clinic, Ali unzipped his trousers and sat with a plastic pot and a sheaf of Western girlie magazines. But although their painted airbrushed moulded flesh turned him on to start with, it was of Diane that he was thinking as he groaned softly and spurted into the pot held beneath his blood-hardened penis. Then he re-zipped, stuffed the pot into a plastic bag, dumped it on the desk of the laboratory and fled.

The following day, Mustafa, sly, lolling back in his chair, tapping his teeth with a gold fountain pen, gave him the news.

'Azoospermia, Ali. No sperm at all.' On Mustafa's face was the exact expression he'd worn that day in the apricot orchard as he'd watched the cats hiss and spit and attack each other.

'You sure about that kid, Ali?' he asked. 'You ever have any illnesses as a kid yourself? Mumps, maybe?'

Then Ali remembered. When he was thirteen, he'd had a bad attack of mumps, he and his youngest brother both. He remembered the pain in his jaw, and some tingling in his balls that he'd been too embarrassed to speak of. Now understanding hit him like a runaway horse. If he was infertile with Muna, he must have been infertile with Diane as well. The boy could not be his. Her affair with David Llewelyn, that wimp of a cardiology registrar, must have started while she was still living with Ali. The child must have been David's. The pregnancy had been nothing to do with him at all.

Mustafa hadn't been too bad, actually. He made his point but didn't press it home. He suggested that Muna could be impregnated with donor sperm and would not even need to know it wasn't Ali's. He, Mustafa, could arrange such things with ease. Which he did. Muna conceived on her second cycle, two embryos, both girls. The eggs were Muna's. The sperm were — whose? Ali did not even know if his tiny daughters, technically twins, born prematurely by caesarean section in Baghdad in the spring of 1989, had the same father. He just knew it wasn't him.

One child had died within days of her birth, but the other, little Ziena, was strong. Muna, traditional, adored her daughter but believed she must try again for a son. Men must have sons, she knew. Her own mother had given birth to five, Ali's mother to four. Ali had felt he could not face any more deception. From being a man who already had a son, he had become a man who could never have a son.

He took refuge in the worsening political situation. The country, just recovering from the long war with Iran, was convulsed by Saddam's decision to invade Kuwait, and the war with America. He moved his little family out of Baghdad, back to the safety of the countryside. After the war, the Paediatric Hospital was the first to suffer the cuts to the supplies of medicines and equipment that had come with the victors' policy of sanctions, and Ali was struggling just to earn enough for the three of them plus the members of their extended families. This is not a good time for another baby, he had said to Muna.

And then his brother had died.

19

The day his brother died, his father had telephoned Ali in Baghdad. The old man's voice was low, he could barely find the words he needed, and he gave no details of what had happened to Hamid.

'Go,' he said, 'you must go at once, or you will be the next. Go to Jordan, and Muna and Ziena can join you later. Khaled will bring them.' Khaled was the youngest, unmarried brother.

Ali did not understand what his father meant, but there was no mistaking the urgency of his message. '*Dir balak*,' his father said, 'take care, my son.' And Ali had answered, 'Daddy, *Baba*, I will.'

It was the last time he would speak to the old man.

At first it had seemed to Ali, lodging with an uncle he had never met before, in the suburbs of Amman, avoiding direct contact with his family still in Iraq, that this was a temporary arrangement. The break had been so sudden, he could not envisage leaving his country for good. He had imagined that things would be worked out, and that he would return to his post in Baghdad. He owned a good house in the suburbs, leased rooms in a clinic off Mansour Square, was on the staff of the Paediatric Teaching Hospital. He was disturbed by the delayed arrival from Baghdad of Muna and Khaled and the little girl, but felt that soon they would be there. These ideas were shattered by the appearance in Amman of Ali's cousin, Mehmet Ali, with news from home.

Mehmet Ali had put his arms around Ali and, weeping, told him of the accident in the desert. There was no doubt, he said, that Muna, Ziena and Khaled were all dead. A petrol truck had collided with their car, its extra fuel tanks, loaded for the long trip across the desert, had exploded with the impact. With difficulty, Mehmet Ali and a family friend had gone to the village close to where the accident occurred, persuaded villagers to show them the unmarked burial site, and put markers on the graves.

Mehmet Ali also told him, for the first time, the details of his older brother's death. Hamid had been a surgeon. He and his wife Zahra'a lived with Ali's father to the south of Baghdad. Some weeks earlier, about two weeks before Hamid's death, Ali himself had been visiting the family home. A man had come in the night with a sick child, asking first for Hamid. Then Ali had been called to see the child, seriously ill with a fever. The father, in white *dishdash*, his head covered with the red-checked *keffiyeh*, was thin and anxious. It was clear he was a man on the run. The child's breathing was laboured and there were the crackles of pneumonia in his lungs. He should be in hospital, with oxygen and intravenous antibiotics, Ali knew. This was what would happen in England, in Australia. It was what had happened in Baghdad before the Gulf War. Now there were fewer antibiotics even for the rich in Baghdad, and this man was not rich.

The only antibiotic Ali had was chloramphenicol, made in Pakistan, past its use-by date, and considered dangerous for children. With it, the child might still die. Without it, he would certainly do so. 'We can try,' he said to the father.

'*Inshallah*,' the man replied — let us trust in God. The boy did not want to swallow the crushed tablets. Ali had melted honey in warm water, mixed in the bitter medicine and, a spoonful at a time, gently persuaded the child to take it.

The next day, a taxi had come and taken Ali to a house in a distant village. In the back room of a mud house, the child lay on a rug. His mother and aunts, in black *abaya* and veiled, were with him. He was definitely a little better. Ali left more of the antibiotic, with instructions to give fluids and aspirin. The following day he had to return to Baghdad. He never heard what had happened to the boy.

A fortnight later, the same taxi had appeared at the family's door, and the same driver had asked for Hamid: he was to take his surgical instruments and go with the driver, there was an urgent case. It was just after the sunset prayers when Hamid set off. He was not back at midnight, and by the time of the dawn prayers, his wife and father were frantic with anxiety.

At lunchtime of that long next day, while the family were gathered at the table but unable to eat, the bell at the gate had been rung. It was the taxi driver, pale, shaking violently, unable to speak, unable almost to point to the back seat of his taxi where Hamid's body lay. The driver cowered by the wall of the family compound as a brave neighbour helped Ali's father carry his son inside. Hamid had been shot in the back of the head. But his hands were missing. A sack retrieved from the boot of the taxi contained the severed hands and the scalpel used to perform the amputations.

For weeks after Mehmet Ali's arrival in Jordan, Ali felt that his soul had frozen hard inside himself. The family of his uncle were devout. They urged Ali to pray, to seek solace in his faith, to visit the mosque, talk with the imams. '*Inshallah*,' they said gently, 'what has happened, it is God's will.'

Two days in a row Ali went with them to the morning prayers. He heard the familiar words of the opening prayer: *Praise be to God, Most compassionate and merciful. It is you to whom we turn for aid, Guide us on the straight path ...* He soon realised that, though he still had faith, this was not in any way relevant to the rest of his life. God was Great, too great and lofty to be concerned with the troubles of men like himself.

On the third day, and each day thereafter, Ali rose with the family at the dawn call, but instead of praying, he walked the dusty streets of the suburbs of Amman, where apartment blocks four and five storeys tall grew up almost overnight, and were filled with families from the countryside, and from Palestine, before they were even half-finished. He walked unseeing through roadside markets where sheep were butchered besides piles of melons and pomegranates, and where ragged Palestinian children tried to sell him American cigarettes. The news of his father's death, from a massive heart attack, some four months after Ali's arrival in Jordan, came as a strange relief. The old man's heart was literally broken, he could suffer no more. Ali's mother had died some years before. Of his immediate family, only Zahra'a, Hamid's widow, and her son and daughter, now remained in Iraq.

It was the realisation of his precarious financial position that jerked him back into the semblance of a life. He must find himself some work. He had no access to his property or funds in Baghdad. As a foreign doctor, even in Jordan his options were limited. He did some short locums in Amman and other towns. It was clear that he could not anticipate the kind of specialist career he'd had in Baghdad.

He had, however, his British qualifications. He could find a job, not a consultant post, it was true, but a hospital job in his specialty, in England. He spent long hours at the British Embassy, sat a test in spoken English. And was told that yes, if he found a post, he could have a limited visa. He believed that Diane had gone back to live in Wales. So he would confine himself to the south-east of the country, an area he already knew. He would be able to support himself. And from England he could send money to Zahra'a.

Zahra'a. Even now, here in Cairns, he still thought of Zahra'a as the third woman in his life. She would be astounded if she knew this, would burst out laughing, the bracelets jingling on her plump arms, if she knew how many years he had spent thinking of her, imagining a life together. A life of atonement.

For in England, he had come to believe that he should marry his brother's widow. That would provide for her socially as well as financially. Married, she would be able, eventually, to join him in Britain. Her future would be secure. This plan was responsible. It was correct. It was *wajeb*.

And he? He would be less burdened by the blame he felt for his marriage with Muna, and the accident in the desert. It was a plan that covered everything.

He did send money to Zahra'a regularly, and occasional short notes, when friends came and went to Baghdad. She was grateful, always, for the money. It was dangerous for her to communicate at length or too openly with him. She moved with her children to live in the countryside with her mother, who was elderly and slowly dying.

Ali did not immediately tell her of his intentions. He wanted a more permanent post in England, even if he could not become a consultant. And he should wait until the old woman died, when Zahra'a would be free to leave. Then he would present the whole plan to her and she would see its advantages. She would have a husband, her children would have a father. He was more closely related by blood to those children than he had been to his own daughter.

Occasionally, he thought of other benefits a second marriage would bring him: sex was an ever-present problem. He remembered Zahra'a as laughing, dark-eyed, slender. Though she must be older now, that too had its advantages: she would not demand more children. He would not need to have that discussion.

Then, two years ago now, Zahra'a seemed to disappear. Her mother had passed on, but she was no longer at the family house, friends reported. Anxiously he sent faxes to everyone he could think of still in Baghdad, hoping not to compromise them. But nothing was learned in return.

Finally had come the letter from France. He recognised at once the childish wording of the English address, the firmer strokes of her Arabic script. 'My dearest brother-in-law,' Zahra'a had written. 'You will no doubt be surprised to have this letter. I am so happy to tell you that I am now married to a Frenchman. Pierre-Yves is an engineer whom I met when he was working in our country. We were married quietly in Baghdad and so I was able to get a resident visa from France ... I was always so grateful for the help you sent us, but now I am no longer in need. We do hope you will be able to come to visit us in Bellevue ...'

He had gone to Bellevue, last year. Zahra'a had put on weight, a great deal of it. She giggled and jiggled as she talked and moved, and as she reached for the chocolate box, her many bracelets slipped up and down arms that were as pink and soft as Turkish delight. Ali could see little trace of the woman he had once known. The French engineer was a dry little man well into his sixties, bent and bandy-legged, much resembling an amiable tortoise. Clearly he adored Zahra'a, and was delighted to have a woman who would spend her days cooking good Arab food and fussing over him.

Ali could not imagine anything at all sexual in this relationship. The Frenchman spoke Arabic badly, and Zahra'a spoke worse French, but the two of them had a well-developed domestic routine. While Zahra'a cooked lamb kebabs and spiced rice, in just the way Ali remembered from his childhood, Pierre-Yves went shopping. From the Lebanese pastry shop on the corner, he brought back baklava and other sweets that caused his wife to smile and fling her arms around his wrinkled reptilian neck. Zahra'a's daughter, happy to be in Europe, seemed settled, and her son was enrolled in the local lycée.

Briefly, while Pierre-Yves was gone, Zahra'a had turned to him, her frivolity discarded. She had spoken earnestly. 'Cousin,' she said, 'one must do the best one can ... I take French lessons, I hope to become a teacher again. He is kind. And we are safe.'

On the train back to England, Ali had thought hard about his life. For nearly five years now he had been drifting from one job to the next, with this half-baked idea of marrying Zahra'a in his mind. Thank God at least that he had never proposed marriage to her by letter. She was a charming person, eager to help others, but the thought of colliding between the sheets with that mound of wobbling flesh was intolerable. What a fool he had been, alternating between registrar and locum posts, occasionally sharing a bed with a woman whose name he might barely know, with an idealised version of Zahra'a free-floating in his head. He must do something to escape. He must, as they said, 'get a life'.

This was not so easy though for an Arab doctor of a certain age, single and adrift in the United Kingdom at the end of the 1990s.

It was quite by chance that he'd met up again with Colin at a conference in Brighton, a meeting on cystic fibrosis. Colin had slapped him on the back and taken him off to the pub. A little hazy with beer, and half-jokingly, Ali had asked about work in Australia. British qualifications were no longer recognised there, he was sure, and visas nearly impossible to get. Colin answered him seriously.

'You couldn't be employed in the big cities,' he'd said, 'there are enough Australian graduates. But if you were prepared to go to a rural post, and some of the places aren't bad, in Queensland or Western Australia, say, you'd easily get a job. Cairns, for example. Now, that's a decent town in the far north, and they're always looking for people. I'll find out more when I get back home, if you like.'

Cairns. He was here now. The sun shone. He had a job, an income, a place to live, colleagues. He had been invited to lunch. He was acquainted with a detective and his family. This should be enough. Indeed, it was much more than he had dared to hope for. He must not do anything foolish. He must cast aside all notions of involvement with someone like Leah.

Yet he could not lightly cast aside the memory of her fingers as she had reached for his on the beach today, nor her face as she leaned towards him on the wharf this evening, leaned so that he could, fleetingly, kiss her cheek. A polite farewell gesture, nothing more. Crossing back to the mainland on the *Argo*, only the presence of the others had stopped him pressing his fingers to his lips where they had touched her skin. The thought of it now brought the blood rushing, and a familiar longing in his loins. His mind might say one thing, but his body acted differently. It wanted Leah Rookwood.

Ali stood up and leaned across the balcony, looking at the sea. He remembered then the dead girl on the beach. It was clear from their conversation in the tinnie that both Leah and Leslie felt that her death had not been an accident. Ali had little experience of the drowned, but he could see that Leah was right, people here were well adapted to the water. They did not easily submit to drowning. He had also observed, in his two months of work in the hospital, that in Australia, Aboriginal people were sometimes considered more dispensable than whites. So it was quite possible that the girl was murdered.

He'd been impressed by Leah's stories of the blood-stained history of the island. He had no difficulty imagining

Aboriginal people slipping easily through that rainforest, barely visible in the dim light filtering through the huge trees, watching and waiting. Waiting, perhaps for years, until finally the moment came to push that stone. In Iraq, such loyalties, such long-term acts of revenge, had been woven into the very fabric of society. Those wronged by a killing, in the family, in the tribe, even professional people like himself, would take an oath of vengeance. *Thar* ... that was the word for it. Revenge. Blood for blood. If he himself could have avenged his brother's death by waiting patiently until he too could push a stone, he would have done so. As it was, it seemed that Hamid's murderers would go forever unpunished.

The half-moon was now high in the night sky. Ali decided he would walk along the Esplanade before preparing his solitary evening meal.

20

She shouldn't have been there, there on the beach. That wasn't what he thought would happen.

He'd thought she'd go straight to the bottom of the deep muddy channel the river cut beside the mangroves near its north bank. He'd fished all over this area, knew every bit of it. Once he knew what he would do, he knew immediately that was the place. No-one lived near there, no-one would be out there at night.

Weighted down with what was in her billum, the string bag he'd wound around her wrists, she should have gone straight down. Probably not a single bone remaining, if the sharks and codfish did their job. It was a good plan. It was true, there had been that one case of the drowned fisherman whose head turned up inside a potato cod in the Cairns fish-processing plant. That was a one-in-a-million though. That wouldn't happen to her.

But Nature was quirky. Nature had played a different trick on him.

She sank, yes. But the sharks and the cod had no time to get her. Instead, a branch, semi-submerged and floating down from the mountains, snagged her and took her out into the bay, where the tide met her. The river and the sea conspired, and brought her rolling in on the early morning waves to where the rocks met the sand of South Cassowary Beach.

21

Earlier that same evening, Zak had watched Leslie, with his family and Ali, head off down the track towards Cassowary village and the highway. Then he had climbed into the Land Rover and driven off behind them. He'd been apprehensive approaching the wharf again in the *Argo*, then surprised and a little shocked to see that, while there was still police tape where Ebony's body had lain, there were no other signs of the tragedy.

Leslie caught his glance, and reached out a hand to touch Zak's shoulder.

'Zak,' he said, 'the tide's come in, everything has been washed clean and Ebony taken in to the mortuary.'

'Yeah. It just seems wrong that the place is exactly as it was. Unchanged. Unaffected.' Zak was still staring at the outcrop of rocks. 'Like it must have been, the time all those people were killed here,' he added. 'All the blood, just washed away by the sea.'

'There is something,' Ali said, and he pointed to where a large bunch of flowers, heliconias and red hibiscus from Cassowary village gardens, had been laid on the beach well above the high-tide mark.

'I'd say Renee organised that,' Claudine remarked. 'I'm sure there will be a lot more in the next few days. And Zak, people won't forget her. There will be a grave out on country and services for her at the school. Quite apart from the police case. Are you OK to drive in by yourself? Some of us could go with you.'

But he preferred to drive alone. He would go and drop in on his mate John Dollinson on the northern beaches.

He rummaged through the stock of CDs. The car might be old, but Leah had agreed to having a CD player installed. Now he found the first Pearl Jam album and slid it in. He waited until he was well past Cassowary village and turned up the sound above the roar of the engine.

'Alive!' He shouted the words with the band as he drove through the empty countryside. *Yes*, he thought, *I'm still alive* ...

He hadn't known Ebony well, but the terrible and unexpected sight of her body had shocked him deeply. He'd seen cadavers in med school, well, one, but as students they'd all been prepared for that, and anyway, the man had been old and drained of blood, and his veins filled with preservative. No doubt in life he'd been a nice person, nice enough to bequeath his body to the med school, but in death he was more like a model made from some peculiarly pliable plastic than a human being. Zak had also seen surgical operations and not fainted or winced, but there too you knew what you'd come for and what was happening. Finding Ebony had been very different.

The raw emotion of the song poured out over the canefields, and he sang along with the words.

His mother managed to cope with it all. She cut up flesh every day, quite apart from dealing with all those formalin-hardened specimens in her office. He'd never been to an autopsy she'd done here — 'Cairns is too small a town,' she said, 'at least until you're qualified. Too likely to be someone you know or whose family know you.'

He'd talked to her about how she felt about her work several times.

'I've just learned to act professionally and distance myself while I dissect,' she'd said. 'Most of the time. But I still can feel a lot of sadness for some of the people I do.'

'*I'm* still alive,' sang Zak again, after pressing the repeat button on the CD.

The band moved on to 'Black'. It was too much, too close to the day's events. He fumbled in the glove box and found jazz instead. That would soothe him until he reached the Dollinsons.

Another thing he needed time to think about was his mother and the Arab doctor. He was nearly certain there was something going on between them. His mother had dressed up much more than she usually did for a Sunday at home, talking and smiling and turning quite pink. Despite Ebony. And Ali, well, he couldn't keep his eyes off her all afternoon. And they both acted like they thought no-one noticed. The Arab doctor was cool, Zak had no problem with him. He'd been impressed by Ali's running down the beach, his immediate concern for Ebony and then, when he saw she was beyond helping, for Zak himself.

He'd have to report all this to his sister Micky though. They'd often discussed their mother's love life, or rather, the apparent lack of it. Leah would go out once or twice with some bloke, and Zak and Micky would hold their collective breaths, and be on their best behaviour, and then they'd never see the man again, and if asked, Leah would reply vaguely, 'Oh him, he's just a friend.' She was frank about sex generally with her children — sometimes to the point of embarrassment — but it was always in the third person, never with herself in the driving seat. They'd had a few suspicions about some overseas and interstate trips — well, Zak had heard from her about his own conception, starting from when he was six and becoming franker as he grew older. Micky, aged fourteen, had reported that she'd once seen condoms in

Leah's make-up bag; the two of them had giggled that they mustn't have been there the night Zak was conceived, and he could be thankful for that! But there was nothing more to go on.

Zak thought back to the afternoon. The looks on both their faces after they'd kissed goodbye at the wharf — a brief kiss, he had to concede — suggested to him that if they weren't an item already they both wished they were. He would await developments with interest.

Dolly lived in a converted garage behind his parents' house. Days he studied commerce at the university in Cairns, and five nights a week he stacked shelves at Kmart, but Sundays and Mondays he had off.

Mrs Dollinson was watching television in the living room when Zak reached the house. He could see her through the screen door. Normally she would just have called out — 'He's round the back, go straight around, Zak.' But this time she got up and opened the door.

'Zak, hello! I'm really sorry to hear what happened. I saw it on the news, but we heard about it earlier. John's out the back, with a few of the others.'

Dolly, in T-shirt and shorts, lolled back in a chair. Jason Beggs and Ryan Snow were also there, Jason at the controls of PlayStation 2. Metallica was on the CD player, as well as on the walls.

Jason nodded to Zak, his eyes fixed on the screen. *Grand Theft Auto*. The others watched as he sprinted to the nearest set of traffic lights and pulled a brown-suited man from a red sedan. There was a low-slung sports car parked temptingly on the side of the road, but he knew he would need extra room for the two goons he would use to rob the bank for him ... Snowy also nodded to Zak, but did not stop watching Jason's play.

'Don't forget to take the Chinatown shortcut this time!' said Snowy, knowing full well that Chinatown was a notorious area for roadblocks and the chances of Jason's success there were minimal.

Dolly turned down the volume a fraction on Metallica and offered a choice of beer or Coke. Then he spoke.

'Hi Zak. Bad day, eh?' Zak nodded and popped open a Coke.

'We heard you found her,' Jason said. Ignoring Snowy's advice, he directed the car to the nearest re-sprayer, the roller door ascending after a few seconds to reveal a fresh coat of blue paint. His wanted level was reduced to zero while the police continued their search for the red sedan.

'Yeah, that's right,' Zak said.

'Man, that must have been ugly.'

'Yeah, it wasn't good. Nobody could have done anything. There was a doctor there.'

'Want to play?' Dolly asked.

'OK.' Zak sat down.

'There'll be a memorial service at the school,' Snowy said. 'But probably not till the end of next week, so it can be properly organised. Mr Hodgetts has told some people.' Mr Hodgetts was the principal of the high school. Within two weeks, his school had lost a pupil and an ex-pupil, both young Aboriginal people.

'She was doing a line with Kevin Brown,' Zak said. He had picked up a yellow sports car, but now smoke was pouring from the bonnet. He applied the handbrake and skidded to a stop.

'Yeah, but I heard they'd split,' Jason answered.

'Only a while ago,' Snowy said. 'Kev will still be cut up.'

'What about going down to the pub, Zak?' Dolly asked. 'Might be an idea.'

'I thought of finding Kev,' Zak said. On screen, he was now sprinting down the street, the sports car exploding in flames behind him, a tyre flying inches above his head. 'And anyway, I've got to drive back home. But you think he might be in the pub? He sometimes drinks in the Northern.'

'More likely to be at home with his family in town,' Dolly said.

'Well, I might drop by there later, if you want to go to the pub first,' Zak said, selecting a garbage truck for his next theft and returning to his base to save his progress.

'You kidding?' asked Snowy. 'You know Kevin that well?'

'Yeah,' Zak answered. 'I guess I've known him all my life. Not just at school. Even though I haven't seen him in a while. He's got family living around Cassowary. He knows the island, and the sea, all that. We did a bit of fishing together. Say, if I'm going to see him, can anyone give me some weed? And if I'm doing that, I won't come to the pub.'

He did not want to make such a visit empty-handed. He traded two cones off Jason.

'How will you get across to the island?' asked Dolly.

'I'll take the boat, the *Argo*,' he said. 'That's how I got here.' Dolly nodded, fine.

Zak suddenly felt better. Talking to Kevin, with a bit of a smoke, would be good for them both, and he felt like a sail. Instead of using the engine he would run up the mainsail, likely catch the land breeze, and sail home.

22

It was lucky he'd been planning to be shocked when he heard about her disappearance. So it wasn't so hard when he heard what happened, though he couldn't understand it. How the hell could she have got herself onto the beach like that? He'd felt the life go out of her himself, while the water of the river washed over her head and the tinnie drifted, silent, in the direction of the island.

It had been easy, she was only a little thing, and she'd had a bellyful of grog. It had been dark enough, with the half-moon behind clouds — that had been a stroke of luck — so dark he couldn't see her face or her hair streaming behind her in the water. Just as well, if he'd seen that he might have stopped. That would have put him in an even worse situation. And it wasn't like he was feeling good about it all.

But if people argued with him like she'd done, they had to accept the consequences.

When he heard, though, it did come as a shock. Lucky no-one seemed to notice. Hell, he was shaking as he thought about it. Lying on the beach like that, still with all her clothes on. There'd be nothing on her body to link her to him, though. She drowned, definitely she drowned. Probably they'd measure her alcohol level. It would be high.

Who had she been with? No-one could be quite sure. Once she was in the dance group, he'd say, she changed. If he was asked. Others would say it too, she could have been with anyone, they'd say that. From the island, from Cassowary, from the town itself...

Just a sad accident, they'd say.

23

On the Tuesday following their lunch at Rookwood, Leslie was again seated in Leah's office. She had just completed the autopsy on Ebony. From her inspection on the beach, together with today's findings, Leah put the time of death between two and six on Sunday morning, and the cause of death as drowning. There was seawater in the nasal sinuses, and the lungs were heavy and oedematous. Laurie was still preparing sections, though Leah was sure that beneath her microscope she'd find the characteristic salt-water damage to the alveolar cells of the lungs. There were tiny haemorrhages in the brain, but these were due to the lack of oxygen associated with the drowning, and not to trauma to the head, Leah told Leslie.

There was some bruising of Ebony's shoulders and neck, but no strangulation marks, and no damage to her larynx or cervical spine. There were some marks consistent with the body being scraped as it was washed onto the rocks on the beach, and some other abrasions, which Leah had noticed on the beach, which looked like scratches from a stick. And there was some ante-mortem bruising around the wrists consistent with both wrists being held very tightly pressed together, but no definite rope marks. Nothing else. Well, yes, something else, what they had suspected. Her blood alcohol had been 0.18, and a full tox screen would follow. That alcohol reading was certainly enough for a seventeen-year-old girl to have done things she might not have otherwise done, and to take less care of herself than might have been needed on a Saturday night in a place like Mitchells.

Leslie's men had traced Ebony's movements as far as possible on the Saturday night. Drew had briefly interviewed Brian Mitchell who, it turned out, had been at the resort that night. On hearing the news, Drew told Leslie, Brian was visibly distressed, but in suitable measure. He expressed sympathy for the family, and offered as her recent employer to contribute to the cost of her funeral. But he could give no more specific information.

'Of course, I'm only up here occasionally,' Brian had explained to Drew. 'My main business interests are down south. It was pure chance I was here at all Saturday night.' All the organisational details of the resort, Brian said, were handled by his live-in manager Ron Reese.

Ron confirmed that Ebony had danced with all the others — the girls and boys, Ron called them, though many were well into their twenties — in two sessions as usual on Saturday night. 'There was a big party of guests here,' Ron said, 'Americans mostly,' who'd been taken fishing during the day, and Brian had gone with them. All of them had watched the entertainment at the resort, and then most of them had been taken by launch into the casino afterwards, although Brian had not joined them for that. Ebony should have gone back to town in one of the resort's smaller boast with the rest of the group. That was what usually happened. The skipper of that boat had told Drew that he took the troupe back to Cairns but did not count heads. He never bothered with that anyway, he just took all those who turned up back to town once their shows had finished. He was absolutely certain nobody fell overboard during the trip.

Other dancers had said that Ebony told them she was meeting someone there and would get a lift back by boat later. Ebony had done this before and always turned up at home by the following morning. They didn't question it this time. Whether it was always the same person or not they did not know. How many times had this happened? Maybe five or six. Was it someone who worked at the resort or a guest? They didn't know this either, but probably not a guest, or at least, not always the same one because the guests usually only stayed two weeks at most. Ron Reese, Drew told Leslie, understandably took the view that these kids were big enough to look after themselves, he was sorry, very sorry, about what had happened, whatever that was, but he couldn't see that the resort was in any way to blame. They paid good wages, gave the kids work they might not be able to find otherwise. Ron had finished up about two am and gone to bed with his partner in their shared apartment in the employees' complex. The partner had corroborated his story, and said they'd heard nothing about Ebony's death until Sunday afternoon.

Ron Reese had also been quick to ask Drew if he'd talked to Ebony's boyfriend Kevin.

'He should know what she was up to that night,' Ron said.

'Indeed we have,' Drew had replied, though he didn't offer to share the contents of this conversation with Ron. Kevin, Drew explained to Leslie, hasn't been part of the performances on the island, he's been with the group currently performing at the tourist centre in town, and as well he's been occupied with family sorry business for the death of his cousin.

'He's related to the kid who died on the Esplanade the other day, you know, Leslie. Garry Brown.' Drew told Leslie that Kevin seemed very, very angry about Ebony's death.

'Ebony's boyfriend?' Leah said to Leslie, after listening to all this. 'That must have been him outside the mortuary when I went in today. Quite tall, very striking looking, holds himself very well? I spoke to everyone there, but I wasn't sure who they all were. Yes, he is very angry. And very sad.'

'That's him,' answered Leslie, 'Kevin Brown. I noticed him the other day, in the same place, waiting for Garry. I've also seen him perform. He has talent. It's tragic for him, for all the family.'

'So he wasn't with Ebony later on, after the show finished at Mitchells?' Leah asked.

'He says not,' Leslie replied. 'It seems he'd broken up with her lately, and he was fully involved with family business in Cairns on Saturday night. He danced in town in the afternoon and went back home afterwards. There are half a dozen family members willing to swear he was with them all night. But we're not ruling Kevin out of this. He could have got himself to Cassowary beach and found a boat, late at night, and met up with her. And an argument escalated into an accident, out on the water.'

Leah nodded. This was plausible.

'None of the girls who danced with Ebony will say much more at the moment,' Leslie went on. They all agree that Ebony was with them on Saturday night until the end of the performance. They all agree she went into the change room, and got changed into the clothes we found her in the next day. They all agree that she didn't get on the boat with them to come back to Cairns. And that's it ... We've questioned all the guests. Some of them are very hesitant about answering questions, but that mainly seems to be for their own reasons, not wanting their identity in the papers, being there with people not their wives, that type of thing. There's nothing that seems to link any of them to a young Aboriginal girl. There were twenty-two members of staff at the resort on Saturday night. They've all been questioned. None saw Ebony anywhere and all the men have alibis –they were either still working, up until two o'clock, or in bed with other staff members.'

'Did she have a bag with her?' Leah asked.

'Right,' said Leslie, 'I'm coming to that. All the girls said that Ebony owned a very distinctive netted bag, a billum from a relative from further up on the Cape, in yellow, black and red. But no-one could remember if they'd seen her with it on Saturday night. Ebony sometimes had a backpack, too, with costumes and other things she needed for the show, although most of the costumes and props stayed in baskets in the resort's restaurant, where they always perform. What we do know about the billum is that it's not in her family's house here and hasn't been found anywhere else yet, whereas the backpack is in the bedroom she shared in the house.'

'Well, Leslie,' Leah said, 'isn't it perfectly possible that she did go somewhere with somebody, for whatever reason — and yes, I've taken vaginal samples, though the vagina was full of water like the rest of her — and then was taken back by some other boat. There are several boats there, by the way, you probably know that, not just the launches, and some of the staff have tinnies with outboards. If she was drunk, she could have just fallen overboard near the wharf on the mainland, and it would be nobody's fault.'

'Queensland's Chappaquiddick, you think? Yes and no. Even postulating that someone had sex with her and wanted to keep it quiet, if there was an accident as you describe, that person would be much better off saying so. Rather than risking a manslaughter or murder charge.'

Leah was silent for a long moment. Then she said, 'Leslie, you were sounding me out about Brian Mitchell the other day, and now there's a body washed up not far from his resort, at a time when he's there, and she's closely associated with his operation. What's going through your mind?'

Leslie also took his time replying. 'I think I can tell you the gist of what we know so far, Leah. Or what's been alleged, I should say. But I had the feeling, the other day, that you also know something more about Mitchell, maybe something that you don't think is relevant. If that's the case, I'd ask you to tell me. We just aren't sure whether there's something major going on here or not. And now we have the girl — maybe an accident, maybe not. And maybe linked to what we already have been told.

He thought for a while longer, and then said, 'There are two allegations. One is that Brian, or someone who works for Brian, possibly Charlie Angell, runs sly grog into communities further north that have restricted alcohol sales. I know what you're going to say, why would someone like Brian bother? The answer would have to be that he's getting something in return. Some people from those communities have been picked up and charged, and this is what has been suggested. But I'd have to say that so far our information is rather vague.

'The other allegation is much bigger. You've probably heard of Justus Lee, he lives in Manila, but he often comes down here to the casino and to Mitchells.' Leah nodded. 'Recently there was a suggestion that his boat, it's an ocean-going cruiser, was carrying rather more than Mr Lee's personal possessions on its trips down here. When the boat was in Australian waters, a proper search warrant was obtained and the boat searched, but nothing was found on that occasion. Lee complained bitterly. The boat makes regular trips, a look at its log is suspicious enough, and we've had snippets of information from different sources. But that's all. Mitchells is always the first port of call when the boat comes here though. It's just possible that Mitchell and Lee are in on something together.'

'And if that's the case, you think Ebony's death is somehow linked as well?' Leah asked.

'I said that the girls Ebony danced with had nothing more to add to their joint accounts. That's not quite true. One girl, Jade, who is Ebony's cousin, has told us something more.

Firstly, she's adamant that Ebony had nothing alcoholic to drink up until the end of the performance. She said that if Ebony was very drunk when she died, then someone must have spiked her drink. Which is something that had occurred to us as well, of course. And secondly, she told us that Ebony had told her that Brian Mitchell was getting her a job dancing in one of his hotels down south, but that Jade should not tell anyone else. Mitchell, though, told Drew that he barely knew her and certainly didn't talk to her on Saturday night. All of which requires further investigation ...'

'So you are thinking that maybe Brian had some kind of sexual relationship with the girl, in exchange for the promise of a job down south?' Leah asked.

Curious, Leslie looked across at her. 'Actually, Leah, I was thinking more of drugs. That perhaps she took stuff into Cairns for him. Maybe just good weed. Maybe something more. Sex? He's a serial marrier, but I'd really not considered that possibility. Ebony is, was, much younger than him ... much younger, although that doesn't rule it out at all ... Do you have some reason for saying that?'

There was a long silence. Then she said, 'Leslie, I'll tell you what I know about Brian Mitchell. I have to say that I'm very sure he is easily capable of sexually using just about any woman. That's a professional opinion, but also based on my own experience. Because when I was thirteen, I was raped by Brian Mitchell.'

24

It had been a warm Saturday evening in the September of 1973. It was the end of the Dry season, six weeks at least since there had been a drop of rain. The leaves crackled on the floor of the rainforest, and running down the steps from her house to the resort, Leah was careful to see where her feet were going. Snakes could be out at this time of day, looking for water. She wore white cotton shorts over her navy blue school Speedos, and she was going down to the resort's pool for a coaching session with Brian Mitchell.

'Yuk,' was Mara's response, when their mother had told them about Brian's offer to coach them both in swimming. 'I'm not going!'

Always until then, when Leah and Mara wanted to swim, they jumped into Turtle Cove, and dared each other to go across to the sharp rocks below the Devil's Pathway, and stand up on them without slipping off. Or they would go down to Mermaids Beach and dive off the wharf. It was six feet deep at least there, a good place to see how long you could hold your breath underwater. At the resort end of the beach, the current was stronger and they were not allowed to swim there.

However, now Leah had started high school. She was in the swimming team. She wanted to be a champion, and she needed to do some serious training.

Brian Mitchell was a tall young man with a deep suntan and dark hair that was almost shoulder length. Leah's father didn't like him, but her mother seemed to think he was really somebody. She talked about how he'd been in the Rugby Firsts at school in Brisbane, and how fortunate Leah was to be offered the coaching. Leah remembered the snake eating Perry, and wasn't so sure about Brian, but the resort had a big pool, a very modern design her mother said, with little concrete mushrooms, coloured bright orange, dotted around the edges, where the guests of the resort could sit with their cocktails, and a twenty-five yard lap lane along one side. Mornings and evenings, Leah could have free access to that lane.

She'd been swimming there for several months. She'd wake each weekday morning at five, when the big alarm clock shrilled, put on the Speedos and her shorts, and run down the hill to the pool. Brian was always up early, there was breakfast to be supervised, and the cook and catering staff were up too. Brian had an office between the pool and the kitchen of the resort, and the office connected directly to the house where he lived with Deborah and their children.

He'd begun by giving her a program to follow. So many laps of freestyle, so many laps of kicking. He'd watch for a few minutes, then disappear back to his office. Leah had been a bit peeved. Wasn't he supposed to be teaching her?

Then he began to watch her for longer. He made her get out of the pool, and demonstrated to her how she should be lifting each arm, raising her elbows, scooping with each palm as she pulled herself through the water. He got her to bend forward, and stood behind her.

'Let your arms go loose, Leah,' he said, and leaning over her, lifted first one arm, then the other, to show her what she should be doing. He knelt down and squeezed her calf muscles. His face when he spoke to her was serious, and she began to feel a challenge — *I'll show him what I can do*, she thought.

One evening he'd called her into his office. She stood beside him, her togs dripping onto the tiled floor. He had talked about her pectoral muscles and how important they were for strength and speed, and as he did so, his hands had strayed across her breasts, which were getting bigger. Her mother was going to buy her a teenage bra, she'd said. Leah didn't want to think about that. But Brian's expression didn't change and it just seemed like a bit more of the coaching. It wasn't like he was touching her breasts.

Then one morning, he just walked in when she was under the shower in the Ladies. No guests ever used the Ladies at that hour, they all had their own bathrooms. It was easier for Leah to shower there, to take her school uniform down with her and get dressed before breakfast. Brian had talked away as if he hadn't even noticed she was stark naked. She'd grabbed a towel, and after that, she always showered at home. It must have just been an accident, she'd decided.

That episode had given her a funny feeling. In a part of her that she knew the written name of, but she didn't know how to say the word. Was it 'va-jina' or 'va-jeena'? Her mother had given her a book. *Growing Up*. It explained how babies were made. And it included that word. Apparently, when she wanted to have a baby, if that ever happened, this was what she would have to do. It seemed impossible that her parents could have done this to make herself and Mara. It was too embarrassing to talk about, even to Mara, anyway, Mara was too young. Leah hid the book at the back of her wardrobe and decided not to think about it either.

Then one particular Saturday evening, she arrived at the resort about five o'clock. Brian appeared at the side of the pool.

'Start off with 400 yards slowly to loosen up,' he said. 'And I've got the Forbes Carlile book for you, you can come in and get it later.'

She'd finished that 400, and when he hadn't reappeared, she'd taken her kick board and begun to work her way vigorously up and down the pool. Then Brian came back out of his office.

'Leah,' he said, 'do you want to come in and get the book? Deborah's away with the children and I've work to do, you can finish off your session yourself tonight.'

She got herself out of the water, wrapped a towel around her waist and went into the office. Brian was sitting at his desk. He stood up.

'I'll get you a Coke,' he said. He knew very well that she and Mara weren't allowed to drink Coke at home, but he'd given it to her a few times before, and it was Saturday evening so she didn't say no. It seemed a bit funny that he locked the office door when he came back with the drink, but she said nothing. She spread her damp towel on a chair opposite him and sat down.

'There's something I want to ask you, Leah,' he said.

He didn't go on, so she replied, 'What?'

Then he said, 'Do you like me touching your breasts?'

She'd felt a hot flush spread from her cheeks to the tips of her ears, and at the same time, that strange feeling between her legs. Uppermost in her mind was the thought that she was drinking Brian's Coca-Cola. Her mother was always telling her how wonderful the Mitchells were and how kind Brian was to be taking an interest in her swimming. It might be rude to say no. So, wishing that she could just be spirited away somewhere else, anywhere, anywhere, she'd just kind of stupidly stared at her bare feet, and muttered, 'Yeah, I don't mind.'

That was a big mistake.

He had been sitting in the chair opposite her, and as she watched she saw that he was unbuttoning his flies. She could see his penis — another word she didn't know how to say, was it 'penn-is' or 'pee-nis'? Brian's penis was small at first, and then to her utter astonishment it began to grow. He had kept stroking it and saying, 'Look at that, Leah, isn't that a beauty?'

She had been stuck to her towel with horror and embarrassment. Horror at the size and shape of the penis, and the colour, which was a kind of puce. Embarrassment as she suddenly realised so much that she hadn't understood before. She was afraid she might suddenly pee all over the chair.

Then Brian stood up and came over and pulled her up against himself, and put his hand inside her swimming costume, and pulled her over onto the couch. His smell of sweat and Old Spice aftershave was mixed with the chlorine of the swimming pool water. He dragged her costume down, and pushed her legs apart, and pulled her down onto him, and then behaved as if she wasn't even there, moaning and groaning. There was a sharp and terrible pain between her legs, but what was even worse was the thought that the kitchen staff might hear the noise. Then Brian shook and groaned even more, and suddenly pulled her aside, and she had felt warm liquid flowing down her legs, although she had no idea what had happened. And confusingly, he then said, 'Oh, Leah, Leah, you're so good!' He put his head against her bare stomach for a moment and she had lain, unable to move away from him, against the back of the couch, when there was a knock on the office door. The cook.

'Mr Mitchell! Mr Mitchell!' she called. 'You're wanted in the dining room!'

'Quiet, Leah,' Brian whispered to her, 'or you'll be in trouble!'

She must be to blame then, it must be her fault … She stayed absolutely quiet, petrified of what the cook might think if she saw Leah there. However, after rattling the door, the cook found it locked and went away again.

'You'd better go out the back way,' Brian said, pushing her aside and standing up. He looked bizarre, he was still wearing his shoes and long socks, his shorts were around his knees and the 'pee-niss'–'penn-iss' flopped against his thighs, but he spoke as if everything was quite normal.

'Finish up your Coke like a good girl now.' She had pulled up her costume, wrapped the towel around herself, swallowed the rest of the Coke so quickly that she almost choked, and fled out the back door.

She climbed back up the steps to her house, but went straight past the house and on to the cemetery. She sat on John Rookwood's flat tombstone and hugged her knees beneath her towel, trying to understand what had happened to her. She'd left her shorts behind at the pool. She would have to go back to get them, not now though. But she would have to go back anyway, she couldn't just stop the swimming, her parents would notice. There was no-one she could talk to. Mara was too young. She would not be able to find the words to tell her parents, and besides, what might happen then? What if her father went down to see Brian, and everybody then found out what she had done? What if she was pregnant? This was for making babies, wasn't it?

Later when it was dark, she slipped into the house through the back door and ran a bath in the big old bathroom. She felt a great need to wash away the ache between her legs. She discovered she was bleeding, though her period wasn't due for a few days. If she was bleeding, did that mean she couldn't be pregnant? She did not know, but the bleeding continued, and seemed to run on into her period, and with every day of bleeding, she told herself with more certainty that she could not be pregnant, but still it was several months until she felt really sure.

Because of the bleeding, she did not go back to the pool for more than a week. Deborah was back by then, and Brian behaved completely as if nothing unusual had happened. She stayed well away from him when he spoke to her, but anyway, he never again tried to touch her or make any suggestions. Which convinced her that it must have been she who was in the wrong.

When the Christmas holidays came that year, she told her parents that she was sick of swimming training and she was giving it up.

25

Now, in Leah's office with its view of the sea, and its piles of journals and array of specimens, Leslie stood up and walked across to her, and put a hand on her shoulder.

'I'm so sorry, Leah,' he said. 'I had no idea. I hadn't intended you to tell me things about your past that you don't want to talk about.'

'It's OK,' she said. 'It was a long time ago and it's something I think I've come to terms with. And I mentioned it only because it might tell you something about what Brian has always been like. Which may be relevant.'

'Did you make a complaint?' Leslie asked. 'What about your parents? There's no record of any charges like that against him that I know of.'

She shook her head. "No, Leslie. I wouldn't have known how to tell my parents, and they wouldn't have known how to respond. Even though my Dad was a doctor. I've talked about it with my sister at times, and she pointed out, more than once, that I could still bring charges. But ... I just can't do that. It was years before I even understood myself what had happened to me. I was a textbook case!

'It was all part of the whole Rookwood–Mitchell story, really. My mother was a Mitchell, my father met her when he was a medical student in Brisbane. By then, Brian's father owned that land on Rookwood, although when he was alive, nothing was ever built on it apart from a fishing shack that he used once in a blue moon.

'Brian, though, decided to build the resort, and my parents differed violently on that. My mother was all for it, the place would be so exclusive, with all these rich Sydney and Brisbane people coming up by flying boat. Finally, there would be some of her own kind on this God-forsaken desert isle. Whereas my father was appalled. Rookwood Island was ours. He argued and argued with Brian, but always by letter or telegram, after the war he hated any face-to-face arguments, though there were a good few with my mother over it all. Anyway, the resort became a reality and Brian was based there then.

'I'm rambling, but I am now getting to the point of this story. Which began when Brian offered to coach me in swimming and let me use the pool in the resort. Of course he made this offer through my mother. I was really on my father's side when it came to the Mitchells, I'd never liked Brian, but I was thirteen, I wasn't all that much into family differences, and I wanted to swim better. So I was keen to take up the offer. Brian was supposed to have been some kind of athlete when he was younger, though it's hard to credit now.'

Leslie was watching her closely. I could tell him everything, she thought, the whole lot, and all at once she realised, that's what makes him so good at his job, he makes people want to tell him everything. She took a deep breath, and continued.

'I must explain that the one thing that was never, ever mentioned in our house was sex. It was partly the times. Even in the late sixties, up here, people just didn't talk about it. And partly my parents. My mother was prudish as well as snobbish. She had a difficult time having me and Mara. She probably was worried about getting pregnant again. I know everyone believes that their parents never had sex except to conceive them, but I think for many years for my parents it was almost true. When I was about eleven, she gave me a book called *Growing Up*, and that was my sex education.'

She stopped to laugh. 'Leslie, that book made me more confused than ever! I kind of understood the animal aspects, from dogs and cats and so on. But I ended up thinking it was something a married couple did once, when they wanted a baby, like, "Hey, let's have a baby now." I grasped that it felt quite nice, but what completely escaped me was that people could do it at other times.' And the book, Leah recalled, also completely failed to mention erections. She'd had no idea that the penis didn't just fit into the vagina when necessary.

'Also, I have to say, I wasn't all that interested. I was quite isolated, just with Mara on the island most of the time, no TV, wireless listening restricted to *The Argonauts* on the ABC, who you've probably never heard of, and we had our own games and places to play. I think we were quite odd children. Other kids didn't often come over to Rookwood. Of course we went to school, but only to that little school in Cassowary village, until high school. I read lots of books, but not the kind of books that told you anything about sex or even hinted that it existed. So I just didn't pick up on any of the signals and the whole thing just kind of passed me by.' That sex was why people danced together, and hugged and kissed, and what a lot of jokes were about, she'd simply had no idea.

'I can't imagine there are kids around today like I was then. I was totally innocent, and of course, Brian knew that.' She shook her head, amazed at the memory of her younger self. 'Nothing in my life had prepared me for what happened. I didn't say no, because I didn't know how to. And he was not, really, violent. But I certainly did not consent. I was like a piece of wet clay.'

'And you couldn't tell your parents ...' Leslie said gently.

'I was absolutely unable to speak to either of my parents. My mother because I couldn't find the words, and she was such a fan of the Mitchells. My father because of pure embarrassment at having to mention parts of my body which were unmentionable, and also I'd have to admit how right he'd been about the Mitchells. But also, in relation to my parents, I felt I'd discovered an aspect of life that they didn't know about — sex apart from procreation.

'Mara was different, she seemed to cotton on to all kinds of things that simply passed me by. When my father died, seventeen years after this all happened, Mara was here, and I told her for the first time about Brian. She was furious, wanted me to proceed with a complaint even then. But I had Zak and Micky to think of and ... it was just something I couldn't do.'

There had been a single occasion, just before she had finished high school, when she had tried to confront her mother with the story. Her parents were divorcing, Leah was going to university, Mara by choice to boarding school, and her mother had seemed aware that she would not see much of her daughters again. She had tried to say that Leah could be proud of her Mitchell connections.

'Proud!' had been Leah's response. She could talk back to her mother by then, since soon she would be gone from home forever. 'Do you know that when I was thirteen, your supposedly holier-than-thou cousin Brian seduced me?' Seduce, that was the word she'd used. She didn't think of it then as rape. Rape, she had believed, happened violently, at gun or knife point. There would be bruises and broken bones. The rapist would be a stranger with a criminal past. Only much later, studying pathology, had she understood the truth.

Her mother had wanted to know the details, so Leah had started to tell her some of what had happened. She didn't get far.

'You went into his house when Deborah wasn't there?' her mother interrupted. 'You had a drink? Obviously you led him on! Leah, you must understand about men. I know Brian, he's a lovely sweet man devoted to his wife and kiddies. He wouldn't have let himself get carried away like that unless you had suggested it. Teenagers! I don't know, I tried to bring you both up properly and look what happens.' Only much later had Leah realised that what her mother understood by seduction was kissing at the most.

I should have told the truth, Leah thought now. *I should have said 'he fucked me and until then I didn't know what it was, because you never told me anything, so how could I say no?'*

She sat for a moment with her chin resting on her hands. Then she stood up and looked straight at Leslie and said, 'Don't think that I still see myself as traumatised by what happened, Leslie. Everyone has some bad experiences, and it would be wrong to say that mine were worse than anybody else's or particularly different from many other girls. But I do know it affected how I was as a teenager, and my life for a good while afterwards. And Leslie, you can see why you caught me off-balance the other day when you asked me about Brian.'

'I certainly did get bad vibes when I brought his name up,' Leslie agreed. He also stood and moved across to where she was looking out through the window of her office.

'And then, when you mentioned Brian and the girl,' she said, 'I immediately thought of sex, not drugs, though of course drugs might be involved too. I do know that Brian's reasons for raping me were the classical ones — power over me and my family, as well as some kind of victory at taking my virginity. And I think he always had the intention, from the very beginning of the coaching sessions, of abusing me if he could. He wouldn't have tried it with Mara, he knew she was much sharper than me. But I've no reason to think that in thirty years his character or his behaviour have changed. My immediate gut feeling is that if he is linked at all to Ebony's death, sex is involved somewhere.'

Later, she could not explain to herself how it happened. She was a pathologist, more than forty years old, in her own office, in control, simply retelling a story from long ago. Yet suddenly tears were pouring down her cheeks, and then Leslie's arms were around her and she could smell the fresh laundry smell of the shirt Claudine had washed for him and beneath it the man-smell that must be so well-known to Claudine, and she felt the longing welling up from deep within her pelvis and knew she wanted, wanted, to go to bed with Ali.

Leslie sat her down and found a box of tissues.

'It's Ebony I'm crying for really, Leslie,' she said, blowing her nose, and he said yes, he understood that. The front of his shirt was streaked wet with her tears.

'My God, Leslie,' she said, 'there's lipstick on your neck!' She took a tissue and wiped it off for him. 'What would Claudine think?'

He smiled at this. 'I could explain,' he said, 'but hell, Leah, that's really a lot you've had to live with. Like you said, rape doesn't have to be violent, it's still rape.' He leaned down and squeezed her shoulder. 'And I must thank you for telling me that. Because it does shed new light on Mitchell, gives us another line we can explore. I have to have a formal interview with him, he's gone down to Brisbane but he's back on Friday, and I've arranged to talk to him then. We'll be talking to a whole lot of other people, too, of course. I'll let you know what I can about what we find.'

He bent forward and briefly kissed her left cheek. 'You'll be OK?' She nodded, yes of course. 'I must be off then — I'll expect your preliminary report on Ebony by fax as usual.'

He was halfway out the door when he turned back. 'I've just remembered,' he said, fishing in his pockets. 'Claudine gave me some tickets she thought you might be able to use. For the Aboriginal Dance Theatre next Saturday night. She got them for us, then it turned out the girls have a music night at school that we need to go to instead.' He found the tickets and handed them to her.

'Well, thanks very much, and thank Claudine,' she responded. 'But there are two, and Zak's gone back to Townsville this morning.'

Leslie considered for a moment. Then he raised an eyebrow, and said, 'Perhaps you could ask Ali Hassan,' before disappearing out the door.

26

Leslie had arranged with Drew that they would talk together with Kevin Brown, backstage in the town's theatre, after the dancers had finished rehearsing. As he passed through the glass doors of the theatre's foyer late on the Wednesday morning following Ebony's autopsy, he studied the large posters advertising the dance group, with Kevin's photo featured. In addition to the group's established repertoire, a new work was promised: *Beach Warrior* would be a fusion of dance and drama, of old and new cultures. Kevin was depicted wearing tights, with his torso bare and painted with traditional markings in white clay. His head was clean-shaven and the skin of his face was smooth, the nose and cheekbones wide, the expression uncompromising. The muscles of his body were individually sculpted by the rigours of his daily dance practice. Face and body both proclaimed him a proud fighter in the long traditions of his people.

Beach Warrior would premiere in Cairns on the following Saturday evening and was soon to transfer to southern capitals. This was the performance that Leslie and Claudine would miss. *But,* Leslie thought, *some gentle encouragement of Ali and Leah would be a damn good thing.*

Drew arrived on Leslie's heels. Drew had already spoken to relatives of Ebony, and to Ina and Ivy. He had told Leslie that Kevin and Ebony had recently split up, that they'd been heard arguing. Some people thought Kevin was very angry. Angry about Garry's death, angry about Ebony's. Garry's death was a tragedy that Kevin could have done nothing about. But Ebony's?

Kevin was waiting for them both in a small windowless dressing room. He was perched on a metal stool, wearing tights as in his photograph but no make-up, and he had pulled a T-shirt over his bare chest. Sweat ran down his face and stained the shirt. It would be easier for Kevin to talk here, Leslie felt, than in the Police Department. He'd also come without a uniformed man. Even with just the two detectives, no white coppers, Kevin looked uneasy. He kept turning to see who else might be listening. Well, that was understandable. Most white people were equally unhappy, talking to detectives. It was clear to Leslie that Kevin was still very angry, though he kept that anger well-controlled. And, as Leah had said, he was very sad.

'Drew will make notes of what we say, Kevin,' Leslie explained, 'and you can read them when they are typed up. What we need to do is ask some questions about Ebony's death. I'm sorry, we have to use her name, there'll be a coronial inquiry and we have to know exactly who we're talking about.' Kevin nodded, that's OK. 'And,' Leslie added, 'I am also sorry, very sorry, that this has happened, to you and your families. It's been a very hard time for you all lately.'

Kevin nodded again. He gave a single sob, then, gaining control of himself, said, 'Yeah, Mr Fernando, we'd all really like to know what happened. To know, who ... how she died.'

'That's exactly what we intend to find out, Kevin.' Leslie settled back as best he could on a hard wooden chair and began. 'Some people have described Ebony as your girlfriend, Kevin. But is this right? Were you still together?'

Kevin shifted on his stool, looked quickly over his shoulder. 'We *were*,' he said. 'From when she first joined the group, when she was fifteen. We were close then. But lately ... not so much. We were kind of drifting apart a bit.'

'Would you say this change dated from since she began dancing in the resort and you were in town? Say about three months ago now?'

Kevin reached for a towel, wiped his face and draped the towel around his neck. Then he said, 'Yeah, well, you could say that.' His face was inscrutable.

'Did you actually break up with her?'

Kevin fixed his gaze on a point in the middle distance. 'Yeah, well, I guess you could say that. We had a bit of an argument.'

'You hit her?'

'*No!* Who said that? *She* hit *me*. Slapped my face in the park the other day! I guess someone overheard us.'

'Yes. A couple of people heard you, Kevin. Over anything in particular, this argument? Something you said? Maybe because of something she told you?'

Kevin did not reply and Leslie leaned forward. 'Kevin, we've heard that Ebony was offered a job dancing in a hotel down south, and that she was planning to accept the offer. Did she tell you that and was that what caused the break-up?'

Kevin flushed and turned towards Leslie, although he did not look up at him. 'So you guys know about that,' he muttered.

'It was true then,' Leslie continued quickly, 'that Brian Mitchell offered her a job on the Gold Coast? And do you think he might have wanted something in return?'

'Yeah,' said Kevin, 'yeah, that's possible.' He stood up and spat into the sink in the corner of the room, then ran the tap, drinking from his hands before sitting down again.

'Did Ebony smoke much weed, Kevin?' Leslie now asked.

Kevin looked at the floor. 'I wouldn't know,' he said.

Leslie persisted. 'Could Brian Mitchell have been giving her weed to sell?'

Kevin considered for a long moment. Then he said, 'Yep, he might have been.'

'There's been a lot of good stuff around in Cairns lately, Kevin, we know that. Coming down from PNG, maybe. I'm not making any assertions here, Kevin, or accusing anyone of anything. Just looking for information. Trying to find out what happened to Ebony. Could there have been any connection with this supply, and Ebony, and was that part of your argument, perhaps?'

Kevin considered this for a long while. Then he nodded silently.

Leslie changed tack again. 'Ebony died from drowning, and she had a very high blood alcohol reading when she died, Kevin. But witnesses say she didn't drink any alcohol at all during the shows. And nobody, staff or guests, saw her drinking socially anywhere afterwards. Did she drink much when she was with you?'

This time Kevin was more forthcoming. 'We never ever drink before a show,' he said fiercely. 'Absolutely never. No alcohol. Anybody who breaks the rules gets chucked out of the dance group. And if she was really drunk, that wouldn't be like her. Grass, maybe. Booze, no. Someone must have spiked her drink.'

Leslie nodded, then asked, 'Do you think she was doing any drugs, Kevin, I mean, apart from weed?'

More relaxed now, Kevin shook his head. 'Not that I ever saw. But I was worried that if she left here, and went down south, she might get mixed up in drugs and that. And more than just weed ... She was ... only seventeen.' His voice shook as he said this.

'She didn't offer you anything yourself, weed or anything else?' Leslie probed.

'If she did, I would have said no. OK, I might have smoked a bit in the past. But I've seen what's happened to my family, to my people. I won't be doing that again. No drugs, no alcohol. Nothing!' He stood up, defiant, and took another drink from the tap. Then turned to face Leslie and said brusquely, 'Mr Fernando, I want to live!'

'Right, Kevin, I understand what you're saying. One more question ... Did you go to meet her when the launch came back to Cairns last Saturday night? Did you walk down to the pier looking for her?'

Kevin took a deep breath, and took his time answering. Finally he said, 'Well, I reckon you guys know I did. Yeah, I waited on the pier, but out of the way, I didn't, you know, want anyone to know I was looking out for her since we'd split up. But I didn't find her anyway. She wasn't on the boat.'

'Wasn't on *that* boat. We know that, Kevin.' Leslie watched Kevin's face. 'She could have come on another boat, Kevin. Later. With someone else. Someone you weren't happy to see her with. Or you could have gone over to Mitchells yourself to find her.'

'No, that didn't happen. I mean, I didn't see her on the pier with the others, so after they'd gone, I went back home. That's all.'

'You're sure? You didn't meet her later, and take her out from the Cassowary beach? You didn't go across to the island in a tinnie and find her? You're sure about all that?'

'Mr Fernando, I'm sure. OK, I was mad at her. For what she was doing. She was too young. But if I'd found her that night, yeah, we might have argued again, but I would never have hurt her. Never!'

'OK, Kevin. One last question. Do you have any idea of anybody that she might have been with, at the resort, or on a boat, any boat, after the shows ended on Saturday night?'

Now Kevin came back towards Leslie and Drew, and stood in front of them, and his anger was palpable, although it was not directed at the detectives.

'Mr Fernando,' he answered, 'I think you should ask Brian Mitchell that.'

Leslie and Drew stood up, and Drew pressed Kevin's shoulder lightly as they left. Outside the room, Drew said, 'That was a long shot, Leslie. Nobody told us that he'd been looking for her on Saturday.'

'No. But I figured he might go quite often, after his show was over, to meet that boat when they were together. And then I figured maybe he did it again, even though they'd split.'

They made their way through the front doors of the theatre, and Leslie looked again at the blown-up photograph of Kevin. At the top of the steps leading from the theatre's foyer, he paused, and Drew turned back to look at him. Though Leslie stood three steps above him Drew's head was level with his boss's.

Leslie narrowed his eyes, then said to Drew, 'So we have an angry young Black man, spurned so it seems by his girlfriend for a rich and powerful white man, looking for that girlfriend just hours before she died. He's got access to any boat he wants on Cassowary wharf. He's got his own ute in Cairns. She's already drunk a lot over at the resort, doing God knows what. And he's got any number of relatives prepared to say he never left them all night.'

Drew shook his head. 'Leslie,' he said, 'Sir, I just don't want that it happened that way.'

27

On Friday afternoon, Leslie and Drew took the water police launch across to Rookwood Island for their appointment with Brian Mitchell.

'There are some perks in this job after all,' Drew remarked as they sat together on the outside deck; the sea was calm and a benevolent sun shone over it. The launch's captain, 'Shorty' Brewer, was at the wheel. On their left were white sand beaches, bordering the sprawling suburbs of Cairns, and alternating with patches of mangrove swamp. Nearing the mouth of the Cassowary River, they turned to port, towards the northern end of Rookwood Island.

Ron Reese met them at the resort's wharf. Ron was from the north of England, a plump and balding man whose slightly camp manner was accentuated by his flowered Hawaiian shirt, ear stud and thick gold neck chain. It was clear he was an efficient deputy for his boss. Since the discovery of Ebony's body, he had been more than helpful to Drew and his men in arranging questioning of resort staff and discreet interviews with guests. But this morning he had telephoned Leslie with a request — 'We have a new group of guests arriving today, Mr Fernando. Mr Mitchell will see you as planned, but could we not have police uniforms on the resort site?' Leslie had been happy to comply.

Ron led them to his boss's office where Brian waited at the door. A man well in control of himself, Leslie thought, studying Brian. A big man, weighty around the middle.

Leslie recalled what Leah had said of him. He had no difficulty imagining someone of Mitchell's size man-handling a woman as slim as Leah. Or Ebony. Mitchell was clean-shaven, tanned, in smart designer casual wear — checked trousers, maroon polo shirt, and what Leslie noted were Gucci loafers.

'Fernando! Come in, have a seat. Yes, I met Drew the other day.' Hands were shaken, seats offered.

Brian's quarters, office and living accommodation, were set slightly apart from the rest of the resort, quite close to Mermaids Beach. He had a view directly across to the mouth of the river, and to a panorama of mangrove forest and beach spreading into the distance from the river's northern shore. Leslie could see a couple of tinnies drawn up on the beach outside Brian's office, well away from the resort's main wharf. The office was panelled with fine tropical hardwoods. Leslie noted that the walls were thick, and no doubt well soundproofed as a result. He also observed that Ron Reese remained in the office, seating himself discreetly in a chair by the door while his boss answered questions.

Brian pressed a switch and a cupboard opened to display a fabulously stocked bar. He offered Scotch, knowing full well both his visitors would decline. Drew, his face a mask, accepted a glass of water.

'Tragic thing this,' said Brian, 'though I'm not sure how I can help you two gentlemen any more than we've already done. Ron tells me you've already spoken to all the staff who were here that night.'

'Just a chat, Brian,' Leslie informed him, 'just a chat. But Drew will make notes and let you see what is written down when it's typed up, as usual.'

'Oh, I'm sure I have nothing to hide,' Brian said smoothly.

'You were here on Saturday night?' Leslie asked.

'Yes, as it happens, I was. We had some special guests. I looked after them personally during the day. Business people, you know. We went fishing. And in the evening, I was around the dining room where the shows are, as well. Of course,' Brian added, looking across to where Ron sat, silent but attentive, 'Ron runs all that side of things, but sometimes I like to be personally involved.'

'Some guests went across to the casino, but you didn't go?'

'No. I believe they came back about one o'clock. I was in my office, then my rooms which adjoin us here' — he waved an arm — 'watching a movie until about one-thirty. I came out to check with Ron that all was well, then went to bed at two.' Ron nodded his head at this. The movie had been a replay of *GoldenEye*, no doubt Brian knew all the action anyway since it had been around since 1995.

'Did you have a drink at all during the evening?'

'I think I had a Scotch or two.'

'Nothing else?'

'No, why?'

'One of your barmen noticed that a nearly full bottle of Polish vodka had gone from the bar during the late evening. Later he found the empty bottle in the kitchen bin. We wondered if you might have picked it up.'

'No,' said Brian. There was a short silence, then he added, 'Of course, anything like that could have been handled by any member of staff from time to time.'

'Meaning?' Leslie raised his eyebrows.

'Well ...' For the first time Brian seemed uncomfortable. 'Just, if you guys were going to take fingerprints, you know.'

'Fingerprints? Brian, Ebony Passmore died of drowning. We believe there was an accident. We're just trying to establish what that accident was.' Leslie knew that Drew was thinking just what he was thinking — that office cupboard has enough grog for an entire army, but probably not many staff fingerprints on the bottles. Whereas the vodka bottle ... He watched Brian's face carefully, and then said, 'One thing about Ebony though. She did have a high blood alcohol reading. She must have had a lot to drink here.'

'Here?' Brian stared. 'Oh, you mean at the resort ... Well, guests buy drinks for the dancers, or they can buy their own.'

'We've heard the group is very strict about no alcohol before and during performances.'

'Well, maybe. But sometimes these kids get around that. And the staff might be over- generous sometimes, although they have orders not to serve underage drinkers.'

'So you know how old Ebony was?'

Brian flushed. 'I ... I just thought she was less than eighteen, someone said that ... Actually, I hardly even remember which one she was, Leslie. She was just one of the kids in the dance group.'

'Did you suggest to her that you might be able to fix her up with a job down south?'

'No ... ah, who told you that?'

'More than one of her friends has told us that, Brian.'

'Well, she was a smart girl and a good dancer — no harm in that, is there? I've got interests on the Gold Coast, hotels that run shows every night. I could easily fix up something for her.' He stopped suddenly, then corrected himself: 'I mean, I could have if ... It was nothing personal. I just like to help these kids.'

'You like young girls, Brian?' asked Drew suddenly.

'Say, what is this?' Brian protested. 'I'm a married man. What are you implying? You two can't talk to me like this!'

'You seem to know quite a lot about her, Brian, considering she was a casual employee,' Leslie said.

'She was just one of the kids who dance in the shows here. I could hardly tell her from any of the others.'

'A smart girl and a good dancer,' Leslie said slowly, 'yet you could hardly tell her from the others ...' He changed tack abruptly. 'What about drugs? Did she smoke dope do you think?'

'I can't tell you the answer to that.'

Can't or won't, Leslie wondered. 'We believe she'd been smoking cannabis the night she died,' he said.

'Well, she's a local kid, many of them do. You'd have to ask those friends of hers,' Brian replied, cool again now. He considered for a moment, then added, 'I'll say this, Leslie — she was good-looking, she did stand out in that group, and I might have mentioned the idea that she could find work down south, and that I could put in a word for her. It's no more than I've done for others. But there was nothing, repeat nothing, more than that. There was nothing going on between me and her, and I did not see her last Saturday after the show, and I don't know what happened to her.'

Leslie stood up. 'Well thanks for your time, Brian. We don't know what happened to her either. But I have to tell you we intend to find out.'

28

Back in his office after his visit to Mitchell, Leslie picked up the phone, dialled the hospital and asked to speak to Dr Ali Hassan.

'Ali! This is Leslie, Leslie Fernando.'

'Ah ... hello, Leslie!'

'Ali — I need to get a short statement from you please. About what happened on Sunday to Ebony Passmore. Just that you were the first medical practitioner on the scene, and that she was already dead. That type of thing.'

'It is necessary?' Ali was wary.

'Yes, if you don't mind. I could come to see you if you like. Perhaps not in the hospital though.'

'Yes, the flat would be better.' Ali sounded relieved.

'Six o'clock then.'

At two minutes to six, Leslie pressed the button for the lift in Leah's apartment building. In his shirt pocket he had the notes he'd made for Ali's statement. Cradled against his left elbow was a six-pack. Sure, he needed the statement. But he was officially off-duty at six, and he was planning another role for himself. On his wife's instructions.

Ali had the door of the flat open when Leslie reached the sixth floor. He led Leslie into a tidy living room, where a tray with juice and glasses were already set out. The doors were open to the terrace.

'I brought something a little stronger,' Leslie said, producing the six-pack, and Ali smiled. While Ali opened two beers, Leslie studied a poster on the wall. It was an enlarged photo taken from the top of a mosque, looking down over myriad richly woven carpets, on each of which a praying figure knelt.

'It's beautiful,' he said.

'Yes,' Ali agreed. 'The mosque is at Najaf. It's one of the holy cities of the Shia people. I am not exactly one of them, but I appreciate the beauty of the mosque.'

Leslie's gaze passed to several framed photos on Leah's sideboard.

'My family,' said Ali. 'By all means you can see them.'

The largest photo was faded, brown and white. Four boys, aged from perhaps fifteen down to five, all dark-eyed and with hair slicked into place with water, stood with a bearded older man and a woman whose flowing silken robe joined a scarf that lightly covered her hair. Behind them, rather distant, was a long, flat house of the kind Leslie associated with the Bible stories of his youth, flanked by palm trees, and beside it an irrigation ditch edged with bushes.

'My parents and my brothers,' Ali said. 'At my family's home south of Baghdad. When we were all still at school.'

Christ, Leslie thought, *everyone of them except Ali is dead.* Leslie's own brothers, all four of them, were alive and well, all married with children, his parents lived comfortably amongst family and friends in Melbourne. 'Do you think you will ever go back to Iraq?' he had asked Ali, driving back from Rookwood the previous Sunday.

'There would have to be great changes,' Ali had said. 'When I first went to England, I was in touch with opposition groups, I thought of trying to do something through them. But it seemed like the people who weren't connected to the CIA were probably from Saddam's security service, and some no doubt were from both. I couldn't trust anyone. I decided I would just work and try to live my life quietly.'

A smaller coloured portrait showed Ali as a new father, serious in suit and tie, with his wife and baby. The baby was almost hidden beneath layers of white lace. The wife, Leslie noted, was dark and pretty. And considerably younger than Ali.

The third photo was a hazy snapshot of a young man in military uniform.

'My brother Ahmed,' Ali explained. 'He died in the war with Iran. He was the first of my family to die.' He shrugged slightly as he held a glass of beer towards Leslie, and Leslie understood this was as much information as he wished to give.

'Would you like to sit on the terrace? It is very pleasant in the evenings.'

They sat down and Leslie produced his notebook. It was very simple, he explained, just a description of what Ali had seen, there would be no need for any court appearances or further interviews.

'Do you have any ideas about what happened?' Ali asked. 'Any clues?'

'At the moment, we're concentrating on the resort,' Leslie answered, 'since that was where she was that night, but we have nothing definite yet. There is also the question of her boyfriend. Her ex-boyfriend. Apparently they had argued, people overheard them. He's also a dancer, performing at the theatre here in town.'

'Ah,' said Ali. 'Yes. Leah has asked me to go to the theatre with her tomorrow night.'

'And you said you would?'

There was a silence. Above the balcony railing, Leslie watched a Qantas jet take off from out at the airport, rise rapidly over the town and swing towards New Zealand, the red kangaroo on the tail disappearing into the dusk. Jazz music began to drift up from a restaurant below on the Esplanade.

He already knew what Ali had said. He had telephoned Leah the previous day. On Claudine's orders. "You must find out, Leslie," she had said. So Leslie had chatted about this and that. The autopsy result. The progress with his case. He had told Leah about the interview with Kevin, and about Brian Mitchell. And finally he'd asked — 'By the way, are you taking Ali Hassan to the theatre?'

'I don't think so,' she had said. 'He didn't sound very keen.'

Now Ali said, 'I was not sure.'

'Not sure?' Leslie asked. 'About what?' And when still Ali did not speak, he said gently, 'She is an attractive woman.'

'Yes,' Ali agreed. Then he added slowly, watching Leslie, 'But I am nobody here, Leslie. I have some savings in England, but no house, not even a car yet. I cannot stay too long in Australia. She will think I am ...' His voice drifted off.

'... gold-digging?' Leslie finished off for him and Ali nodded.

'I don't think so, Ali. I think she can make up her mind pretty well about these things. But you know, despite owning Rookwood, and so on, her life hasn't been all that easy. She's divorced from her husband, years ago. She barely knew Zak's father, as I understand it. She brought those kids up virtually on her own. Maybe she also needs a little ... encouragement.'

Ali took a long draught from his glass.

'Ali,' said Leslie, 'one thing. I take it you didn't marry again? After your wife died in Iraq?'

Ali looked startled. 'No, no,' he said. 'Only one wife. Why?'

'I, um, just wanted to make sure, you know, that you weren't planning to bring anyone else to live here in the flat.

From England, maybe? There's more than enough room for two.'

'No, I have no-one in England or anything like that. And nobody now in Iraq.' Then he looked directly at Leslie. 'Is that what she thinks?'

'It may have passed through her mind.'

'And she? She also has nobody else?'

'I don't believe so.'

Ali finished his beer in one swallow.

'In that case, perhaps I will go with her to the theatre.'

29

He was sure he'd been convincing. That he'd played it with just the right touch. He'd been helpful, told the truth. Well, some of it.

So they knew she'd been promised a job down south. They thought she'd been drinking. That maybe she fell out of a boat and drowned. It didn't seem like they knew much more for certain. Where was her billum? They hadn't mentioned that. Or what was in it. Well, that didn't really matter. VB was a common beer up here, everyone drank it, if they had found that they would simply say it fitted with her drinking earlier. Taking some more home, that's what she was doing.

Leslie Fernando had watched him hard while the other one, Drew, the tall guy, was taking all the notes. Not a muscle in his face had moved while Leslie watched, he was sure — nothing had betrayed him. He'd tried to act normally, to just do the things he'd normally do, but he'd had to think hard about how he'd be, normally. He was a good actor. He was sure he'd succeeded.

30

Leah sat in her living room, an open bottle of merlot and a glass on the table in front of her. She had been planning to work on reports on her computer, but she was finding she could not concentrate at all. It was Friday evening anyway, not really a time for work.

For the first time since she'd moved back to the island, she wondered if she had made the right decision. She had known she would be alone much of the time, but she had not expected that she might be lonely. She was missing Zak, she knew, though she had always known that he would go away to university, and it was totally unreasonable to expect a nineteen-year-old boy to live on an island with his mother. But if she'd stayed in town, there would have been friends she could call up, drop in on, go for coffee with ... *Be honest*, she told herself. *It's not the island. You're upset that Ali said no. You thought there might be something in it, and there wasn't. He's from a different country, a different culture, you were crazy to think about it at all. Find something else to do. And put the top back on that bottle ...*

Then she remembered the letters. There were at least two more to read. She fetched the box and unfolded the fine sheets of a third letter.

Hope Street
Cooktown
30th September 1879

My dear Emily,

Yes, I can tell you as I wrote in my telegram, John and I were married on Tuesday of last week. I am enclosing the account of the event that I have cut from the *Cooktown Herald* that describes better than I could our dress and reception. As you may surmise from this, weddings don't happen every day in Cooktown. The excitement as we drove the whole half-mile from the church to the Sovereign Hotel was quite something to behold, as everyone in town knows 'the Doctor' and most think it's just right and proper that he should marry 'the Irish Nurse'. I was surprised the horses didn't bolt! Drinking men came out from every public house to toast us, and the children were all lined up by Miss Best outside the school. What should have been a stately progression was a regular *hurly-burly*! Many of the Chinese also were cheering, as John sometimes treats them as patients, almost as well as white men in my opinion.

As you know, no bridal trip or 'honeymoon' at present because we will be down in Sydney for six whole weeks with you at Christmas. We are now assured of a *locum tenens* in the person of Dr Hargraves, who arrives soon from home on a direct Royal Mail steamer. It will be far better for us this way because the heat and rain can be so *intolerably* oppressive in January. Whereas the winters here are quite beautiful. We had the whole week to ourselves until Sunday though, John absolutely refused to see any patients unless they needed surgery that could not possibly wait, and said that Mr Kirkpatrick and Mrs Mulligan could manage anything else, and apart from a leg that needed setting on Friday evening, we were pretty much able to make ourselves snug in our own new house on the hill. We are still in need of a sideboard so I have all the silver and plate in boxes on the floor but the dining table and chairs — Queensland maple — did come up in time from Bowen and do us proud. Also the bedroom furniture and wash stands. I have more than enough linen now, what with my own and your *beautiful* gift. John has found a Chinese servant, Lee Chin, and a woman, a miner's wife, to do all the washing. So I could be quite the married lady, except I shall continue for the moment to do my nursing else I should be bored. There is no reason I can see why a married woman should not work for a while and in a place like Cooktown, so new and far from everything else, it seems even more like the right thing to do. (Yes, I know what you are thinking, and if *that* happens, of course I shall be giving up my nursing.)

On Sunday we went for a day picnic to the island with the Chapmans and Mrs Howe, the widow of a ship's captain, leaving very early. It is a comfortable sail in the schooner with a good breeze. I no longer find the sailing boat making me queasy and in fact I am starting to enjoy sailing. John has constructed a wharf on the beach closest to the mainland, and also a cabin he calls the summer-house, and a kitchen, both of planks but quite serviceable. The best beach for swimming is a little sheltered cove he has called Turtle Beach, on the far side of the island. We have to climb a path up to the top of the island, and then down again. I suppose the paths were made by the blacks to get down to the beach, they have left traces of their fires and piles of shells on the beach although thankfully there were no blacks themselves to be seen on the island that day. We all bathed in the sea and then climbed back up to the top for the picnic — ham and cold roast beef, fresh bread and preserves and cakes, and madeira wine, you see we want for nothing in Cooktown! On the top of the island is a flat shelf of rock from which it is possible to see for miles around, and here John says he hopes one day to build a house, though the location seems very remote to me. He asked me to name the beach on the west side of the island, and I have chosen 'Mermaids Beach' which he thought very whimsical. I must admit he is more prosaic than myself.

Anyway, apart from picnics, we are now establishing our household routine. We take breakfast together each morning at eight, and that is very pleasant. Then John departs for morning surgery and I busy myself with my little household, in a few weeks I shall start going down to the surgery around ten each morning, but for the moment I am well occupied at home. I am also anxious to practise my cooking skills as much as possible and I am most grateful for your sending 'Mrs Beeton' up to me. Her 'ten things to do with cold roast beef' are an inspiration! We have dinner at twelve and because of the heat a 'siesta' until three, unless there is an urgent case. Supper is at eight and we usually manage to have a cup of tea together at five-thirty and watch the sunset from our 'veranda' as it is called here. We sit on the veranda again after supper and John smokes his pipe and takes ' a wee drop', we are able to get Powers from home and also stout which as you know I like to take a bottle of in the mornings at least twice a week. After ten days you see we are really very settled-in and I think that makes John happy.

Well, Emily, you ask me frankly, *do I love him*? (I have destroyed that letter of yours now, he is not I am sure a man to read his wife's private letters but I did think it best.) I was surprised at how acute you are! I have always taken pains to praise his many good qualities to you when I write. But Emily, please do not think that because I am over thirty I felt I had to marry. And yes, it is less than a year since my arrival here, but I do not think our decision was at all rushed. For some years before I took this position I was quite equably resigned to being busily single all my days, and perhaps eventually becoming the matron of a hospital in some large city (I see you smiling at that). Emily, I thought a great deal about my decision, and told John what I thought. I believe I shall grow to love him. He is a good man, and very fair. Of course I have now been initiated into certain delicate matters which have been familiar to you for some time. Luckily my training had me well prepared and I came through tolerably well I think. I believe this aspect will develop over time also.

I am sending in a separate parcel some of my wedding cake for the 'little maid' — it is Mother's fruit cake recipe with extra currants, so not suitable for baby Cecily. Give both of them lots of hugs from me and Uncle John (yes, I can truly write that now!) The wedding photograph is being framed for you and will be dispatched next week when I shall send my next instalment of married life!

Affectionately, Addie

Folded into the pages of the letter, much creased, was a smaller copy of the wedding photograph of John and Adeline that stood on Leah's piano.

Well, Leah thought. *Well now*. Clearly Adeline had not been bowled over by John's advances, although she sounded quite happy with her decision. At least, at the beginning. She had gone into the marriage with her eyes wide open. What about John? He had advertised for a nurse — had he also thought he might find a wife? He would have known before he engaged her that Adeline Horton was from the same Irish Protestant background as himself, genteel but not rich. Quite probably Adeline had come to New South Wales together with her sister — it seemed that Emily had quickly found a husband, while Adeline had continued to practise her profession.

As Adeline had herself observed, the arrival of Nurse Horton in Cooktown, and her courting, engagement and marriage had all taken place in less than a year. John would have been well aware that it was unlikely that many suitable single women would turn up spontaneously in a frontier town like Cooktown. Probably there had been no shortage of unsuitable women, as Adeline had hinted in her earlier letter. Indeed John's concise medical records had included the treatment of syphilitic ulcers and gonorrhoea. The pox and the clap had come off the same boats as the earliest arrivals in Cooktown. But it would have been difficult, if not impossible, for an unmarried doctor in a small place like Cooktown to avail himself of such women and still maintain his professional position. How had the relationship with Adeline fared with the passing years? Was it greatly affected by the incident on the island, and the terrible massacre?

'I will grow to love him,' Adeline had hoped. She could be critical of Addie, Leah thought. Respectability must have played a part in her decision. But then it had for John too. And how many people did Leah know who had married for reasons that couldn't be criticised? Maybe Leslie and Claudine? Not many others ... She herself had been sexually bewitched by Gareth — when the spell wore off, there was nothing else. Ali's marriage had been traditionally arranged. It seemed that it had not been happy, though many such marriages were successful.

Ali again. She must stop thinking about him. There was little need to come across him in the course of her work, especially if she did much of it at home. She must just forget the whole incident.

She uncorked the wine bottle and was pouring herself another 'wee drop' when her mobile rang. It was Ali himself.

'Leah,' he said. 'Leah. Is it too late to change my mind? May I come to the theatre?'

'Oh!' she said. 'Oh Ali, yes. Yes.'

31

The theatre and its gardens occupied a whole block in the centre of town. By seven on Saturday evening, dozens of glowing Japanese lanterns and tiny coloured bulbs had given the place a festive air not apparent in daylight hours, and a full moon hung low above the palm trees surrounding the building. In front of the theatre meandered a pond, with a wooden bridge in the style of Monet. Lily pads floated on the water and the colours of the fairylights were reflected back onto the crowd gathering to watch the Cairns Dance group.

Across the road from the theatre was a large park, the buffalo grass studded with big old fig trees and eucalypts. Little groups of people huddled together beneath the figs, all of them with casks of wine or stubbies of beer. They slurped the wine directly from the casks, or ripped the tops off the glass stubby bottles and tipped their heads back to drink. Cigarettes glowed in the darkness. Some of these people would later trudge to spend the night in one of the shelters or hostels the town provided. Others would sleep rough, in the open, backs up against the trunks of the figs. Many of these people were from distant communities, but they did not want to stay in those communities now because the communities' dry policy made their lives difficult, and there was nowhere else for them to go.

Cars drew up and people began to arrive on foot as well. By seven, the foyer of the theatre was packed with people laughing and talking, and drinking bottled wine and beer from clean, washed glasses. Last minute tickets were collected, mobile phones switched off. The bells began to ring, the show would soon begin, and the people finished their drinks, put down their glasses and made their way into the auditorium. Among them were Leah and Ali. As they edged toward their seats, Ali saw Leah wave to at least a dozen people she knew. The lights dimmed, and the soft moan of a didgeridoo began to tell a story.

The first part of the program consisted of dances that were well known to Leah, part of the daily dance performances for the tourists who flocked to Cairns. They were loosely based on the origins of the people who had once occupied not only the land on which Cairns had been built, but also the region –the mountains that sent trickling streams into tributaries that formed the Barron River, the scrub plains and the palm-edged beaches, the mangrove swamps teaming with fish, the dense rainforest filled with so many fruits, berries and medicinal herbs. People who for 40,000 years had found their livelihood in harmony with the land, who for centuries had gone across in their canoes to Rookwood Island, to fish, trap turtle, light fires and cook their haul on the beaches. People who knew how to move silently through the rainforest catching birds, lizards and larger animals for tucker.

Only some of the people who now lived in Cairns identified with these original people of the country around them. Many other people were descended from tribes who had been moved steadily east by various government agencies and missions, away from farming land, until they had come to the sea, and could be moved no further.

With light and movement, the dancers told stories of the creation of their country. Of the spirits who have always lived there — one in the shape of a crocodile, another of a turtle, the third a big trout. Spirits who were sometimes helpful, sometimes not. Who sometimes needed to be appeased and sometimes avoided altogether.

With music from the didgeridoo and the synthesiser combined, these tales were portrayed on stage. The troupe enjoyed themselves. They hopped about, imitating animals – kangaroo, cassowary, crocodile. They poked fun at each other and at the audience. Only Kevin Brown, who took some of the lead roles, seemed aloof. *Well*, thought Leah, *that's understandable.*

Ali had not seen it before, nor indeed any Indigenous culture. He watched carefully, consulting the program between items. Of course, Leah knew, it was designed for tourists. Many of the traditional stories had been altered to Western, or Japanese, taste. The music and scenery were an eclectic mixture, not typical of any one country. But it was a positive celebration nevertheless.

At interval, Leah and Ali stood on the Monet bridge, drinks in hand. Around them the comments of the audience could be heard: 'Charming!' '*Wunderschön!*' '*Cho berigu!*'

Across the road in the park, two police cars and a paddy wagon had drawn up. A fight had broken out. Two men and a woman were being escorted into the wagon. 'Fuck you!' shouted the woman at the uniformed man slamming the wagon door, 'you pinched my grog.'

A few people from the audience turned briefly at the sound, and turned away again. Leah glanced at the people around her. Among the people in the auditorium she'd seen scarcely one black face.

But there was one young woman standing slightly apart from a small group of white people, mostly men, all with glasses in their hands. An Aboriginal woman, perhaps in her mid-twenties, with glossy black curls tumbling down her back. The woman watched the scene across the road intently. Then one of the men broke away from the group, spoke to her and took her arm, bringing her back to the others. A man considerably older than her. There was something disturbing, proprietorial, in his gesture, Leah thought.

She thought she recognised him, but she was sure he was not from Cairns. Then it dawned on her. He was a sociologist, a professor from some southern city, often in the news for his support for Indigenous causes. Rufus ... Rufus Forbes, that was his name. Was the woman his assistant? His student? His wife? But Leah didn't know him and she did not know the woman. Other people were drifting past and she and Ali joined them for the second half of the performance.

Back in the theatre after the interval, it was clear the mood had changed. The auditorium was plunged into a profound darkness. *Beach Warrior!* a screen across the front of the stage proclaimed. A new work, choreographed by and featuring Kevin Brown.

Gradually, the theatre lightened and Kevin was first seen lying centre-stage, a sleeping rock. Then the morning sky appeared as a moving image behind him — on film, which changed as the dance progressed. Kevin slowly awoke, stood up and stretched, and then became, one after the other, the totems of the clans into which his people were divided — the snake, the turtle, the eel, the crocodile. In the film behind him, people appeared, black people, tattooed or luminously painted. They began to hunt, fish, make camp, cook, hold ceremonial dances of their own, walk together, laugh and be happy. Around Kevin, other dancers appeared briefly, swirling about him, but all the power, the tension of the story was concentrated in the elastic figure of Kevin, the Warrior, at the end of the most powerful spotlight.

Now in the background film, dark clouds moved across the sky, rain began to sputter, the mood became sombre. New men arrived, white men in clothes, miners, men on horses, who cut at the bush and dug in the rivers. The black people in the film gathered together, afraid. On the stage, more dancers appeared around Kevin. Some were painted white, and as they danced they pulled on shirts and trousers. Some carried Bibles, others held bottles. The remaining dancers were covered in war paint and held spears. Now the white men held rifles. They shot blindly at those with spears, who cried out loudly as they fell. Some of the tribespeople tried to flee but were intercepted by the white men. More and more people filled the stage, and the spotlight probed, picking out one dancer after another, each individual a Goya-esque cartoon of tragedy. The central figure continued to be Kevin, black and with his war paint smeared, holding a spear, desperately battling until he, too, was felled by a gunshot and blood flowed.

Then the background screen shifted to a different scene. The beach at Cassowary River, the sea, the white sand, and the forest at its edge. And the sign, red, black and yellow, marking the site of the massacre.

The stage dimmed for perhaps thirty seconds, while the didgeridoo softly roared. Then Kevin reappeared. Painted like a warrior, he leapt back and forth the across the stage, twisting and diving, the light intermittently catching him at the height of each leap so that he appeared to fly across the scene, first as a bird, then as an eel or fish, and finally as an exuberant black warrior, throwing his arms back, his head high, exhorting his ancestors to protect him.

As he flew, exultant, through the air, Leah was overwhelmed with emotion. This was a proud man, determined to fight for his people, she thought.

But could this same powerful emotion have led him to murder?

As suddenly as it had begun, Kevin executed one final swoop, and an hour of concentrated performance was done. The stage was in darkness again. And throughout the auditorium was an uneasy hum.

Then some people began to clap, Leah among them. Ali joined in and others followed. The applause was enthusiastic. The dancers came out to take their bows. Kevin especially was applauded, but still Leah sensed uncertainty in those around her, in people used to the digestible, fairytale pieces of the first half of the program. Were they being mocked? On the other side of the theatre Leah could see Rufus Forbes and his friends, and he was talking volubly. No doubt he held strong opinions, but he was too far away for Leah to hear what they might be.

She and Ali joined the stream of people leaving the theatre. The conversation around them was muted. Across the road, the park was in darkness. A few people were curled up, sleeping on the grass. The cop cars and the paddy wagon had gone.

32

Ali said, 'It was the beach story, that same story you told me! But it was too hard for them, the audience. They liked the simple stories better!' He was anxious — *what would happen now?* He wanted to reach out and touch her, but he could not. They were moving slowly towards her parked car.

'Yes. The first half was much less confronting,' Leah answered. 'I wonder how it will go, down south. It's appearing in Brisbane and Sydney. The dancing and the choreography are first-class. But it was challenging for white people. No-one could mistake its meaning.'

'Kevin is a very powerful dancer,' Ali ventured, wondering: *should he make a move before they reached the car?*

'Superb. He has great strength of character to be able to continue with this after Ebony's death — and Garry's.'

'Ah — he is a relative of my little patient, Benjy?' *And what if she said no to his advances?*

'Yes, I think so. The families are close to each other. They lost both Garry and Ebony within two weeks. He has great natural ability, but now there's a sense of purpose and power that I haven't seen before. I've seen him several times dancing with the group that does the usual tourist performances. What he's been through has been very rough, but it seems to have made his work stronger.'

She was speaking hurriedly to fill the space between them, she realised. She was as jittery as a cat on hot bricks. They were walking slowly but definitely towards her car. Her pulse was racing, she was excited by the dance, tormented by not knowing what was to come.

'Shall I drop you home?' she asked nervously, searching for her keys.

'Please.' And then he reached across and touched her hand and asked, 'Why don't you come in for some coffee?'

'Yes,' she said, 'yes. I'd like that.' Her legs felt weak and she trembled as she turned the key in the ignition. She knew that if he leaned over and touched her again she would have to stop the car. But he kept still and somehow she negotiated the car park exit and the drive along the Esplanade.

The moon was a huge orange globe above the sea, its light a golden ladder down from the sky and across the water to the very edge of the shore. She parked, and they moved towards the foyer of the apartment building. Hell, there were butterflies in her stomach. In the lift, he pressed the button for the sixth floor, then turned.

'Leah!' he said, and then he did touch her again, she found his arms around her, his mouth against hers. *My God*, she thought, *how much I want this man* ... They were still locked together and her hands were inside his shirt when the lift reached the sixth floor, stopped, the doors opened and shut again, and the lift began its descent. Leah raised her head and giggled. 'We'll have to go back down and up again!'

At ground level waited the elderly Bennetts from the fourth floor, visibly startled by the sight of Dr Rookwood and that Middle Eastern fellow who had rented her flat clutching one another. Mrs Bennett held a litre of milk.

'Bob and I just went out for the milk,' she said, firmly pressing the button for the fourth. 'Not like the old days when you could depend on the milko to deliver it for you each morning, is it, Doctor?' She couldn't help noticing that Dr Rookwood's lipstick was smeared around that man's mouth.

At the fourth floor, the lift doors opened and then closed behind the venerable couple, and as they once again ascended, Leah burst into helpless laughter.

'Everyone in the building will hear about this first thing tomorrow,' she said.

'That matters?' he asked.

'No, no, no, not at all,' she answered, leaning against him. They emerged onto their own floor and she said, 'There's something I've just realised I must tell you.'

'Yes?' He was hesitant.

'Since my divorce, I have never shared my bed in this flat with anyone else.'

'Ah!' He thought for a moment and then said, 'Well, neither have I!'

And he opened the front door.

33

Early on Sunday morning, Leslie drove himself out to the Cassowary River. He always enjoyed this drive through the canefields and the rainforest. Reaching the river, he stopped at the Big Croc to find Renee.

Drew had already interviewed Renee and Bill. The two of them had lived in Cassowary village for more than twenty years, and knew everyone for miles around. But nobody had any ideas about how Ebony might have come to be drowned. Nobody had seen or heard a boat late that night, and anyway, the dwellings and businesses that made up Cassowary were more than half a mile from the mouth of the river.

Renee confirmed this again for Leslie.

'Often on Sundays, I'll take the dogs on the beach real early for a run,' she said, 'or Bill rides his horse down on the sand. But that day we slept in.'

Renee shook her head. 'I knew that little girl when she was in primary school. The family moved into Cairns about the time she started at the high school. I remember when she would walk past on the way to school in the mornings. Always laughing and dancing about. Couldn't keep still.' Renee would go to the funeral in Cairns later in the week. 'Ina is taking it hard, as hard as her own family I think. Ina tries so much for the kids. And I heard her boyfriend has been real upset too.'

'Kevin?' Leslie asked. 'But they weren't still together?'

'I heard they had a bit of a bust-up,' Renee conceded.

'Do you know why?' Leslie asked, and when Renee did not reply he said quite sharply, 'Renee, the girl's dead. If you know anything, you should say it. It won't be anything that involves you, I know that.'

'Well. Maybe over drugs. Drugs I'm talking just grass, weed, you understand, nothing big.'

'Yes, well, I can tell you we're looking at that angle. Drugs involving Kevin, would you say?'

Renee was adamant. 'No. Definitely not,' she said. 'I never heard of him dealing.'

From his pocket Leslie produced a photo of Justus Lee.

'Did you ever see him here?' he asked Renee, and Bill, who by now had joined them on the riverbank.

'No. Not him. But I did once see a couple of men rather like him. From the Philippines, is it? Asian but not exactly Chinese looking? They went to the island for something."

'I don't remember that,' Bill said.

'I don't think you were here, I think you went into town that day, darl,' Renee said.

Leslie turned to Bill. Had he particularly noticed anything about Ebony?

Bill looked uncomfortable. Well, as it happened, a couple of times during the day, she'd turned up from the island and called for a taxi to town from the café. Which had surprised him. There was a bus service — the Big Croc was the end of the bus route. The buses didn't run often, but local people knew the timetable. Taxis were expensive. Once when Bill had asked her, casually, where she was going, Ebony had been quick to explain that she was in a show in town, her costume was in the bag she was carrying, and she was making enough money to take taxis now. He'd not thought any more about it then.

'A couple of times?'

'Well, probably three at least.'

'All in the last couple of months, would you say?' Leslie asked.

'Yes,' said Bill, 'about that.'

'So someone from the resort would have brought her across from the island, then she'd walked up from the wharf?'

'She must have done. It takes about twenty minutes. But also a tinnie could have come further up the river and dropped her off on the bank. Someone from the resort could have done that. I didn't ask her.'

Leslie thanked them both, and said goodbye. He drove slowly down the dirt road, through the paperbark scrub, to the wharf and the beach. There were a few houses and shacks dotted between the trees. Most of them were fenced, and most had dogs — big dogs — running around in the yards. It was a safe road for a teenage girl to walk along in daylight, he thought. But at night?

The very last house was Charlie Angell's. It was on the riverbank; there was a tinnie tied to the bank and another upside down in the front yard. Charlie himself was nowhere to be seen.

He drove on, reached the beach, parked the car, and walked to the end of the wharf. There was the *Argo*, tied up. That was interesting, Leah must be still in town. There were also several tinnies, tied up or riding at anchor slightly away from the wharf. Some belonged to people in town, and one at least to the resort.

The beach was deserted. In the morning sunlight, washed clean by the outgoing tide, it was a place of absolute calm. Only the memorial notice for the fifteen nameless people, and the renewed flowers that Renee must have placed near the rocks the day before, told a different story.

Leslie returned to his car and headed back to town himself.

34

Through a haze of sleep, Leah heard her mobile phone ringing. Coming slowly into consciousness, she opened her eyes and found sunlight spilling between the curtains. Reaching across to the phone, she was aware that she was in a familiar place, though not where she had expected to be.

She heard Zak's voice in her ear. 'Hello, Mum.' Then it all came flooding back — she was in the bed of her former bedroom in the flat. In Ali's bed. And Ali himself appeared in the doorway with steaming coffee.

'Oh Zak!' How the hell would she deal with this? Though her own children had brought partners to the flat, and to the island, there had never been any occasion when she had done so herself.

'Mum, you OK? You sound strange. Where are you? I tried Rookwood but there was no answer. So I thought trying the mobile would be OK ..'

'Um ... I'm in the flat.'

'Oh, the flat.' A moment's silence. Then, 'But you've let the flat to the doctor. To Ali Hassan.'

'That's right. He's here too, Zak.'

'Oh.' Further silence. Then, 'That's good, Mum. He's a great guy. I told Micky about him, and how I thought you two might have it on for one another. And we both think that's OK.'

Despite his words, Leah thought he sounded slightly miffed — perhaps he believed she should have sought their permission first. The ways of the younger generation were strange indeed. Did one, at forty-four ,require the approval of one's children to conduct an affair? If this was in fact an affair ...

However, she simply said, 'Thanks for that, Zak,' and smiled at Ali, who was placing the coffee cup at her elbow and bending to kiss her forehead. She realised he already knew how she liked her coffee. He was dressed only in one of her own bath towels, and at the sight of the dark hairs across his chest, she was seized with a great need to pull him back into the bed with her. But realising that she was talking to her son, he put his finger to his lips, smiled, then turned and went back into the kitchen.

'Well, um, I'll be quick,' Zak was saying, 'I know it's early.' By the bedside clock, Leah saw it was half past eight.

'I found a cheap Virgin flight on the net,' Zak continued. 'There's a memorial service for Ebony on Friday at the high school, I'd like to go if I could, but I'd have to get you to pay the fare. I have only one class on Friday anyway, and I could stay over until Tuesday.'

'Yes, that's OK — put it on your Visacard and I'll give you the money.'

'Thanks Mum.' Then he asked, 'Is there any more news about what happened? Have you spoken to Leslie?'

Leah hesitated a moment. Then she thought that she might as well tell him. They'd be talking about it when he came up anyway. And he'd have to see Leslie, Leslie had said that he'd need a formal statement from Zak at some point.

'There seem to be two possibilities that Leslie's pursuing. I have to say that I think Leslie is suspicious of Brian Mitchell, suspicious that Brian may know something, or have seen something, that he's not telling the police about.'

'Brian Mitchell? The guy at the resort. But isn't he your cousin or something?'

'Yes. But, well, just because he's distantly related doesn't mean he's above reproach.'

'But hey, Mum, I just realised. I *saw* him. At the Cassowary wharf. When I came back from seeing Kev. I'd forgotten who he is, I hardly know him, but I thought I recognised him. Brian Mitchell!'

'What are you talking about, Zak? Kev? You mean Kevin Brown? And when did you see Brian Mitchell?'

'The night ... last Sunday. The night after I found Ebony. Remember I took the Fernandos and Ali — say hello to Ali for me, won't you — across to the wharf. Then I took the car into town to see a few people. I was feeling pretty cut-up about Ebony. I went to Dolly's house, and he wanted to go to the pub, but I didn't want to drink a lot. I wanted to talk to Kevin — I hadn't seen him in a while, but he'd been going with Ebony for a long time and I felt really bad for him. Dolly said that he mostly stayed in town during the week now, and he'd certainly be at home after what had happened.

'So I drove into town and went to his place. He was there, and we went and sat out the back in the yard to talk. It's been really hard for him. He was with Ebony more than two years, they'd broken up but he still cared a lot about her. He reckoned he was to blame, said if he'd made her dance in town instead it wouldn't have happened.

'I told him not to think like that. And what really surprised me, he's not only stopped drinking alcohol, he also reckoned he wouldn't smoke at all from now on, not even cigarettes. "It's just bad for me," he said, "bad for all of us".'

Kevin had asked Zak a lot of questions. He had wanted to know how Ebony had looked, what she was wearing when Zak found her.

'Did they find her bag? She always had that billum, y'know, red and yellow and black.'

'I don't know,' Zak had said, 'I didn't see it, but I'll ask Leslie.'

Finally Kevin had asked Zak, 'Man, did she look like she had, y'know, suffered a lot?'

'Kev, I can't tell you the answer to that,' Zak had said. 'Too much had happened to her since then, if you get what I mean.' Kevin had nodded and then tears had poured down his cheeks and he'd buried his head in his hands. Zak had put his arm around him and gradually the sobs had subsided.

Then Kevin had said, 'Thanks, thanks bro for coming, especially to a place like this at night.'

'Whaddayamean?' Zak had said, 'I came to see you, mate, of course I did.' He'd slapped Kevin on the shoulder and they'd walked together around the house and back to the car.

Zak told Leah some of this, and then said, 'So I drove back to the wharf and sat down in the *Argo*. It was dark, but there was a half moon and I just sat there thinking for a while.'

'Thinking about the day?' Leah suggested.

'Yes.' That was partly true. Zak had decided to sit for a while in the boat, just thinking, and smoking the weed he'd bought from Jason, and which Kevin had declined. It seemed a pity to waste it, and his mother was not keen on cannabis being kept in the house of a registered medical practitioner.

He was just about to light up, already enjoying the peace of the night and the sound of the waves lapping at the sides of the *Argo*. So he was completely hidden from view when two things happened.

He heard the faint putter of a Suzuki outboard motor growing louder, and into the wharf came a single tinnie. The boat had no lights on it, and there seemed to be just one man aboard.

At the same time, he heard a car speeding along the road from the village. Zak stayed sitting in the *Argo* after concealing his two cones in a locker.

The car stopped, and a man got out and spoke very quietly to the man who'd arrived in the tinnie. Then he too untied a tinnie that was tied to the wharf, got in and started the motor, and the two little boats headed up the river. As they did so, Zak stood up and looked over the edge of the wharf.

'The man from the road was Charlie Angell, y'know, he lives on the edge of the village. He'd parked his ute at the wharf.' He didn't need to tell his mother that Charlie was a well-known supplier of weed.

Zak had thought that the meeting might have been about drugs, although they could just be fishing in one of the river's tributaries that crossed the mangrove swamp. The man who'd come in the first tinnie was a white man, Zak had managed to see that, and he was vaguely familiar. Zak thought maybe he lived on one of the beaches further up the coast. He retrieved his smoke from the locker and sat on in the darkness.

The smoko had the desired mellowing effect — he began to feel calmer about Ebony now, and pleased that he had gone to see Kevin. It was late, well past midnight, but he sat on for a while longer.

He was about to turn on the *Argo*'s lights and start the crossing to the island when he heard the tinnies coming back down the river. He sat down again — he had no wish to run into Charlie Angell in the middle of the night. He was glad the breeze had blown away his own smoke.

But there was just one tinnie now, and it didn't come into the wharf. It headed across to the island, to the resort end, and without lights, although there was enough moonlight for Zak to see that there were two men in it.

So Charlie must have a stash somewhere up the river and be supplying someone at the resort, some staff member, Zak decided. However, he still didn't want to run into Charlie, or even be seen there, if what Charlie was doing was dropping the white bloke back to the resort, then coming back to get into his own ute and go home.

So he sat on in the darkness for a while, thinking about the beach, and Ebony, and Kevin, and was almost asleep when he heard the tinnie coming back again. Charlie jumped up onto the wharf, tied up the boat, and got into his ute — as the interior lights of the ute came on, Zak could see that it was indeed Charlie. The ute disappeared up the road, and in a few minutes Zak decided it was safe for him to move. Forgetting about the sailing, he untied the *Argo's* lines, started up her engine and headed back towards the Rookwood Island wharf. He'd have to find a quiet moment to finish the other cone before he got the plane back to Townsville.

'Well, Zak,' Leah said, after listening to Zak's account, which had omitted all mention of smoke, 'that's very interesting. I might just let Leslie know. He wants a statement, a formal statement, from you anyway, so I'll tell him you'll do that when you're here. Don't worry, it won't be too stressful. And I'll be back on Rookwood later today. I'll ring you this evening.'

'OK Mum. But who's the other person Leslie's suspicious of?'

She hesitated. 'Well, I have to say it's Kevin himself.'

'Kevin? No! Not possible,' Zak began, and then his voice tailed off as he thought this over.

'Well,' Leah answered, 'he has alibis. But he'd broken up with Ebony and he might have been unhappy about it.'

'He'd got his whole life together,' Zak said. 'He wouldn't do something like that to her, no way.'

'Maybe not deliberately,' Leah said unhappily. She thought of Kevin the night before, soaring above the stage. 'But you know, Zak, maybe there was an accident, maybe things went horribly wrong ... so that she died ... but he doesn't feel he'll be believed if he tells the police.' There was silence at Zak's end of the phone, and she knew her son could see that this was possible.

'Mum,' he said finally, 'I really really hope that's not what happened. And the sooner Leslie finds out the truth, the better.'

35

Leslie slowed down as he reached the edge of suburban Cairns, and turned off to the right towards the western suburbs. He would visit Ebony's family first, then Ina and Ivy in the house they shared. At Violet's front gate, he waited while Violet tied up a large brown and white mongrel. Panes of glass were missing from the front window of the house, which was in urgent need of paint, and a bed sheet strung on a rope served as a curtain, though the yard was swept clean. Two small children played near where pumpkins grew in a patch by the veranda. Grandpa Farrell dozed in a chair at the top of the veranda steps.

Leslie and Drew had already talked to Ebony's family. What was she like, they had wanted to know. They all said she was a good girl, did well in school when she was there, and as soon as she quit she joined the dance troupe. True, she didn't go to the church any more, but she hardly drank at all.

'Sure about that?' Drew asked Violet.

'Yeah, true, she might go weeks without a drink, only social. She wouldn't have been drinking before or during the show. They didn't allow that at all.'

Now Leslie sat with Violet and Grandpa Farrell on the veranda. The old man woke up and, seeing Leslie, the tears flowed down his cheeks. She was a good girl, pretty girl, he said. Now Mum dead, daughter dead. Grandpa rocked back and forth on his veranda with his memories.

Through the door came Ebony's cousin Jade. She'd danced with Ebony that night, but come home without her. She was adamant: Ebony had not been drinking during the show, not even a light beer or a cooler. No-one drank until after the shows, except water. It was an absolute rule. And the dance group management discouraged drinking with the guests or staff even after the show, but sometimes some kids, girls, mostly, did stay on. How often?

'Often enough...I wasn't surprised when she didn't turn up for the boat,' said Jade. 'She didn't tell me anything and I didn't ask her. I just didn't see her again after the show.'

'And how would she have got back home to Cairns, if she chose to stay on and socialise?' Leslie asked.

Well, it might not be till next morning, when the staff launch might drop her at the wharf near Cassowary beach, or if she was lucky, at the wharf in Cairns itself. There was always somewhere kids could doss down around the resort for the night if they had to ... maybe even on the beach.

'Did Kevin sometimes come down to the Cairns wharf to meet Ebony from the launch, the regular launch after the show? After he'd finished working in town? Did he ever come and find she hadn't come back from the resort with the others?'

Jade studied her fingernails. 'I can't remember,' she said.

'Did he once meet her, last week perhaps, and argue with her?'

'I don't remember that,' Jade said.

Did Ebony do drugs at all? No, definitely not. Not even weed? Well ... Jade smiled a little, looking at her feet. Well, maybe some weed, perhaps.

'She never offered you anything to smoke?'

Jade appeared to think about the question, then shook her head.

Leslie stood up, shook hands with Jade and Violet. Grandpa Farrell was asleep again.

'I promise to let you know about any progress,' Leslie said. He climbed back in his car and followed the street towards Ina's house two blocks away. He drove slowly, many kids were out on the road and the footpaths, riding bikes or skateboards or kicking balls.

A big mango tree occupied much of the front yard of the house, which was a lowset Queenslander. There was a neat fence of timber pickets. A clump of heliconias grew by the front steps, and there were cane chairs and a table on the wide front veranda.

Leslie sat on that veranda with the twins, drinking the black bush tea they offered. Despite being in their sixties now, and having been separated for many years, the twins were still amazingly alike in mannerisms as well as physical appearance. He'd first got to know Ina well when he'd been investigating a case back in 1993. Ina worked hard in her community, a Mum and Aunty to just about everyone, while Ivy was still a fulltime health worker in the local Aboriginal-run clinic.

'Leslie, we lost two of our best kids in just two weeks,' Ina said.' Her face was deeply etched with grief. She moved back and forth in her rocking chair, planting wide black feet on the bare boards of the veranda with each forward roll. The boards were warm from the morning sun.

'Yes this is a very bad business, Ina, Ivy,' Leslie said, stirring in sugar. 'Ebony, so young. It seems she drowned, but why was she in the water? Her blood alcohol was very high, high enough that she'd hardly know what she was doing if she wasn't used to alcohol, and it seems she'd smoked some grass too. But she had nothing to drink with her friends. And no-one seems to have seen her with anyone else that night. Ina, Ivy, can you shed any light on this?' Leslie asked.

'She was a beautiful kid, very talented, maybe a little wild, but lots of kids are at that age. She was ... thinking maybe to get a job working down south. She had some kind of offer,' Ina ventured.

'An offer by whom?' Leslie quickly asked, but Ina was vague. Just a rumour, was all that she would say. Ivy nodded, but she too said nothing.

'From Brian Mitchell perhaps?' Leslie probed.

'Maybe ...' Ina said. Brian Mitchell had given other kids a start there, he had connections down south and owned some hotel on the Gold Coast, Ina had heard.

'So if Brian Mitchell had made a suggestion like that to Ebony, she would have believed it?' Leslie asked.

'Yes.

'The other kids — were they boys and girls, Ina?'

'Always girls. Yes, I understand what you're saying Leslie, and maybe there's something to it. But that's how things are for young people up here. They want to get away and have a life elsewhere, that might be the price a girl has to pay.'

'And what might her boyfriend have thought about that? Kevin?'

'Mmm ... I think he would have wanted that she stay up here. Where her family is. Maybe not just for himself. For what might happen to her down south.'

'You told Detective Borgese you heard them arguing. Ebony and Kevin.'

'Just so he'd know they'd broken up,' Ina said quickly. 'So he'd know Kevin wouldn't have been with her that night she died. They were together much less the last few weeks anyway. The last couple of weeks it seemed like he was mostly just worried about looking out for her. Specially after Garry died.'

Leslie nodded at this, and then changed tack. 'Does Brian Mitchell have much to do with the community here?' he asked casually.

'What way do you mean?' countered Ina.

'Any way ... helping out. Employing people.'

She shook her head. 'He employs the dance group. Sometimes he shows some artwork over there. One person from here worked a while there, cleaning. No-one ever worked at anything else, on tables or fixing stuff. All the guides, people who take the tours out to the reef, the fishing, all that, they're all white people from Cairns or down south.'

'So if I'd heard that from time to time he, or someone working for him, brought grog into communities, dry communities, that would be wrong, very wrong?'

She was silent for a while. Ivy watched them both, impassive, then seemed to nod at her sister. Finally, Ina said, 'No. I reckon if you'd heard that you heard right.'

'It's a problem?'

'Yes, it's a problem we've been trying to fix. In the councils. Some people, blokes, used to make a lot of money out of grog in the canteens, it came through the council back into the community and certain people got their share. When communities went dry, most of the time, especially weekends, those people thought they lost out. They couldn't drink, and they weren't getting any profit neither. And there's some people who are so addicted to the grog, Leslie, nothing's going to stop them. Some of them move into Cairns. Other people try to help them, but they don't want that help. But some stay and just try to get around the bans any way they can.'

'Ina, why would Brian Mitchell, a rich man who doesn't even live here a lot of the time, be into something small-time like bringing grog to remote communities?'

'Well — I reckon he charges a good bit for it ... and it might be the people working for him who get most of the money anyway.'

'He wouldn't be getting something in return, something that was useful to him?'

Leslie saw Ina catch Ivy's eye. When she realised that Leslie was watching her intently, she looked away. Ina wore strong glasses as thick as the bottoms of Coke bottles. Ivy's sight was better. Ina must have had recurrent eye infections in the time she was a child out in the dusty Gulf country, Leslie thought.

At last Ina said, 'Well, I reckon I could ask about a bit ... sure don't want anything bad happening to any more of our kids.'

Leslie nodded, swallowed the rest of the tea, stood up and shook Ina's hand, then Ivy's, and said, 'If you hear anything more, you just let me know. Especially anything about Kevin Brown and Ebony.'

He climbed into his car, which was an unmarked Mazda, but knowing everyone in the street was watching from their yards or verandas as he drove away. Everyone knew who he had talked with, and why.

37

To the boats below it, the Beechcraft seemed just a speck in the azure sky. The Coastwatch on a routine Tuesday morning patrol. Purely routine. Those guys flew up and down this coast twice a day. You could set your watch by them.

From the cockpit, the view was as usual, a tropical travel advertisement. Far out to the left lay the deep blue of the Pacific. Then there was the Great Barrier Reef itself, the breakers white against the ocean side, on the land side shallows so brightly turquoise that they pained the eyes. The atolls and tiny islands formed a line of arabesques. From this height, the great branching colonies of coral appeared uniformly greenish-brown. If the pilot came in lower, he knew, the colours would become more distinct, pinks and yellows and waving fronds of mauve. There would be sharks and dolphins, and whole schools of fish. Boats could be seen, too, even quite small boats. From a height, they could be photographed and their names and identities fed into the pilot's computer.

The pilot flew steadily southward, looking at nothing in particular and everything in particular. Nobody watching on Lizard Island, for example, or the adjacent string of tiny islets, would have detected anything remarkable as the Beechcraft flew overhead.

Reaching the mouth of the Endeavour River, the pilot banked to the right and began to descend over Cooktown. From this height, it was easy to see the layout of the original town. Whole streets that had been laid out in a grid pattern, had been lined with houses at the height of the goldrush, had crumbled to dust. Grass grew thickly over them now, and yet the lines of the streets were still there, straggling out into the bush. In the settled streets that remained, well-tended houses had verandas with views across the river. There were caravan parks and motels, and at the edge of the town the old cemetery and several fruit farms, and then the Endeavour River again, winding inland. In front of him now, the pilot could see the looming shape of Black Mountain. Thousands of black basalt boulders were scattered down the sides of that mountain. People had disappeared up there, vanished clean off the face of the earth. Nobody in their right mind would walk up Black Mountain. The pilot had seen it hundreds of times, but every time he flew into Cooktown it spooked him. He swung away from the mountain and further around to the right to make his approach to the runway of the Cooktown aerodrome. He brought the plane down lightly, bounced a little, taxied to the end of the runway, then more slowly turned to a parking spot near the airfield gate.

He climbed down from the cockpit, the sunlight catching the gold thread in his epaulets, and walked across to where his boss waited.

'Morning, Tom.'

'Morning, mate. You see our man?'

'About ten miles north of Lizard Island. They're just meandering around out there.'

'Like tourists?'

'Just like tourists. And also, just like someone waiting for instructions to make a drop.'

'Yeah. Well, Cairns says do nothing but watch him for the moment. So that's just what we'll do.'

36

Leah put down the phone and stretched in bed, enjoying her nakedness against the sheets.

'Ali?' she called. He came to the door, hesitated a little. She looked up and smiled.

'You're OK?' she asked.

'Yes,' he said. 'But I just wondered if you thought it was a mistake?'

'Last night?'

'Yes.'

Leah roared with laughter. 'A mistake? No! It was the best thing I've done for years. I'd almost forgotten how much I like sex.'

She stretched out both arms. 'Neither of us has to be at work today. Come back to bed. But I'd better switch off my mobile. I'd forgotten all about it last night.'

Much later, she rolled over on her back and curled like a cat against Ali's crooked arm. For a few moments neither spoke. Then Ali asked, 'That was your son on the phone?'

'Yes. He sends you his regards. And apparently approves of you. I'll bet he's talking to his sister right now with the news!'

She turned to look directly at him, to answer the unasked question. 'Yes,' she said, 'I've had relationships since my divorce, but always casual, never anyone I wanted to get to know my children.' And it was too soon for him to ask, or even think: *So am I casual too? A passing Arab?*

'Also,' she said,' I must tell you about Zak's father. You've probably wondered ...'

Ali nodded. It had been a question he felt he could not ask Leslie, and Leslie hadn't volunteered much information.

So she told him about Ted.

At the end, he looked at her in amazement. 'So he left no family — no blood family?'

'Not as far as I know. When I was in London, when Zak was ten, after his wife — widow — would have nothing to do with me, I hired a private agency to see if any relatives could be located in England or the West Indies, but they couldn't find anybody. A couple of people who looked like they might be related turned out to be dead, and one couldn't be located at all.

'I was thinking, when I took Zak to London that time, that if there were relatives they might like to meet him, and he might like to meet them, but I didn't tell him what I was going to do, because if I didn't find anyone he might be disappointed. He knows who his father was, and as much as I know about him, which is mostly his work, and so far he's never wanted to know much more.'

'And so you've brought him up by yourself? While you were always working?'

'Well, yes. It was just ... what I wanted to do, I guess! And also what I had to do. I had to support myself and my kids.'

'You have done a very good job!' Ali said firmly.

'Thank you!' Leah laughed. 'So anyway, Zak was calling because he's coming back up here later in the week. There's to be a memorial service for the girl, Ebony, and he wants to go. And Leslie wants a statement from him, like the one he took from you. And he told me something interesting. He saw Brian Mitchell over at the Cassowary beach on Sunday night, really late, apparently with a man who's known for drug dealing, who lives over there.'

'Brian Mitchell? He is the man from Mitchells Resort?'

'He started it, yes. He's a relative of my mother's family.'

'He's your cousin then? Your family?'

'Very distant. Not somebody I see often. Cousins in Australia aren't always the same as cousins in Iraq. He lives down near Brisbane most of the time.'

'And this Mr Mitchell, Leslie suspects him of doing something to the girl?

'It seems he does.'

Ali was silent a moment. Then he said, 'Leah, your face changes a lot when you talk about this Mitchell. I think you don't like him at all.'

'No,' she said slowly, 'I don't. I told you the other day how the Mitchells held onto their land on the island and built the resort. My father argued a lot with Brian Mitchell over that, he didn't want the resort there. But Brian just went ahead. And ... once he did something bad to me, when I was a child. Not something to tell you now, one day maybe. I mostly don't have to see him these days. But just because of all that, or because I don't like him, doesn't mean he did harm Ebony.'

'If he was bad to you then I could believe he is bad now,' said Ali, 'and I wouldn't like him either. That is the Arab way. Land, honour, those things are very important. They must be held onto. But I am sure if there is truth to be uncovered, your Leslie will find it.'

'Yes,' she agreed. Then she said, 'Oh Ali, come out to Rookwood with me today. I want to show you all over the island. Last week, we were so saddened by Ebony's death. And I was thinking of you all the time then, but I was quite sure you weren't interested in me.'

'I was the same. Yes, I will come with you with pleasure. But first, I have another idea.'

38

Midday on Wednesday, and it seemed like the whole of Cassowary village, population ninety, had turned out to see what was going on. People watched from their verandas, Renee and Bill from the front of the Big Croc. Two cop cars had come from Cairns, followed by another with the tall detective, Drew, and they'd all gone down the road to where Charlie Angell lived. Walked down, not driving. Well, it wasn't much more than two hundred metres. Charlie had been a bit slow to come to the door. Two men had to go round the back and bang hard. Not breaking-the-door-down hard, but hard. Then Charlie had come out the front, he must have got dressed in a hurry because his shirt was inside out. The cops were quite polite to Charlie, but he moved at a smart pace down the road with them. The whole lot disappeared into the cars and headed off toward the beach. By this time, every kid in the place who wasn't in school, and a good many adults, were lined up on the road watching.

So a few of the men, including Bill, got in their utes and followed the cavalcade down to the beach, where they discovered that a big police launch from Cairns had come in close near the wharf and a large policeman was rowing the launch's dinghy towards the wharf where the police waited with Charlie. So large was the policeman that the bows of the dinghy were almost below the surface, while the stern was lifted out of the water. But he was strong — he quickly reached the wharf, and Charlie and Detective Drew Borgese and two coppers got in and the large policeman rowed back to the launch, where all five got aboard.

The engine of the launch had been turning over, and now it revved up and the launch turned and headed towards the river. But then it suddenly stopped, and it seemed like the skipper must have decided that the river was too shallow for his craft. Because then Charlie and the two cops and the detective came back ashore in the dinghy and got into Charlie's bigger tinnie at the wharf, and headed up the river in the direction of the mangrove swamp. The skipper slowly turned the launch and edged it back to stand off-shore by the wharf. The remaining policemen all got back into their cars and disappeared back up the road in the direction of the village, no doubt for a cuppa in the Big Croc, leaving the entire community in a state of amazement. Charlie had been busted before, but it had only ever required one or two cops to do the job. What the hell was happening here?

Aboard the tinnie, the policemen and the detective had been silent, but Charlie was talking flat out.

'You know me, you know I wouldn't be mixed up in anything like that. I was just doing him a favour. Who told you anyway? I didn't know it had anything to do with the girl.'

'Just shut up for the moment and show us where you branched off from the river, Charlie,' Drew said pleasantly. 'You can talk as much as you want later. You're not under arrest, you know, you're just a person helping the police with their inquiries. We always appreciate help, you know that, Charlie.'

Beyond the northern side of the Cassowary stretched a vast area of mangroves. Small rivers emptied into large ones at regular intervals, but among the closely entwined roots and branches of the mangroves, their mouths were hard to see. Charlie, having accepted Drew's advice and fallen silent, looked grim as he manoeuvred his tinnie slowly between tree roots and muddy banks,

Then, after about ten minutes, he said 'There, boss, in there by that big old mangrove root.'

The tinnie slowed as Drew stuck an oar in to test the depth, and Charlie decided he could proceed cautiously. They passed into a narrow channel beneath a tunnel of mangrove branches. The only movement was the occasional plopping of twigs into the water and the scurrying of crabs on the surface of mudbanks. Drew watched carefully as the tinnie nosed its way forward. It would not be a good move to run aground here. Very likely several crocodiles who called the place home were watching them even now.

'There,' said Charlie, 'over there.'

And he was right. Part of another tinnie could be seen pushed up against the bank, but otherwise it had all sunk.

'We shot holes in it,' Charlie had said back on the launch. 'It was the easiest way to get it to take water. Nobody was around.' Well, that was easy to believe. Drew raised an eyebrow. Did Charlie Angell have a gun licence? He made a note to himself to check.

One of the uniformed police took a grappling hook and leaned across the bows of their boat, prodding the tinnie. Though filled with water, there was not yet too much mud weighing it down.

'Take us a bit closer, Charlie,' he said. 'I reckon if we get a hold on it with the cable, we can pull it out,' he said.

'OK,' Drew said, 'we'll give it a go. One go.'

While Charlie kept the tinnie stationary, ticking over, Drew leaned far forward and slipped the cable through the metal ring on the sunken tinnie's stern. Then Charlie slowly inched back down the channel. The motor whined and strained under the load.

'Slowly, mate, slowly, or we'll all be in the drink with the crocs.'

Reluctantly, the sunken tinnie began to move, then suddenly was freed with a glugging sound like a giant gumboot being pulled from a mud puddle. Their own boat jerked, but then began to move freely, bringing the muddied tinnie with it. Slowly the procession returned to the wharf, where the tinnie was attached so it could be towed behind the launch.

'We'll drop you here,' Drew told Charlie. 'I'm going back to Cairns on the launch. And just remember every little thing we've told you today.' Charlie nodded, quite silent now. He was sweating profusely, and not from the heat. His immediate future looked decidedly cloudy.

39

On Friday morning, Ali came in early for his round in the Children's Ward.

'Benjy's back in,' the charge nurse told him. 'Benjy who was here before. He came in last night with a chest infection and asthma. We have him just inside the door, 2B.'

'I'll see him first,' Ali said, taking the chart. He glanced briefly at her name badge. *Diane.* It was nothing to him now.

Ali was expecting to see Benjy's mother with him, or perhaps Ina and Ivy again. But sitting on the bed was a young Black man, in a basketball singlet and jeans. Ali didn't recall seeing him here before, yet he looked familiar. Slim, tall, sitting very straight. Then Ali remembered. The dancer. Kevin Brown.

Kevin stood up. He was taller than Ali, though not quite six feet, and from him radiated a sense of self-confidence that Ali had not seen before in an Aboriginal person. Ali held out his hand.

'Hello. I'm Dr Ali. I saw you in the theatre last Saturday. It was wonderful.'

'Thanks. Yeah, I'm Kevin. I know who you are, Doc. My Mum and Zak both told me.'

'Zak?'

'Yes. He came to see me ... that Sunday night ... two weeks ago. I've known him a long time. We were at school together.'

When Ali said nothing, waiting, trying to follow this, Kevin went on. 'He just came to, well, be with me a little bit.

After she died. Zak wanted, well, he was the one who found her ... He told me you'd been there.'

Then Ali remembered. Leah had told him. Kevin had been Ebony's boyfriend. So Zak had known him at school. Ali nodded. 'I understand now,' he said.

Kevin watched him intently. He seemed to be summing him up. Slightly intimidated, Ali turned to Benjy.

'How are you, Benjy?' he asked. 'You've come back to see us again!'

'I was sick, but I'm good now,' answered Benjy. His eyes never left Kevin. 'Can I go home now with Kev?'

'Maybe tomorrow,' Ali replied. 'We need to fix up this sickness for you properly. Get rid of those bugs that keep making it hard for you to breathe, Benjy. I'll need to talk to your mother.'

'You can talk to me,' Kevin said. 'I'm family too.'

'Yes, well ... OK. Benjy's been seen by the ear, nose and throat specialist. Although we've got him on a new antibiotic that's helping, it seems like a good idea for him to have his tonsils out. Tonsils and adenoids.' Ali turned to Benjy. 'That doctor with the red hair and glasses, he saw you last time you were here, thinks you should have your tonsils out. What do you think about that?'

'Today?'

'No, not today.' Ali smiled. 'Probably in a few weeks.'

'Will it hurt?'

'Not while it's happening. You'll be asleep. When you wake up, you'll have a sore throat. Unfortunately, you won't be able to eat anything except ice-cream for at least a week.'

A big smile spread across Benjy's face.

'He'll be OK?' Kevin asked anxiously, and Ali saw the muscles in his neck tense. 'Having an operation, like, that's a big thing, being asleep. He's only six.'

'He'll be fine,' Ali said firmly.

Kevin looked into the distance for a moment and then murmured low, 'No chance he'll die from it?'

'Well,' Ali answered slowly, turning so that the conversation was out of Benjy's hearing. 'I can't promise you that one hundred per cent. Nobody could.' Kevin nodded. 'But it's very, very unlikely. Anaesthetics now are very safe. And you have to think about how he is now. Twice in the last month he's been in here really very sick.'

He moved slightly more out of Benjy's hearing, aware that the little boy was closely watching the conversation between the foreign doctor and his big, bright cousin.

'He could die from an asthma attack brought on by an infection, you know, sometimes it happens to children.' Then he saw he had frightened Kevin, despite his strength and bravado. He leaned over and pressed Kevin on the shoulder. 'I don't think that will happen, but we must try to reduce the chances. And it doesn't have to be straight away, your family can talk about it. But remember, all the time he's in hospital, he's missing school, and if he has ear infections, he can't hear so well and maybe that affects his schoolwork. Not to forget that he doesn't eat and grow so well when he's sick.'

Kevin nodded. He could see that this last statement was certainly true. He muttered, 'Yeah, thanks Doc.'

Ali was turning back to Benjy when Kevin said, looking at his feet, 'Doc — Zak told me ... that you tried to help ...'

'To help?'

'When she died. On the beach.'

'Oh.' Of course. Ebony again.

'I'm sorry,' Ali said gently. 'We were far too late. There was nothing anyone could have done by then.'

Kevin nodded again. Then slammed his right fist into his open left palm. 'The bastard!' he said.

Ali stared at Kevin. Then asked slowly: 'What do you mean?'

'Mitchell!' Kevin said.

'Mitchell? Brian Mitchell?' Ali remembered what Leah had said. Leslie was suspicious of Mitchell. And he thought of how Leah's own face had closed over as she mentioned Mitchell's name. *She's afraid of that man*, Ali thought now.

He asked, 'You think he knows what happened? You don't think it was an accident?'

'Nah, no accident. He filled her up with grog, like he'd been doing for weeks. Maybe spiked the drinks with something. He wasn't interested in her career neither. Just using her. Though she couldn't see that.'

'But why would he kill her? You mean he was taking advantage of her, sleeping with her?'

'Yeah, well, not much sleeping about it, I'd say. And I don't know, but I reckon she found out too much about him, or he wanted her to do something she didn't want to do. He's clever, Mitchell. She was coming there nights anyway, drinking, very easy to give her more grog than she's realised then offer to take her home in any of the boats they've got over there. Then push her off, maybe hold her head under so no-one hears her scream.'

Ali, remembering the brilliant figure that had spun through the darkness of the stage on Saturday, was surprised to see that Kevin's eyes glistened with tears.

'But for sure he's got an alibi,' Kevin said, 'no-one's gonna catch him. Mr Big Money, with his friends in the casino and Brisbane. Guys like him, they've got everything. Money, lawyers, fancy cars, lotta' people working for them. You can't pin nothin' on them.'

Ali stood considering all this carefully for some moments. He thought of Hamid, of the last time he had seen his brother. Hamid had been sitting with the family at dinner, laughing and peeling an orange for his daughter, his fingers deftly removing the skin of the fruit so it became a long, coloured snake for the child. It was how Ali always tried to think of his brother now, so that he didn't have to imagine those hands, severed and bleeding, in the boot of the taxi.

Ali looked around him. Nobody was there but himself, Kevin and Benjy. He took Kevin's arm and, not watching him directly, said, 'Kevin, maybe this is not something the police can fix for you. Maybe this is something you need to fix yourself. I'm not saying you should or you shouldn't, or telling you how to do it. In my country, we have a system of payback. It is the Arab way. For families or for tribes. Sometimes it's a very bad thing. Especially if an *innocent* person were to be wrongly punished. But sometimes it's the only way we know of getting justice.'

Kevin looked away slightly too, and his eyes narrowed. Then he nodded slowly. He brought his fist into his palm again.

'Yeah,' he said softly, 'I hear you, Dr Ali. Yeah, there might be a way.'

40

'Fish and chips!' Leah said to Ali. 'Now we must have fish and chips! The best fish and chips in the world is made right here on the pier in Cooktown.'

She was riding her bike along in front of him down the main street of Cooktown, Charlotte Street. She'd already pointed out to him the granite gutters edging the wide streets that the founding fathers had laid out for the original town, the elegant brick building that had been the Bank of New South Wales and was now a restaurant, and the deep well the town council had sunk in 1876. They'd walked hand-in-hand up Grassy Hill above the town, where there was a red and white lighthouse that exactly matched her own on Rookwood. From the top of the hill, they had looked across a landscape of sand dunes, river, low forest and distant smoky mountains, Aboriginal land that had been unchanged for 60,000 years. To their left was the sinister shape of Black Mountain.

Then she'd taken him down the hill, past the two-storeyed convent that now housed Cooktown's museum, and past the old hospital where her great-grandfather had worked.

'Tomorrow,' Leah had said to him on Friday evening, in the house on the island, 'we should go to Cooktown. You must see it. We'll leave very early, sail up, and come back on Sunday. Can you ride a bicycle?'

'Of course,' he said, 'but why?'

'We have to get around the town,' she said.

They'd risen at five, just as the first rays of the sun streaked an oyster-coloured sky. It was the perfect time to start out on the sea, Leah had told him. She had made a thermos of coffee and, leaving Zak sleeping, they'd carried the two bikes from Leah's veranda down to the *Dolphin*.

Zak had arrived on Friday morning for Ebony's memorial service, and would stay until Tuesday. 'Thanks,' he'd said when asked, 'but I've been to Cooktown a thousand times. Weekend mornings I'm planning to sleep in.'

So under Leah's guidance Ali was going to learn to sail.

Leah used the engine to get them out of Turtle Cove and away from the island. Then she instructed Ali how to grind the winch and run up the mainsail while she held the tiller. Ali wound as hard as he could, sweating in his yellow life-jacket and watching the sail slowly climb the mast. Leah cut the engine.

'Keep going,' she called, 'it has to get to the top.' The sail flapped violently — luffing, Leah called it — and then with one final tug became taut, and Ali realised they were moving by the sail alone, speeding through the water at a remarkable six knots in the direction of Cooktown. His instructor seemed pleased with his efforts.

'Now we can have some coffee,' she said. 'And you'll see, we do the same thing with the jib in a moment, and then use the sails, altering course whenever we have to, so that we make best use of the wind. It's quite simple really.'

Ali didn't feel it was simple at all, but he decided to agree with his captain. And in fact, he found, as he followed her orders — now we tack, now we jibe — as he took the tiller while she slackened some lines and tightened others, as he ground on the winches until he'd felt his arms would break, that it was logical. And fun.

Reaching Cooktown, they rounded the point into the mouth of the Endeavour River and dropped anchor offshore.

Several other sailing boats were moored in the river, and there were houseboats permanently in place against the bank on the town side.

Leah brought Ali in the *Dolphin's* little dinghy across to the wharf, and they sat at a late lunch in a café by the water's edge. Around them were other tables filled with weekend boaters. As they ate, they watched a fishing trawler unloading live coral trout at the Cooktown wharf. Three white men, tanned to the colour of coconut husks, and wearing nothing but Stubbies and thongs, stood on the wharf, sorting the trout by size into deep troughs. By this time tomorrow, the biggest fish would be on tables in Japan.

Then she took him along Hope Street on their bikes.

'This is where John Rookwood lived and practised,' she said, 'with Adeline. But the house is gone now.' In its place stood an unremarkable motel where they would spend the night.

They'd ridden out past rambling gardens and orchards to the cemetery. Dismounting, they propped the bikes against the cemetery railings and walked among the old graves. Whole families were buried together. Deaths had been frequent in the 1870s and 80s, peaking in the 90s then slackening off as the town's numbers dwindled and there were no newcomers. Many babies and children, sometimes whole families, had succumbed to infectious diseases. Leah pointed out where three children under six from the Wrightson family had died in an epidemic of spinal fever, the same disease John Rookwood had treated the day he'd left his own family on the island.

She led Ali on the bush track that meandered past groves of eucalyptus to the Chinese shrine.

'We know many Chinese are buried here,' she said, 'but the graves are unmarked. Probably Lee Chin is here. The shrine was built much later.'

The shrine was an elegant structure, lacquered red and inscribed with Chinese characters in gold. There were recent flowers placed at its foot and the remains of offerings of incense. It faced a small stream, no doubt the result of favourable *feng shui*.

Then they'd ridden slowly back into the town and up the hill to the old convent. The Sisters of Mercy had arrived in the town in the 1880s, and for a hundred years they'd worked away solidly, educating the girls of the region to be good Catholic wives and mothers. Now the nuns were gone and the high-ceilinged Victorian rooms were filled with glass cases. A whole new wing at the back was dedicated to the captain, James Cook, and his voyages, but especially to the voyage of 1770 when he'd run aground on the Reef and come into the Endeavour River. He'd stayed for more than one hundred days while his crew repaired the hole in the vessel's bottom (the *Endeavour*, the river was named for her, Leah explained to Ali.) The ship was alone, she was their only means of return to England, so they had to get it right.

'Cook was a great navigator,' she said, 'and brave. But he also did what he'd been told to do, back in London, and claimed the whole continent for Britain. To stop the French getting it.' Ali nodded.

'That happened in Iraq also,' he told her.

On the first floor of the convent were rooms devoted to old Cooktown. A whole display case was given over to the Rookwood Island 'incident' and the massacre that had followed. There were sepia photographs of Adeline and John, and their wedding photo again, a tiny photo of Skipper Jackson, and a report of the incident, though not the massacre, from the Cooktown *Herald*. There was a tinted portrait of Thomas in later life as a doctor in Cairns. No picture, though, of Lee Chin.

As Leah had told Ali, the Aboriginal side of the story was also now told for all to read: the island was a traditional spot for fishing and turtle-hunting, no harm had been intended to the Rookwood family or their servant, and in fact it had been Aboriginal people who had suffered, fifteen at least of them dead. There were photos from the era, of people from the district, traditional owners for thousands of years, lined up uncertainly for the camera, their nakedness concealed beneath lap-laps or bunched grass.

Also behind glass were memorabilia of the Rookwood family, and here Leah pointed out for Ali items that had belonged to John: forceps and needle holders, a steriliser lit by a spirit lamp, an ink stand, a breakfast cup and saucer. There was a photo of the old doctor, formally attired in the operating room of the first Cooktown hospital, dated 1899, the year before his death. He was undeniably stout in this portrait, and his hair and moustache were grey. More than anything, he looked resigned. A man who accepted what life had given him and no longer sought to change it.

'He worked in Cooktown for twenty-four years,' Ali said, after studying all this. 'It was his whole world.'

'Yes,' she said, 'I think he gave the town good service.'

Now they were back in the main street, cycling slowly back towards the wharf, and Leah was talking about dinner.

She was right, Ali found, about the fish and chips. Mackerel caught in the ocean that morning, battered and fried to perfection. He had never found any as good anywhere in England, a place where he'd eaten plenty of fish and chips. They sat at a table by the river, sharing the meal directly from the paper wrapping.

'It is a wonderful thing to know where you belong, Leah,' he said. 'I would like to take you like this to show you parts of Iraq. But I don't believe it will be possible in my lifetime.'

'If you could show me one thing,' she asked, 'what would it be? The mosque in Najaf that you have in your photo? Or the desert?'

'I think I would show you the view from my grandparents' home. In the evening, just as the sun is setting over the Euphrates River, which is not far away. It is very peaceful, there are fields in front of the house and people are making their way home from these fields. The men are in white robes, what we call *dishdash*, and the women, they are in black, because these are country people. There are lots of kids running about, and donkeys and goats. It is very green there because of the water from the river, irrigation channels run between the fields and asparagus fern grows there. There are groves of palm trees and orchards. There is one white mosque in the distance, with a tall and narrow minaret. And low houses, especially my grandfather's house, which was built of mud bricks. That is what I would show you.'

He was silent for a moment. Then laughed. 'Nostalgia is deceptive,' he said. 'I haven't lived in that place for more than thirty years. Most of my life in Iraq I lived in Baghdad.'

She asked, 'That's where you lived with your wife, and your daughter? Tell me about your daughter.'

'Ziena. She should have been thirteen by now. The last time I saw her, she was not quite four. Very healthy, reaching all her milestones. She was just learning to read a little, in Arabic of course. She had a red tricycle — my last view of her was sitting on that tricycle in the courtyard of our house, waving goodbye. I had just kissed her for the last time.'

He stopped for a moment. Then he said: 'But Leah, I must tell you something. She was not really my daughter.'

And he told her about Mustafa.

When he had finished, they sat together for some time in silence. Then she reached over for his hand.

'Ali, she *was* your daughter. You were her father for all the time she was on this earth. You kissed her goodbye. That's what matters. And ...' She struggled to find the right words. 'Ali, I don't know what the future holds for us. We're just getting to know each other. We have a long way to go. But I do know that your fertility is absolutely irrelevant to what's happened between us so far. Ali ... I think if you want to, you can make a new life here.'

'With you?'

'I can't promise that yet. But I do want to see if it's possible for me. Ali, you've transformed my life in the past couple of weeks, but I ... I need time to think about the future. We can't change the past, but we can live in the present, and for the moment, yes, I want to do that with you.'

He looked across at this woman who had so changed his own life in the same short time, and who now spoke so frankly.

'That is what I want also,' he said quietly.

41

The following morning, they were up at six and took an early breakfast on the wharf. They would use the engine to get back to the island, but this would still take several hours. It was a sunny morning, though cool, and the wide flat river in front of the café flowed smoothly into the Coral Sea. A thoughtful heron perched on a branch over the water, and on the mudflats on the far side, yellow-beaked white egrets bent their necks, searching for their own breakfast.

Ali had just ordered second coffees for them when there was a squeal of brakes from the street. They looked up and saw two police cars, Cooktown's entire fleet, stop beside the wharf and four uniformed men emerge. A moment later, a paddy wagon arrived. Soon a total of six policemen were standing on the wharf looking expectantly out towards the sea, and rapidly gathering a crowd of curious Cooktown residents.

Then around the corner from the north, into the mouth of the river and across toward the wharf, came two boats. The first was a grey launch with the navy-blue insignia of the Australian Customs Service. The second was a large luxury cruiser. The *Hyacinth*.

'That's Justus Lee's boat!' exclaimed Leah. 'The man who Leslie thinks is working with Brian Mitchell. They've seized his boat — I wonder what they've found. And whether he's aboard?'

As the two boats approached they could see that a uniformed Customs officer stood on the bridge of the cruiser with the captain. The *Hyacinth* came to a halt out in the middle of the river. The Customs boat came up beside her and a ladder was lowered from the deck of the *Hyacinth*. As the crowd watched, six crew members, dark-skinned and glum, made their way down the ladder, followed by the captain. Apparently Justus Lee himself had not been on board. The Customs boat chugged across to the wharf where the police waited, and the sailors and captain were loaded into the paddy wagon. Also brought ashore was a large jute sack labelled RAW ARABICA COFFEE BEANS, PRODUCE OF PAPUA NEW GUINEA, which seemed to be of great interest to the sergeant in charge. This was carefully signed for and placed into the front of one of the police cars. Then all the police and their prisoners disappeared in the direction of the little Cooktown police station, leaving just the one Customs officer guarding the *Hyacinth*.

'Hey, Jimmy, aren't you going to tell us what's in the sack?' someone shouted at the departing cars, but the sergeant just grinned and said, 'Stan, you'll have to read about it in the paper tomorrow!'

'Interesting!' Leah said. 'I wonder if anything's happened back in Cairns. It's time to be heading home anyway. We'll be back on Rookwood in a few hours.'

42

O n Sunday afternoon, Leslie was at work again. He was in the water police launch, which was cutting its way through the smooth turquoise sea as easily as scissors might rip through silk. The launch was travelling north from Cairns, heading for Rookwood Island. Leslie leaned over the railings on the starboard side. The water was so clear that in many places he could see right through to the sand below, every rock and contour. Fish, two and three feet long, flicked their way through the depths, and once he saw a spotted shark, maybe six feet long, cruising among them.

With Leslie were two uniformed men, plus the skipper, Shorty Brewer, and three crew. Drew was off-duty today, but these numbers seemed perfectly adequate to Leslie for the task in hand. Having ascertained that Brian Mitchell had returned to the island from a week of business meetings in Brisbane, Leslie had an appointment with him for three o'clock, and an arrest warrant in his shirt pocket.

The launch came up closer to the mouth of the Cassowary River and Leslie looked across at the beach and the rocky outcrop where Ebony's body had been found. There were no people here today apart from a woman walking a dog. Leah's Land Rover was parked by the wharf, and down at the other end of the island he could see the *Argo* at Leah's wharf. Leah was home then, although he doubted he'd be calling on her today. He must remember to give her the photo his mother had sent to Claudine from Melbourne (clearly showing her lack of trust in her own son's ability to remember family matters).

Horton's Guesthouse (she'd written in her letter), about 1925. The house itself is still there outside Kurunegala. Myself aged five on the top step next to the two ladies. They were the Horton sisters, Emily and Addie. They'd both been married and widowed at least twice, that I do remember, but I don't recall their married names. We went there every year to stay before we were taken up to see the Kandy Temple Elephants in the Perehara Procession. Addie and Emily must have been in their late seventies then, but they both lived well into their eighties and ran the guesthouse themselves until they died.

The launch slowed a little, rocking as it changed course toward the island and took the stream of the Cassowary across the bows. Shorty made a further turn around to the right to the north of the island and came up close beside the resort's private wharf. He found a mooring between two large cabin cruisers, and his crew jumped onto the wharf and fastened the lines.

'I'll take both of you with me,' Leslie said to Constables Stephens and Doughty. To Shorty he said, 'I don't expect to be long. It's just a matter of producing the warrant and letting him get a few things together, make a phone call. But keep a close eye on him on the crossing back. He's a somewhat unpredictable character and more aggressive than you might think. And he won't be a happy camper.'

With the uniformed men, he made his way down the wharf and across the manicured gardens of the resort towards reception. On the previous visit, he had bowed to Ron Reese's request to have no uniformed men alarming the guests. Today was different.

At the reception desk stood a soignée blonde woman in a Polynesian sarong and top. Leslie had met this woman before, when she had been the picture of cool chic. Now she seemed flustered. And behind her, Ron Reese was even more agitated, a red flush spreading from his plump cheeks all the way to the top of his shaven head.

'Mr Fernando! I know Mr Mitchell had an appointment with you. But he took a call about fifteen minutes ago in his office. Then, when I went in just now to remind him about your coming, he wasn't in the office or his apartment, and the back door to the apartment's wide open. I had a look around but I can't find him. It's not at all like him.'

'The back door? Leading to the beach on that side?'

'Yes.'

'Just show me where he went out,' he told Ron, and then followed the man through the buildings to Mitchell's apartment. Mitchell was definitely not there. But nor was he on the water, making his escape in one of the tinnies — they were all still on Mermaids Beach, and Leslie could see straight across the sea to the river and the northern shore, and there were no boats there.

Leslie thought quickly. Certainly Mitchell had not passed the resort wharf as the launch had come in, nor had he been seen on the North Beach path, which led away on the left side of the wharf. If he'd gone by the back door of his apartment, he could have hidden behind palms when he'd seen the police launch approaching. Leslie had to admit that he had not been scanning the beach there particularly acutely. He had not really anticipated Mitchell trying to flee.

'Doughty,' he said, 'go back to the wharf, keep a look-out for our man. If you see him, nab him. If you don't, get Shorty to start the launch up and just idle off-shore until I see what's going on. I may need him in a hurry. Stephens — you stay here and scout around the cabins, he may be still here. Stay ready, I may need you too. I'm going along Mermaids Beach to look for Mitchell. If I need help, I'll call or fall back here.'

He went out the door and across more well-tended gardens. Two Japanese men in bright Hawaiian shirts stared at him from a balcony. Leslie reached the edge of the sand and slid behind the red trunk of a lipstick palm. There was a good view of Mermaids Beach all the way down to where the *Argo* was moored, and it was completely deserted.

He decided the best approach was an overt one and stepped onto the edge of the beach. Immediately, he sank to his calves in the fine sand, and his leather brogues, so suitable for the Cairns street detective, filled with the stuff. It trickled into his socks and covered his trouser bottoms. Cursing softly, he extracted both feet and began to hop along the beach from one firmer grassed patch to the next. In the distance, the *Argo* rocked gently on the water.

He was suddenly aware that he might be placing himself in a dangerous situation. The timing of the Cooktown arrests had been meant to make the Mitchell arrest straightforward, but if Mitchell had somehow got wind of them, or simply turned panicky, he could do something quite irrational and dangerous. He could well be armed. If he decided to take a hostage or hostages, the result could be atrocious. Leslie was not carrying a gun, although Doughty and Stephens were armed, and Shorty would have guns aboard.

'Mitchell!' he called. 'Mitchell — if you're here, show yourself.'

There was a rustling behind a large tree fern and Leslie turned sharply. A young Japanese woman in shorts emerged with a net on the end of a stick. What the hell? Then he realised she was collecting butterflies — she had a superb brilliant blue specimen of a Ulysses in the net.

'You look someone?' she asked.

'Er, yes, did you happen to see the owner, Mr Mitchell, go past here just now?'

'Mr Mitchell? Big man? Ah yes. I think ... that way.' She pointed up the beach towards the *Argo*.

'Thanks. Sorry to disturb you. M'am, could I ask you to go back to the resort for just a few moments?'

She looked at him with obvious doubts about his sanity let alone his authority, but complied. When she was safely out of the way, he continued his painful progress along the beach. It occurred to him that Mitchell might be in the *Argo*, preparing to escape that way. If he saw Leslie and he had a gun, he might decide to use it. Leslie edged slowly along using the palms beside the beach as cover. Once he was past the stairs that led directly up to the top of the island, he would be able to see straight into the *Argo*. A crab with claws the size of boxing gloves darted out from a sand-hole between his feet, and he jumped. *Hell, don't lose your nerve now*, he told himself. But the *Argo* was completely empty.

The stairs! The concrete steps led to the top of the island, and also to Leah's house. But Mitchell almost never went up there, why would he do so now? Hell ... *Leah*. Had Mitchell gone up there, armed, to take Leah hostage? Her house would be the perfect place for such a drama — high on the island, fortified, well-stocked with provisions so that Mitchell could withstand a siege while he bargained with police outside.

Immediately, Leslie could see the scene unfolding and how it would catch the attention of the media. Against a perfect tropical background, prominent local businessman holds besieging police at bay ... Ending in the shooting deaths of the hostage and several of Leslie's own men. Shit — he should have been better prepared than this. Should have had Drew with him ...

He ran the distance to the bottom of the steps awkwardly — he was fit, he ran on the Esplanade nearly every day with his daughters, but here, with every step, the soft ground gave way under his feet. He must hurry, though, if Mitchell really was at Leah's.

He took the stairs two at a time, but it was difficult. The climb was a stiff one, and the stairs were irregular and rough in places. Strands of lawyer vine and wait-a-while snapped across his face. He should be going slower, watching out for Mitchell on each side in the trees and undergrowth as he passed, but his instinct told him that Mitchell had not stopped, that if he had come this way at all, he was intent on getting to the top. He paused for a moment, pulled off his shoes and stumbled on in bare feet up the stairs.

43

So now everything had changed. They knew it was him. They knew about everything. Not just the girl.

He'd been jumpy all day, starting in the morning. He'd tried to call Justus on the satellite phone and couldn't get through, although the man had promised to stay in touch throughout the operation. Couldn't get an answer from the Hyacinth *either*.

Then had come Fernando's phone call. Wanting to see him again. A few more questions, that's all, was what Fernando said. But he was coming personally. On a Sunday. That was a big worry. He hadn't been asked to go to Cairns, though, they hadn't sent police in uniforms to arrest him or anything like that.

He couldn't eat anything. He poured a half glass of Scotch and swallowed it in a single gulp, went into the bathroom and swilled water around his mouth. He would brazen it out, he told himself. Deny everything. But when he looked in the bathroom mirror, he saw a frightened man sweating in the air-conditioning. A muscle just below his left eye was twitching rapidly.

He paced around the apartment. Thank God Deb was in Brisbane. His passport was there too, though, with her. He pulled open a drawer, found the Colt, checked the chamber and pushed the gun into his trouser pocket. Just in case.

Then came the second call. A male voice, telling him to meet a girl on North Beach. She had some information for him.

Then the voice rang off. Information about what? Had Justus arranged an escape for him? Was there a boat waiting for him somewhere?

He had to get away. Before Fernando arrived. There was no time to arrange anything with Ron. He'd leave by the back door, go around to the wharf, take a tinnie, go into Cairns and call Deb from there. Get a flight down south.

He ran across the garden and stopped just behind a palm at the edge of the sand, catching sight of the police launch nosing its way around to the resort's wharf with uniformed cops on board, as well as Fernando.

He was too late.

What the hell could he do? He remembered the voice on the phone. He could get up to the top of the island and look down on North Beach from there. See if there was anyone on the beach. There might be a spare tinnie or a rubber boat he could take. Leah Rookwood had boats, too, at the wharf and on Turtle Beach. Maybe he could take one of them. He mustn't be seen. He must be quick. He couldn't risk running along Mermaids Beach. He'd have to get to the top of the island, and then see where the boats were moored.

He stumbled through the undergrowth by the edge of the sand, recoiled when he saw a bending figure, then realised it was a Japanese woman, one of his own guests. Not stopping, he crashed onwards, sideways and upwards, wherever the forest thinned out and he could make his way between the trees and the clinging, stinging vines. He was breathing heavily, but he knew he had to run, to get away, to get to Cairns, find Deb, get his passport. He had friends overseas, friends in lots of places — Manila, Dubai, the Canaries ... lots of friends, money in Switzerland, he just had to get away from this bloody island first and he'd be right. Christ it had been a mistake to get involved in this, he should have stuck to what he knew.

He pushed on upwards through the jungle. Once he thought he glimpsed a slim black figure and he called out, but just as quickly the image vanished. Towards the top of the island, the trees were more scattered, and he could see the domed roof of the lighthouse above them. He stopped for a moment, his breath coming in hard painful gasps. His shirt was torn, and sticky vines were tangled across his shoulders. He saw that he had come up close to the old cemetery and away from the Rookwood house. He hadn't been up here for years, but he knew where the Devil's Path was and how it led down to North Beach. From the start of it, he'd be able to see down to North Beach, and to Turtle Cove as well. He'd see if anything was happening on either of them. And then decide.

44

At the top of the stairs, Leslie emerged onto the flat ground behind Leah's house. To his left above the roof of the house, he could see the cemetery railings, and beyond that, the lighthouse, with no sign of Mitchell. He edged his way forward along the south end of the house. He thought he could hear voices, indistinct, inside.

He decided to make his way along the back of the house between the wall and the raised ground a few feet behind it. He bent double as he passed a couple of curtained windows in this wall. He could distinguish no voices at this distance. He kept a watch to the left and above himself — if Mitchell suddenly appeared above him from the direction of the cemetery, he would have Leslie at his mercy. Leslie knew he would be sensible to stop this, to retreat and get at least one of the uniformed men up here with him. On the other hand, if Brian was in the act of capturing Leah, maybe even tying her up right now, he might just be in time. Reaching the edge of the veranda on the north side of the house, he stopped to listen. He could make out faint sounds within the house, otherwise all was still.

There was the abrupt banging of a door up at the lighthouse and footsteps. Leslie turned, every muscle taut, ready for action.

It was Zak.

'Leslie!' Zak said. 'What *are* you doing?'

Leslie was suddenly conscious of how he must look. The climb had caused him to pant heavily, his bare feet were covered with sand, and his hand was bleeding where he'd grabbed at a vine on the way up. But maybe Zak's mother's life was in danger, maybe even now Brian Mitchell was inside stuffing her mouth with a tea towel and binding her hands. He gestured for Zak to join him and keep silent. When Zak reached him, Leslie pulled him close to the veranda post, behind the rainwater tank, leaned forward and hissed into his ear, 'I'm looking for Brian Mitchell. I think he may be in there with Leah. I've come to arrest him.'

Zak looked at Leslie as if he had completely lost his mind.

'But Mum's not there,' he said. 'She's gone to Cooktown. With Ali. In the *Dolphin*.'

'Who *is* in the house then?'

'No-one. At least, I don't think so. They'll be back soon, but ...' he peered towards Turtle Beach until Leslie hastily pulled him back into the safety of the veranda, 'they aren't back yet.'

'I heard voices.'

Zak laughed. 'Leslie, the footy's on. The score was so atrocious that I decided to go and put some of Mum's junk up in the lighthouse.'

'You haven't seen Mitchell?'

'No. At least, I thought there was someone behind the lighthouse while I was inside, but there's no-one there now. I thought it was one of the guests from the resort. They do sometimes come up here to have a look.'

'Zak, I want you to stay here. I don't know where Mitchell is, but he just may be armed and he may be dangerous. Keep out of sight here and don't move until I come back to get you.'

'Well ... OK, Leslie.'

The highest ground on Rookwood was the flat rock behind the cemetery. From that he would have a view right around the island. If Mitchell were anywhere in the open, Leslie should be able to see him. Of course, Mitchell could be hidden among trees or rocks. He could even be calmly back at the resort office. Leslie decided that it was best to reach the vantage point on the rock, then, if he saw nothing, to call Stephens and Doughty to come up before they tackled Leah's house together. He still felt it was quite possible that Mitchell was inside.

Keeping a good eye open, he edged up the path to the cemetery, skirted the railings and climbed onto the rock. Below him the green roof of Leah's house lay peacefully in the afternoon sunshine. He could no longer see Zak, hidden behind the tank. There was nothing visible on the lawns in front of the house or on what he could see of the cliff path on the south side. There was nobody on Turtle Beach. Then he saw the *Dolphin*. She was just coming around the north side of Turtle Beach. Leah was at the tiller and Ali was with her.

Leslie turned toward the north side of the island. He could see where the rainforest began again beyond the lighthouse. An area of bushes and scattered boulders led down to the track Leah called the Devil's Path. He could see the start of the track, and how close it was to the cliff edge on the right side. Then the track disappeared beneath a rocky overhang and around the corner, as it began to descend towards North Beach. Further away, he could see right down to North Beach itself, its full length.

Someone was on that beach, a solitary figure. A girl. An Aboriginal girl. She was fishing in the shallows at the end of the beach, where a couple of tinnies were drawn up on the sand. From this distance he could not be sure, but she looked quite like that girl, Ebony's cousin. Jade. Yes, it looked like Jade. Well, she was one of the dancers at the resort, she probably had some free time, there wasn't anything too unusual about that. Otherwise, as far as Leslie could see, nothing stirred.

But as Leslie stood considering his next move on the rock platform, a figure emerged from the low trees near the start of the Devil's Path. Mitchell. He was alone. His blue sports shirt was torn, he was strewn with leaves and tangled vines, and he was panting like a dog. He paused for a moment, looking around him and down at North Beach, but not up at Leslie.

What happened next took a matter of eight seconds, but when Leslie saw it all in his mind again later, it was in a series of freeze-frames, each lasting an eternity.

First the girl, Jade, turned, looked up at the pathway, and seemed to wave to Mitchell. Mitchell hesitated a moment, then began to walk along the Devil's Path. No, not to walk. To run.

In the next scene, Leslie became aware of a rustling in the forest beside the rock shelf and saw a shower of boulders, large and small, moving, gathering speed as they slid down towards the rock overhanging the path below.

Then cut to Leslie shouting 'Mitchell!' and Brian Mitchell turning slightly back towards him as he ran. Turning back so that his right foot seemed to splay out towards the cliff edge just as he reached the corner of the path.

The next frame was blurred. Did Leslie's call startle Mitchell so that he missed his footing and fell, with rocks hitting him and accelerating his flight over the cliff edge? Did the boulders push him down? Or was it actually Mitchell's intention, as he began to run, to throw himself clean off the Devil's Path?

Either way, the final picture was acutely clear. Leslie was simultaneously aware of Leah and Ali, both aboard the *Dolphin* as she sailed into Turtle Beach, looking up at his cry of Mitchell's name, and of his own relief as he realised that Zak could not see what was happening. He heard Mitchell scream, *Jesus!* Mitchell's back was arched, his arms flailing in front of him, and his mouth wide open with that single scream as he plunged onto the rocks below.

45

Two hours later, Leslie sat in Leah's living room drinking tea. Also present were Leah herself, Ali Hassan, Zak and Constables Stephens and Doughty. Leslie had emptied the sand from his shoes and socks onto the edge of Leah's lawn, but his trousers were crumpled and torn. Leah had bandaged his bleeding hand.

'Well, Leslie,' said Leah, passing around biscuits, 'perhaps you can tell us a bit more now about what happened. What on earth was he doing on the Devil's Path in the first place?'

'I can tell you what we know,' said Leslie, 'and also what I think. But I'm not sure we'll ever have the full story. As you saw in Cooktown, Justus Lee's boat was taken into custody this morning with all the crew. And this time we found, not heroin, which is what we expected, but methamphetamine. At least, that's what it looks like — we'll need lab reports. Enough to make about three million dollars on the street. Produced somewhere up around Hong Kong no doubt, easier to do that than depend on heroin coming across from Burma and Thailand, and much more lucrative.'

Leah remembered Adeline's words. 'Opium is very freely imported from China,' she had written. *Not much has changed then*, Leah thought.

'Coastwatch has been trailing the boat for a couple of weeks now,' Leslie continued. 'PNG reported a possible transfer at sea off the coast of Madang with another vessel belonging to Lee. Lee himself has been arrested in Manila, hopefully there's enough evidence to charge him this time.

'It seems likely that Lee arranged for Mitchell to get the stuff from here across to Cassowary, where Charlie Angell was to hold it. Charlie had done small jobs with Mitchell before, we know that. With this one, Ebony was to act as a courier from here to Charlie, and then with most of the stash into Cairns, where it would be passed on to the big cities down south. She'd already done several runs with marijuana from PNG. A neat operation, it kept Mitchell and Charlie at arm's length. We don't think they'd done a successful run yet with anything more than weed. Charlie's house was swabbed and the sniffer dogs went in, but they didn't turn up anything to suggest there'd been heroin or meth or anything else there at all, and Charlie swears it never happened. Of course he would say that.

'After we heard what Zak had to say about seeing Charlie and Mitchell on the Sunday night, we got Charlie to show us what they'd been doing. He was happy to cooperate. Mitchell had come across and said he needed to get rid of a tinnie. So Charlie went with him up to a remote creek he knew off the Cassowary and scuttled the boat, then brought Brian back and dropped him off at the resort. Charlie, of course, says he thought it was just something to do with dope, nothing more, didn't link it to Ebony at all until our men came to talk to him. A story I'm sure he'll stick to. Anyway, rather than arrest Charlie on Tuesday, we let him go provided he didn't tell Mitchell what had happened, and made sure no-one else did either. If he complied, we wouldn't press too many charges. I rather think he did.

'Mitchell's motive in scuttling the tinnie must have been to get rid of any evidence, fingerprints, hairs and so on, that might have linked himself and Ebony to that boat.

'Because I think he took her in that tinnie from Mermaids Beach, which is just outside his apartment and pretty much out of sight of the rest of the resort, ostensibly back to Cassowary beach. But somewhere between here and there, he pushed her out. Probably close to the north bank of the river where the water's deep and muddy and full of predators, and there's less risk of being seen because there are no houses there. What did he tell her? That he had a car and would drive her back to Cairns? That he'd call a taxi? I don't know. I do know that he'd already filled her up with vodka and probably she couldn't think straight.

'I think he took her as far as the river mouth on the north side, just kept the engine running, pushed her over and held her under until she stopped struggling. He was much stronger than she was and probably almost sober. And I think he probably tried to weigh her down with something, maybe a six-pack or two, inside her billum, with the straps of the billum wrapped around her wrists.

'Although his plan had mostly worked and the river had washed away all traces of any other clues inside the tinnie, there was one thing it hadn't altered. Caught in the outboard's engine were strands, red and black and yellow, of her billum. She probably struggled, and the propeller tore a hole in the billum. So that as she sank, whatever was in the billum slid out through the hole and the billum detached itself from where he had wound it around her wrists.

'And then something else happened, something he hadn't counted on. A big tree branch floating down the river snagged her. Ebony's body should have gone straight to the bottom, but the snag held onto her so that she got picked up by the current from the river and then brought back in to the beach by the tide, where her clothes were caught by the rocks. We found the snag further down the beach, with a couple of threads from the billum on it too, although the billum itself was gone. Leah, you thought that there had been something around her wrists, and there were scratches, probably from the branch.'

Leah nodded, yes, this reconstruction was plausible.

'Why did he kill her?' Leslie continued. 'I think he panicked because she refused to carry the meth, having previously taken the weed. Maybe she had originally agreed to do it and changed her mind, maybe she refused from the start. He certainly must have arranged to meet her that night after the show — he'd spent all day fishing with resort guests he said were important business contacts, yet he didn't go with them to the casino. The reason must have been something major. When she said she wouldn't do the run, he might have told her she could forget about the job down south — and she might have threatened to turn him in.

'So then he decided to kill her, before she came to us herself or talked to anyone in Cairns about him. One step up from the kinds of things he's done before, but then so were the drugs. Unfortunately, you don't have to be down in the big city to get mixed up in stuff like this, which was what Kevin was afraid of for her.' Kevin, Leslie was sure, knew something of what Lee and Mitchell were up to. It had probably been Kevin, or one of his mates, who made the call to Crime Stoppers, but this opinion Leslie would keep to himself.

At the mention of Kevin's name, Ali looked down, studying his feet. Would Leslie have anything to say of Kevin's possible role in Mitchell's death?

Forever afterwards, Leslie would think of his decision to race down to Turtle Beach after he saw Brian go over the cliff. In one way, this was an understandable reaction. A coroner would see it so — Mitchell must be rescued. In another, he knew he had made a conscious decision not to go straight away to look in the rainforest above the Devil's Path. After all, there had been two qualified medical practitioners already on the beach, well able to deal with Brian given the remote possibility that he was still alive. As soon as Leah and Ali had seen Brian fall, they had gone across to the rocks, but as in John Rookwood's case, death had been instant.

So that when Leslie did finally climb back up from Turtle Beach, having summoned the launch to pick up the body, and two very surprised constables to join their boss, there was no sign of any human input into the movement of the boulders. The remaining rocks lay warm in the afternoon sun and the bushes were still. Had someone been there, someone who had then glided, slid, danced even, away through a rainforest they knew well? As Leah had said, sometimes rocks just fell on their own onto the Devil's Path. Now she planned to close off the whole track before another death occurred.

That still didn't answer why Brian had been on the path.

He had received a phone call, Ron Reese said. A young male voice, was all Ron could say about it. 'Mr Mitchell, please, I need to talk to him about Ebony Passmore.' Brian had taken the call at once.

'We'll put a trace on the caller, of course,' Leslie said, 'but it will almost certainly turn out to be from a public phone somewhere in Cairns and therefore untraceable.' Like the Crime Stoppers call.

'But it could have been a request for Mitchell to go to a meeting on North Beach. Maybe avoiding passing through the resort, where his staff would see him...'

Constable Stephens had questioned the girl, Jade. She'd gone on peaceably fishing, in fact had several cod and a parrotfish in her bucket. When asked why she'd waved at Mitchell, she'd replied simply that she'd seen him on the path and he was the boss of the resort. No, she hadn't intended to meet him on the beach, of course not. She hadn't called him, she wouldn't even know how to do that. And she hadn't seen him fall, she was shocked to hear what had happened. When the constable suggested it was odd she was fishing alone, she retorted that North Beach was a traditional fishing place for her people, they'd been fishing there for hundreds of years, and she'd promised Grandpa Farrell she'd bring him fish for dinner.

In Mitchell's pocket, Shorty had found a Colt .45, loaded. Why, exactly? Did someone tell Mitchell that Jade was on the beach with important information for him, knowing that Mitchell was likely to take the Devil's Path? And so had Mitchell taken the gun as a precaution or to bargain? Or did Mitchell see the launch from his apartment window, maybe after a call from someone in the know in Cairns, and decide to make a bid to escape, perhaps using one of Leah's boats, running up the steps to see if he could take the *Dolphin*? Another possibility: had he grabbed the gun, deciding that suicide was the only way out, and opting for the Devil's Path only at the moment he saw the track in front of him?

'Of course,' said Leslie, 'we'll investigate all these things very fully. Now that their boss is dead, we might find some members of staff at the resort who did glimpse Ebony heading towards Brian's apartment on that Saturday night. And I'm sure Ron Reese knows a few things he hasn't told us yet, though I doubt he was involved himself. But I think that, just exactly as happened with John Rookwood, we might never know the whole truth.'

He wouldn't ask Leah to do the autopsy. Not this one. He would point out to the authorities that Leah and Mitchell were distant relations, and get a police pathologist up from Townsville instead.

46

Some hours later, Leah lay in the bath in the huge old bathroom at the centre of the house. She'd filled the bath almost to the brim and poured in a good dose of lemon bath oil.

Earlier in the evening, she had taken Ali and Zak, and Leslie and his men, across to the Cassowary beach in the *Argo*. Shorty and the police launch had already returned to Cairns with the body of Brian Mitchell. A police car was waiting for Leslie at the wharf, and Zak had taken the Land Rover to drop Ali at the hospital, where he was on call for the night, and to make visits himself in town.

Leah was grateful for the time alone. She felt a great need to cleanse herself of the afternoon's events. To wash away the memory of Brian Mitchell.

From the *Dolphin*, entering Turtle Beach, she had watched his fall with an extraordinary feeling of inevitability. It seemed as if she had known all her life that this would happen. In a matter of a couple of seconds, she had thought of herself as a young child, in awe of Brian, of her father arguing with Brian and her mother, of Brian proudly displaying his penis, and of a photo of Brian, grinning, beside a huge marlin, which she must have once seen, years ago, in the foyer of the resort. She imagined similar scenes flooding through Brian's mind. Then he had hit the wet rocks with a sound like nothing she had ever heard before.

She had known what she must do, and she did it. She gave the tiller to Ali, who was surprisingly calm at the turn of events, stripped off the T-shirt she wore over her swimsuit, and swam towards the rocks where Brian lay absolutely still. Closer to those rocks, she could see that he had fractured his spine and skull, his chest was stoved in, and he was dead.

She had been enormously relieved to hear Leslie's voice at just that moment, and to turn and see Leslie himself running down the path from her house.

'The water police launch is coming around,' he called, 'there's no need for you to do anything. Shorty's men will pick him up.' And within minutes the launch had come into the cove at full throttle and Shorty had taken charge of the operation, dispatching two of his men in a dinghy with a camera and a body bag. The body was stowed away in the launch and the waves washed over the rocks. In ten minutes, all traces of Brian Mitchell had disappeared.

Leah had been able to climb aboard, bring the *Dolphin* back to her normal anchorage and weigh the anchor, and get herself and Ali onto the beach in the dinghy. Then she had turned to Ali and buried herself in his arms, weeping unashamedly while he soothed her.

'Leah, Leah!' he said. 'You could do nothing. And I believe he was not a good man.'

Tactfully, Leslie had stepped down the beach and busied himself discussing details with Shorty, but he'd been pleased to see that Ali had taken his advice to heart.

At much the same time, Constables Doughty and Stephens had appeared on Turtle Beach, both breathing hard, having run from different parts of the island at Leslie's call. Leslie sent one to tell Ron Reese what had happened, the other to walk along the bottom path to North Beach to interview Jade. Then he himself had climbed back up the cliff to the house. Zak was still standing, goggle-eyed, by the veranda post.

'I'll explain it all in a minute,' Leslie had called, 'you're quite safe now.' Leslie walked on and up to the area above the Devil's Path. There was no-one there, and Zak had seen no-one pass back down the steps to Mermaids Beach.

All of this Leah thought over as she lay in the warm water, adding more hot with the pressure of her toes on the tap. She'd scrubbed herself vigorously with the loofah and shampooed her hair twice.

This was the first night she'd spent apart from Ali since the evening of the concert. She felt that this was right. She would lie here a while longer, and then let the water out, and with it as far as possible the memory of Brian's battered corpse on the rocks.

There was something else to think of as well. The letter.

She'd climbed up the cliff path after tying up the *Argo* at the wharf this evening, and as she'd done so, she'd remembered the last letter in the brass box. When she got back to the house, she'd poured herself a glass of wine and sat down with the box.

At first she'd thought that this one had not been written by Adeline. There were several sheets of a different notepaper, and the writing was firmer, the down strokes more definite, the t's more firmly crossed. But yes, it was Adeline's hand, except it was dated some twenty years after the others in the box. Then Leah saw that it was addressed, not to Emily, but to John. 'My dear John,' began Adeline. How had it come to be among Emily's possessions? Certainly Leah knew of no other letters to John that had been preserved.

Then she understood. The letter was written in Sydney and dated 23 April 1900. Two days after John's mysterious death on the Devil's Path. As Leah had thought, Adeline was in Sydney when John died. And turning over the pages, Leah saw that the letter broke off mid-sentence and was not signed. Perhaps she had even been writing the letter when the telegram had come with the news that she was now a widow. The letter had never been sent from Sydney. Leah sat back and slowly began to read.

My dear John,

It is only after much thought and with some trepidation that I take up my pen to write to you on this occasion. Our previous correspondence, I am happy to say, once it was established that I would stay in Sydney and keep Emily company after Robert's death, has been civil and largely concerned with the upbringing and affairs of Thomas. We have come to accept without speaking of it a situation that could not have been otherwise. I have not been unhappy here, working in nursing in Sydney, and I have reason to believe that you have established a tolerable pattern of existence for yourself in Cooktown. I know how much you like an orderly routine in your days. I say that with no irony whatsoever.

Now I write with a different purpose and feel that, in doing so, I must, for the sake of truth, expose much more of myself to you than I ever have done. I have met another man who wishes me to be his wife, and I ask you to release me from our marriage bond. I am willing to be the guilty party if you do not wish to put Mrs Howe to any indignity (you see, I do know a great deal about you). In fact, I have no qualms in saying that I am in fact guilty in this respect. I now realise that no shame should attach to such expressions of love between a man and a woman.

John, there was so much that we never said, could never say, after the events on the island. I cannot tell you everything, partly because there is much that I still could not put into words, but I shall try to explain some of it.

On that first night we were together again in our home, after the incident on the island and the rescue of myself and Lee Chin, after Mrs Mulligan and yourself had nursed me back to health, that night when I first, as you called it, 'became a proper wife to you', the first time I could truly take pleasure in our marriage bed, it was Lee Chin's touch I was thinking of. And on those other occasions also. I believe, too, John, that in your heart of hearts you have always understood that.

Please do not misunderstand me. At no time, ever, on Rookwood or on the cay on which we were stranded, or at any time later in Cooktown, did I do anything whatsoever to bring dishonour to you or our marriage or our family.

Up until the time of the attack on the island, I had not thought much about Lee Chin, although I did think he was exceptional for a Chinese. His knowledge of English was very good, but made difficult by his accent and his shyness. I do believe he was very intelligent and, had he been a white man, I am sure he would have succeeded in any academic field he chose. I believe his knowledge of Chinese characters and history was quite exceptional for someone who did not come from their educated classes. He often spoke to me, when we lived in Hope Street, of his mother and sisters and wife, for he had indeed a wife, and how he hoped to go back to them. I believe he sent almost all the money he earned back to China.

He had been to the diggings, but on his second trip back to Cooktown, when he had a large amount of gold to send off to China, he was in one of those parties that was attacked by the blacks. Several of his comrades including his own cousin were killed. That was one reason he was so anxious when he saw the blacks approaching us that day on the island. It was also the reason he was willing to go into domestic service with us instead of back to the diggings at the Palmer or elsewhere. (Did you know that he taught himself English letters while he was with us at Hope Street, and could read the headlines on our *Sydney Morning Heralds*? Not many other 'Chows' who could do that!)

You know the history of what happened that afternoon and of how we launched the rowboat. He began to row, we thought of course that we would be helped by the winds towards Cooktown, and most of all that we would meet you on your way back — not knowing about the cases of spinal fever and the fact that you would stay on to help Dr Fitzgerald. Nor did we anticipate the storm, which blew up so quickly and took us away and out to sea despite Lee Chin's best efforts.

I realised that he was growing weaker and that the towel I had found in the bottom of the boat and pressed to his chest wound was soaked with blood. It was then that I ripped off my petticoat and made a pressure bandage for his wound, which seemed to work — fortunately, it was just a flesh wound and the clot had come away from it. We were drifting further and further out to sea, I was having to keep a firm hold on Thomas too, it was getting dark rapidly, and I was in despair when Lee Chin sighted the cay and managed to guide the boat toward it. Lee Chin and I both were suffering from thirst by then, he particularly because he had lost so much blood.

We were both exhausted. I took another strip of my petticoat and tied it around Thomas and around myself so that he could not wander off even if I fell asleep myself. Lee Chin indicated that if I wished to perform certain bodily functions he would turn his back, and I did the same for him. (I tell you this because I have heard it is one of the things gossiped about in Cooktown since.) There was a little rainwater in the bottom of the boat and we gave it to Thomas, as you know, and I have told you how he screwed up his face but then drank it without a murmur. Also that I was able to breastfeed him a little — I sat at one side of the cay and kept myself covered.

We all three lay down on the cay, close together for safety, but with Thomas between myself and Lee Chin, and we slept for a long while, worn out. Our fear after leaving the island was that the blacks would follow us and kill us, but they did not. That fear, as well as the realisation of our terrible position, was overcome by the exhaustion of the journey and we slept for a long time. Thomas was hungry and cried, but Lee Chin sang softly to him and he fell asleep before we did.

I was awakened just before dawn by the sound of Lee Chin groaning with pain. The wound had opened again. I took a final piece of petticoat and pressed it firmly, and the bleeding stopped. Then I looked around and could see nothing but the sea, the cay was only a few inches above the sea level, the sun would soon be coming up and I was sure we would die of thirst before anyone found us. My lips were terribly dry and swollen. And I'm afraid I broke down and wept at the prospect of dying slowly and horribly on that deserted isle.

Then Lee Chin put his arms around me and I felt an inexpressible peace and a certainty that we would be saved. I looked up at him and thought, I am in the arms of another man, and realised that yes, Lee Chin was a man, not a Chow, or a Chinese, but a human being it was possible to relate to. I had never thought of him as a man before. It was a revelation.

I fell asleep, deeply comforted by him, and I believe it was just after nine o'clock when Lee Chin sighted the *Ariadne*, and put Thomas' shirt on the end of one of the oars and waved it, and Skipper Jackson rescued us. But I could not believe my ears when Mr Jackson turned on Lee Chin, and shook him roughly, and said to me, 'He didn't harm you, M'am?' I was disgusted, in fact, but I could barely speak, my lips were so parched, just saying, 'No, no, please give him water at once, he saved our lives yesterday, on the island.' And I knew then that I loved Lee Chin.

I do not know what Lee Chin felt in those few hours on the cay. About myself, I mean. Perhaps nothing at all. After all, he had a wife already, perhaps he loved her. I never knew any of those things. When I came home from Mrs Mulligan's, he had gone, you told me he had been severely frightened by the experience, as was very credible, that you had given him some money, and he had left. I know he worked for a time in Ahmat's store. I would see him about the town, and he would bow, and we would say a few words together. Nothing more. But from that, and the fact that I was not wearing my petticoat when I was rescued, grew those rumours that became so persistent in the town. And yes, I will admit, that the night he died from the typhus the following year, I did go to the Asiatic Ward of the hospital, but he was already dead, and yes, it is true that I was weeping in the garden by the church, weeping for a dear friend whom I could never mourn in public in Cooktown.

And so I had the worst of both aspects of it. My name, and yours, were compromised by gossip to which there was no substance, while I had to conceal my love — for it was love, that I knew — from the whole world, including Lee Chin himself.

John, when we married, I had thought I would come to love you, and I did not hide that from you.

And indeed it might have come about, a different kind of love, to be sure, lower key, less intense, had it not been for Lee Chin. Through Lee Chin, I glimpsed the fiercer kind of love. I have found that, once one knows of this love, one can never return to a zone of comfort only. And thus it was that I could not adapt to my old life with you again. My days revolved around the possibility that I might just glimpse him in the street or store, or exchange a few words in a passageway, and when he died, and I had not even that, life in Cooktown was intolerable for me. I could not live with you and share your bed, living, as I knew it, with a lie. For I could take pleasure in the act with you only by thinking of him. I do not know how you have fared in love since Mrs Howe came into your life, but I sincerely hope that you have perhaps known something of the love that you did not know with myself.

I have truly loved our son with a mother's love, and brought him up, when he has been with me, to the best of my ability, as I know you have done too. He is a fine young man. He is fully grown now, and I do not think will be too harmed by an irreversible break between his parents, who have anyway for so long been physically separated. He is happy to be following your own profession, though do not, John, count too much on his taking over your practice, at least not before he has seen a bit more of the world.

The man I have now met is a planter, a Ceylonese of Portuguese background who has an estate in the hill country of that island. He has been in Sydney having some treatment in our hospital. He returns in four weeks to Colombo by P&O. I should like to give him an answer before he leaves. I would anticipate a divorce taking six months to complete. I ask nothing of you, having an adequate wage for the moment and a little savings. I will continue staying with Emily until then. Of course, she is quite put out at the thought that I shall leave her house finally, but I have suggested that she may come to join us in Ceylon. I would ...'

Here the letter ended abruptly, though Leah felt she knew exactly what Adeline had been about to say — that she would welcome her sister to her home in Ceylon, and would not have married any man who would not have warmly welcomed his sister-in-law. For she knew now that this was what had happened. Sometime after Adeline had arrived in Colombo, Emily had come to join her, and she too had found a second husband there. Both sturdy Irish nurses, they had outlived the second husbands as well, and together they had run the guesthouse, where Leslie's mother had stayed, until they died.

The fiercer kind of love ... Lying now in warm bath water, Leah thought of the past nights she had spent with Ali, the pleasure they both took in learning new things about each other, the ascending ecstasy of every encounter. She understood well what Adeline had meant. She was glad that it seemed that Addie herself had finally, in her fifties, found happiness with her planter.

And what of John Rookwood?

It certainly sounded as though John had taken up abode with Mrs Howe in Cooktown once Adeline had settled permanently in Sydney. Mrs Howe, Leah recalled, was 'the captain's widow' of Adeline's earlier letters. Of course, it must have been Mrs Howe who had been on the picnic, probably she who had seen 'the rustling in the bushes'. From the beach in Turtle Cove, Mrs Howe had heard John's cry, and would have looked up from the picnic spread just in time to see her lover fall to his death. Despite the warmth of the bath, Leah shivered as she imagined that scene.

But if the reserved Irish doctor who was so attached to his routines had found a fiercer kind of love with the captain's widow, the knowledge of it had died with him. He had recorded no word of such emotions. He must, thought Leah, have been a man who could feel a great many things, or he would never have got himself from the Irish countryside up to Dublin, let alone through medical school and across the world to where he found and bought an island. Yet it seemed that he had accepted a marriage based on affection and respectability only, that in bed with Adeline, he had been unable to kindle the joy she later found with another.

Adeline, at thirty, having come across the world herself and seen many exotic sights, and, in the course of her profession, many less exotic ones too, had nevertheless been a virgin on her wedding night. A Victorian gentlewoman. She must have felt that John Rookwood was as much as the world had to offer her. That this was as good as it got, and that her decision to marry was a reasonable one. Leah understood this too. It was very much what she herself had once decided, for different reasons, about Gareth.

Leah tried to visualise Lee Chin, and could not. All the photos and pictures of the time showed the Chinese as entirely two-dimensional, as they showed Aboriginal people to be less than human. Small packs of identical Chows shuffling in lines with baskets over their shoulders, taking supplies to the diggings. Or standing smiling with drooping moustaches in the doors of their shops. Dismissed by the white men, that dismissiveness had percolated down even to Leah. The shrine in the cemetery at Cooktown, the foreign gold of the lettered words, the dusty incense sticks, were exotic, but did not evoke warm flesh and hot blood. Yet Lee Chin had stirred Adeline's flesh exactly as Ali now stirred Leah's own.

Ali. Leah did not know what the future held for them both. The situation in the Middle East was worsening, and it seemed that the Americans might soon invade Iraq. What this might mean for an exiled Iraqi doctor in Australia, no-one could predict. And there was anyway a great deal more for them both to learn about each other. For the moment, she knew only that when she was with him, she was happier than she had ever been in her life before.

She stepped out of the bath, wrapped herself in a towel and let the water drain away. Tonight she would send a long email to her sister Mara. And tomorrow, she would see Ali again.

ACKNOWLEDGEMENTS

I would like to thank my editor Gail Cartwright, who has been a great pleasure to work with on the manuscript of 'Hidden Lives' and who has gently but thoroughly directed me to improve the original text. My grateful thanks also to Annie Chance, Michele Moore, Jane Patrick, Jan Walker and my daughter Naomi, all of whom read and critiqued the manuscript in its various stages of development, and to my son Javed for musical and gaming advice.

ABOUT THE AUTHOR

Caroline de Costa is a Cairns-based doctor and professor at James Cook University who has published numerous healthcare books for women. Since 2015 she has also published three novels in the Detective Cass Diamond crime-fiction series; all are set in Cairns. The first, *Double Madness*, was shortlisted for the Davitt Awards of Sisters-in-Crime in 2016. Caroline's short story *Screwed* won the Kerry Greenwood Award of the 2019 Sisters-in-Crime Scarlet Stiletto award, and two other stories were highly commended in the 2020 Scarlet Stiletto awards. *Hidden Lives* is the prequel to her Cass Diamond series.

THE CASS DIAMOND CRIME SERIES

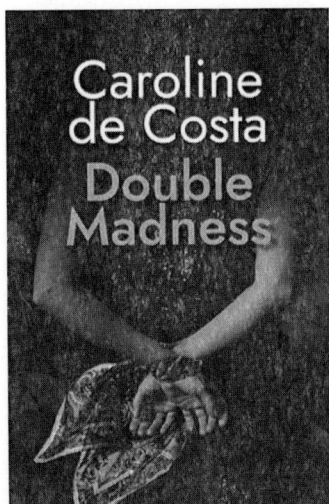

Caroline
de Costa
Double
Madness

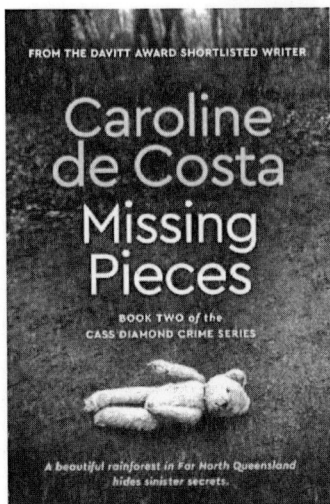

FROM THE DAVITT AWARD SHORTLISTED WRITER

Caroline
de Costa
Missing
Pieces

BOOK TWO of the
CASS DIAMOND CRIME SERIES

A beautiful rainforest in Far North Queensland
hides sinister secrets.

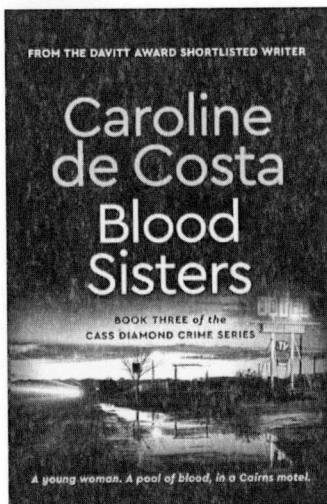

FROM THE DAVITT AWARD SHORTLISTED WRITER

Caroline
de Costa
Blood
Sisters

BOOK THREE of the
CASS DIAMOND CRIME SERIES

A young woman. A pool of blood, in a Cairns motel.